HEIR TO MURDER

English detective fiction at its best

TONY BASSETT

THE
BOOK
FOLKS

Published by The Book Folks

London, 2023

ISBN 978-1-80462-142-4

www.thebookfolks.com

HEIR TO MURDER *is the fifth standalone mystery in the Detectives Roy and Roscoe crime fiction series by Tony Bassett.*

The full list of books is as follows:

Details about these books can be found at the back of this one.

Chapter 1

The young couple were cuddling up together on the settee, trying to watch television. But, from time to time, the sound of heavy rock music blared out from the flat below.

Now it started again.

'I can't take any more of this,' said the man, Jake Harris, shouting above the stomping beat. 'He's been told time and again to keep it down. He just doesn't listen.'

'He's bloody selfish,' said his girlfriend, Hannah, whose mousy blonde hair he had been fondling. 'It was after midnight the other night. The council's noise patrol came round a month ago, but he doesn't take a blind bit of notice of anyone.'

'Well, I'm not having this anymore,' he shouted.

He stormed into their hallway and rummaged around in the coat cupboard by the front door.

Hannah followed him apprehensively. 'What are you looking for?'

'My old cricket bat.'

'Jake, don't do anything foolish. He's not worth it.'

'I'm sorry, Hannah,' he replied, as he collected his English willow bat from the cupboard. 'He's pushed me to the bloody limit. I'm going to sort this out once and for all.'

The deafening sound of the beat and bass seemed to rise to even greater levels as Harris opened the door of their first-floor flat in the Warwickshire market town of Queensbridge and peered out.

'Don't do this, Jake. He's got a fearful temper,' she called from behind.

None of the other residents seemed to be around as he stepped along the landing and climbed down the concrete stairs that led to the floor below.

'Come back,' Hannah hissed. 'You'll get yourself into trouble.'

But Harris, who had been drinking beer and rum all evening, was determined to confront the man.

Hadn't he personally spoken to Miles Kenworth just a few days earlier, explaining the effects his loud music was having on all the residents? Hadn't he mentioned how Hannah had been missing sleep because of the times Kenworth had played music until two in the morning?

She had been late for work on occasion and had to take days off to catch up with her sleep.

It was time for someone to stand up to the noise-loving bully.

After charging down the stairs like a prop forward within sight of the touchline, Harris thumped hard with his fist on the door of Flat 1. Then he waited. There was no response.

'Come out, Miles,' he bellowed. 'I know you're in there.'

He was going to shout, 'Come out and face the music,' but realised how ridiculous that would have sounded in the circumstances – even if the man could hear him above the din.

'Open the bloody door!' he screamed.

Was it his imagination? It seemed the volume had been turned up even more – as though the occupant was mocking him.

Harris felt the noisemaker was having fun at his expense. The man must have heard him knocking. Yet he was steadfastly refusing to open the door. He was happy to let his aggrieved neighbour linger outside in the main foyer of the flats while he continued to indulge in his passion for raucous music.

Well, this could be a day when the music died, thought Harris, as he banged several times more on the door.

'Right,' Harris told himself. 'There's only one thing for it.'

He screamed at the top of his voice, 'You've been warned.'

Then he brandished the cricket bat in the air and struck the upper part of the door. Nothing happened. He swung it over his shoulder twice more. The door didn't budge.

So he dropped the bat on the floor and took a step back from the doorway. Then he kicked hard just to the left of the latch and finally the door flew open.

He had half-expected the rock fan to come dashing helter-skelter towards him through his pale-green hallway, fists flailing and his mouth yelling abuse. But, as the music continued unabated, there was no sign of the occupant.

Harris angrily picked up his bat from the floor and marched into the hall of the modern one-bed flat.

The sound grew louder as he passed the bedroom on the left. He glanced inside it. The dark-green curtains were drawn. The bed was unmade. Clothing was scattered on the floor.

Then he proceeded into the living room. There was no sign of their neighbour. But there, to the side, was the source of all the residents' anguish – Miles Kenworth's sound system.

'Don't say the bastard's gone out and left the music on to torture us,' he muttered to himself.

Without wasting a second, Harris reached down to the nearby plug socket and flicked up the switch. The music stopped at once.

Harris heaved a sigh of relief as blessed silence reigned. Then a smile flickered across his face. Maybe this was his chance to bring an end, once and for all, to the nightly misery which had afflicted them.

He raised his bat again and thrashed about wildly at Kenworth's hi-fi equipment. Within minutes, his neighbour's expensive sound system – including his CD and DVD collection, his CD player, tuner, amplifier and two speakers, were lying in pieces on the oak floor.

Harris stood up. He thought he'd heard something. He looked around the light, airy, open-plan room. He stepped back into the hall and looked inside the bedroom. No, he was alone.

Perhaps it was time for him to go back upstairs. Perhaps the sound had been his girlfriend calling from the first-floor landing.

As he glanced back into the living room, his eyes rested on a brown jacket strewn across an armchair.

'Strange I didn't see that before,' he told himself. Then, protruding from behind the settee, he saw what appeared to be a black shoe.

Surely the noisy neighbour hadn't fallen asleep on the floor while that cacophony was shaking the building?

His curiosity was aroused now. Still clutching his trusty bat, he ventured across the floor, stepping past a coffee table piled with music magazines and empty beer cans.

Peering behind the settee, all he could do was stare at something lying on a red, patterned rug. And he recoiled in horror.

Chapter 2

Like other residents of Waverley Court, Aimee Granville-Cole was irritated by the continual noise they had all been suffering from since her next-door neighbour moved in.

The former model had tried a gentle approach. When Miles Kenworth had played his first loud session, she had called round, introduced herself and asked if he could turn the music down.

For half an hour, he had acceded to her request. After that, the volume had crept up and the loud thumping had returned.

There had been a few occasions since, when she had called on him to reduce the sound level and, again, he had only complied for a short time.

Then, two Sundays ago, she had snapped. She banged on his door and warned him that, if he didn't keep the racket down, she would call the police or Queensbridge Borough Council. And if that failed, she would call the managing agents of the block or the freeholder. This tougher approach also failed to work.

She was becoming depressed about the problem. She had mentioned it to colleagues at the modelling agency in Birmingham where she worked as a secretary. They had been sympathetic, but felt that, ultimately, she might have to consider moving out.

Aimee loved her two-bedroom flat in tree-lined Fishpond Lane where she had lived for three years, and the thought of a fresh upheaval was anathema to her.

She tried reading a book but it was no good. She couldn't settle. She looked at her watch. It was nearly ten o'clock. She stepped into her living room and began watching the television news.

A few minutes later, she heard someone knocking loudly on her neighbour's door.

Then she heard a man's voice shout, 'Come out, Miles.'

Aimee tiptoed to her front door and stood there, listening. All she could hear was the steady thump of the music.

The words were clearer now.

'Open the bloody door!'

She recognised the Black Country tones of a man who lived in one of the upstairs flats. She knew his name was Jake Harris and that he had a bad temper. She knew his partner, Hannah, slightly better.

As quietly as she could, she released the chain on her door and opened it a fraction. She watched as the man kicked Kenworth's door open and burst in.

She was shocked that one of her fellow residents would brazenly break into a neighbour's property in that way, despite the obvious provocation. She wondered if her friends were right. Perhaps she should consider moving.

Then the music suddenly died and, for the next few minutes, all she could hear was the sound of property being damaged.

'All that rock music,' she told herself. 'Mr Harris must have completely lost it. I knew he was hot-tempered. Maybe the next thing is he's going to attack Miles.'

She closed her door and returned to the bedroom where she found her mobile phone.

Moments later, she was speaking to the emergency operator, asking to be put through to Heart of England Police.

The seconds ticked by. Eventually, her call was passed to the control room in North Warwickshire.

She informed the duty sergeant that she lived at the block of flats in Fishpond Lane, on the southern side of Queensbridge.

'We've got a problem neighbour who's always playing loud music,' she said. 'I just saw a guy who lives in one of the flats above break down his door. He's got a cricket bat, and it sounds like he's wrecking the place.'

'What's your name, Miss?'

'I'm Aimee. Aimee Granville-Cole. I live in Flat 3, but, if you come, don't tell anyone it was me that tipped you off or give out my address, will you?'

'Don't worry, Miss,' he assured her. 'This is completely confidential. We've sent a patrol car and officers should be with you within fifteen minutes. It's Flat 1 you say?'

'Yes. It's Miles Kenworth's place, Flat 1, Waverley Court.'

'And you say you recognised the intruder?'

'Yes, it's the man who lives directly above Mr Kenworth's flat.'

'What's his name?'

'Jake Harris.'

The sergeant asked, 'Could you describe him?'

'You won't mention my name, will you?'

'No.'

'Well, he's tall – nearly six foot. He's got short, black hair and a beard, and he's quite stocky.'

'And you say he's in an aggressive mood?'

'Yes, he was holding a cricket bat. Come quickly, won't you? I'm worried someone's going to get hurt.'

'Stay where you are, Miss, and two of our officers will be with you shortly.'

Aimee ended the call. But during her conversation with the officer, she thought she heard a woman's voice on the landing outside.

She rushed back to her front door, peered out and saw Hannah Taylor, Jake's partner.

Aimee had been reluctant to leave her flat after witnessing the break-in. But, seeing Hannah and knowing police were on the way, she felt emboldened.

Taking her front door key from a hook in her hallway, she stepped outside and greeted Hannah.

'What's going on?' she inquired.

'I'm not sure,' replied Hannah. 'My boyfriend came down to have a word with Miles. The music's stopped, but Jake hasn't returned.'

Hannah poked her head inside the open doorway to Flat 1. 'Jake!' she called. 'Are you all right?'

At first, there was silence. But then came a nervous voice from several metres away inside the flat.

'I'm all right, Hannah,' he assured her. 'But something really awful has happened. It's best if you don't come in – I'm coming out.'

Hannah took a few steps inside the hallway. 'Where are you, Jake?' she asked.

'You heard what I said. Don't come in,' said her partner.

These words had piqued her interest. Despite her boyfriend's request, Hannah headed towards the living room with Aimee directly behind her. The pair looked around the hallway nervously as they stepped closer like two gazelles approaching a lion's den.

They reached the open living room door to find Harris standing behind the settee, staring down at the floor with a shocked expression and still grasping his bat.

Joining him behind the settee, they gazed in horror at a shape lying spread-eagled on the rug. It was the body of a man.

As they looked more closely, they could see an axe embedded in the victim's skull.

Chapter 3

The white envelope was lying on Sunita Roy's doormat when she returned from work. She sensed it might be important.

Postmarked Leicester, it was addressed to 'Miss S. Roy' and stamped 'private and confidential'.

After reading the lengthy contents and smiling enigmatically, she placed the letter and envelope on her coffee table before stepping into the kitchen and preparing an evening meal.

She glanced at her watch. It was nearly eight o'clock. Her boyfriend, Samir Banerjee, would be arriving at any moment.

Finally, at around a quarter past eight, lights from an approaching car flickered round the open-plan room. She gazed through the blinds. The black Volkswagen Golf she had been watching out for drew up outside and her boyfriend stepped out.

After quickly brushing her long, dark, flowing hair in the mirror and tying it behind her head, she ran downstairs and opened the front door, greeting Samir warmly with a kiss on the lips.

'Good day?' she asked as they climbed the stairs.

'Yes, a lot of people seem to have broken their computers this week,' said Samir, a slim, educated man that she had met after he saved her ex-boyfriend's life following a shooting.

'Hey, that fish smells good,' he remarked as he helped her set the dining table.

'You like salmon, don't you?' she said as she served the food.

'Love it,' he said, taking his seat at the table.

'I've got some news,' she said.

'What's that?' he asked as he sampled the salmon.

'You know I was telling you about my uncle Ramit who died six months ago? I've just heard from his solicitor. He's left some money to my sister and me.'

He smiled. 'That's very nice, Sunita,' he said.

'I'm not sure how much. But he was a good businessman.'

Sunita walked over to the coffee table and returned with the letter. Samir slipped his black-framed glasses from his trouser pocket and put them on so he could read it.

'So you could be in for a nice payout,' he observed.

'Maybe. The thing is, if it's a lot of money, I'm not sure what I'd do with it. I mean, you don't get much return from a building society account these days. I suppose a wise thing would be for me to invest in some kind of property.'

'When will you find out more?' he asked.

'Tulika and I have been invited to visit the solicitor in Leicester next week. I'll know more after that.'

'So you'll have to take a day off work?'

'Yes. It's unavoidable. I hope the DCI is understanding about it.'

Samir smiled. 'That boss of yours, Mr Roscoe; he expects a lot from you. He sends you hundreds of miles across Britain to interview witnesses and you sometimes have to work a fifteen-hour day.'

She nodded. 'He just believes that hard work and being thorough are important to police work. I suppose long hours go with the turf in my job. If you're on a murder inquiry, you can't say, "Right, it's six o'clock. I'm off home." It's not like a normal job.'

At that moment, Sunita's mobile phone began to ring. She had left it in the pocket of her fawn jacket in the hall and hurried to retrieve it.

'It's my boss, Sam,' she shouted.

'Talk of the devil,' he replied.

'Yes, sir?' said Sunita as she answered the call.

'Sergeant, sorry to trouble you so late,' DCI Gavin Roscoe said in his broad Birmingham accent. 'There's been a brutal murder in Queensbridge. A man's been found with an axe in his head.'

'Oh my God! How terrible,' said Sunita.

'Yes, he was found just over two hours ago,' he continued. 'Young man by the name of Miles Kenworth. Have you got a pen?'

The chief inspector read out the address to her, which she wrote down in her small, black notebook.

'The next-door neighbour, a woman called Aimee, has given us some vital information. She claims to have seen a man who lives on the first floor break into the flat belonging to the deceased, and minutes later found the same man, Jake Harris, standing over the corpse.'

'Good God! Caught in the act.'

'Looks that way.'

'Where's that man, Harris, now?'

'He's in custody at Queensbridge. Omar Khalid's been interviewing him.'

'Hopefully a straightforward case then, sir.'

'Never say that, Sergeant. We don't want to tempt fate. Look, are you prepared for an early start? I'd like us to get over there to Fishpond Lane at seven o'clock and see what the state of play is. We can interview the neighbour, Aimee. Then we can get over to Queensbridge nick and see what Jake Harris has got to say for himself. How does that sound, Sergeant?'

'Sounds good. I'll see you tomorrow.'

Chapter 4

Waverley Court was a modern, three-storey apartment block set in a quiet, country lane on the southern edge of Queensbridge.

The modern, red-brick building, which altogether contained sixteen flats, commanded a prominent position at the top of Fishpond Lane and overlooked open fields and ancient woodland.

Sunita Roy parked her white Peugeot 208 on the far side of the street and stepped out. White and yellow daffodils had sprung up on the grass verge beside a brook which trickled down the gentle hillside towards a pond at the end.

She glanced across at the nearby entrance – double doors providing access to eight of the flats, where a policeman was standing beside blue-and-white tape.

She immediately recognised him as PC Derek Underhill, a conscientious, hard-working officer based in the town.

'The DCI here yet, Derek?' she asked while glancing at the electronic bell pushes, speakerphones, and mailboxes on the wall behind him.

'Yes, he's been here for about ten minutes,' Underhill replied. 'He's gone inside to look at the body. I suppose you'll be wanting to join him?'

'That's right.'

'A word of warning: it's not a pretty sight. I had a quick glance inside and it was enough to turn my stomach.'

'Derek, I didn't become a detective expecting a life of unbridled fun.'

He lowered his voice. 'No? You surprise me. What did you join for then? No, but seriously, be warned. It's grim in there. The stuff of nightmares.'

'I'm sure I've been confronted with worse. I've been in the job for more than eight years.'

'Well, you've been warned.'

Sunita climbed the two stone steps to the glass doors and let herself in. Then she crossed the foyer and saw the entrance to Miles Kenworth's flat.

She noticed the splintered wood on both the door and the architrave as she stepped inside.

Two scenes-of-crime staff were working in the hall, examining the oak floor. She recognised the sound of the chief inspector's voice coming from the room at the end of the corridor and negotiated her way round them.

'Morning, sir,' she called. 'Is it all right for me to come in?'

'Yes, but mind where you put your feet,' the chief inspector replied.

As Derek Underhill had predicted, she was shocked to the core by the sight that met her eyes.

A man in a white coverall suit, Home Office pathologist Dr Silas Reynolds, was crouching over the body of a man with a mutilated head. Her boss, DCI Roscoe – tall, grey-haired, in a navy-blue coat – was standing beside him. Usually genial, he looked as gloomy as a Norwegian winter.

A photographer, also in a white forensic suit, was capturing still pictures of the scene. The dead man's clothing, the floor and some parts of the furniture were drenched in blood. A cricket bat and an empty whisky bottle lay a short distance away.

Disquietingly, an axe remained embedded in the centre of the man's forehead, while the entire head was caked in gore.

For a moment, she thought she would be sick and turned her head away. The middle-aged chief inspector noticed her reaction.

'Not a pleasant sight, is it?' he said as she stepped across the room.

Someone had opened the curtains, allowing light to flood in through the large casement window. She formed a gap with her hand in the venetian blinds and peered out at the garden and the residents' car park beyond. Some daffodils were swaying in the breeze beneath the sill.

She stepped back and immediately her attention was drawn to the centre of the window. Something was odd, but at first she could not decide what it was. Then she realised and called out to the chief inspector.

'Have you got a moment, sir?' she asked.

'What is it, Sergeant?' he replied as he took a few steps towards her.

'This window is not properly fastened,' she said. 'Do you see? It's been pulled to with the handle still in the horizontal position. Maybe someone came in or out through here.'

He moved to the side of the window and pulled a cord, raising the blinds. Then he gazed at the handle.

'You're right,' he said, pushing the pane open and leaning outside. He peered down at the flowers and the mixed coloured pebbles on the ground outside.

'Might be worth getting one of the forensic team to see if there are signs of entry through here,' he agreed.

Her eyes darted round the room like fireflies in a cave, seeking out any object that might seem out of place. They finally rested on a grey metal box in the far corner.

'Any idea what that is?' she asked.

'Yes. It's his toolbox,' he replied. 'Don't worry. The team have gone through it thoroughly. Nothing unusual in it. Just workman's tools. I tell you what though – this might be of interest.'

He produced a small black book from his pocket. It was inside a transparent evidence bag.

'What's that, sir?'

'It's Mr Kenworth's diary. I'm going to let Dr Ling and her people give it the once-over, then you can pore over it and see if you can find any clues about his private life. They haven't been able to find his phone, which is annoying.'

'There's a lot of blood,' she remarked, glancing at the chief inspector.

'Yes, whoever it was must have gone absolutely berserk. Luckily, we've got this key witness who saw Jake Harris breaking in at just gone ten. She dialled 999 at once.'

'Jake Harris – that's the man you told me about last night, sir?'

'Yes, he lives upstairs. Apparently, this guy here was a rock fan who kept other residents awake with his loud music.'

Just then the stocky, grey-haired pathologist looked up from his work.

'Sorry business, Sergeant,' he said. 'Very sorry business. The victim's male, Caucasian, in his mid-thirties with long, dark-brown hair. He's a hundred and eighty-two centimetres tall. He's wearing a blue shirt and grey trousers. He's got tattoos of guitars, drums and sheet music on his arms.'

Roscoe folded his arms. 'Tell us about the injuries, Silas.'

'The guy's suffered from a great number of slash, stab and cut wounds. There are also a number of superficial abrasions and bruises on the skin.'

Sunita was writing furiously in a small notebook with her head bowed. She glanced up at the pathologist.

'Dr Reynolds, can you tell us about the axe?'

'Yes. It's a sixteen-inch-long wood-handled axe. It's got a forged head of carbon steel and double bevel blade measuring seven and a half centimetres. Looks like it was imported from Scandinavia by a firm called Better Age (Midlands) Limited.'

'Dr Reynolds, is it too early to suggest an actual cause of death?'

Roscoe quipped, 'I'm guessing the axe played a part.'

Reynolds shrugged his shoulders. 'It appears the immediate cause of death was shock and haemorrhage to the head from multiple wounds,' he said.

'I'm assuming he's largely suffered what the man in the street would call a brain injury,' said Roscoe.

'Precisely,' said Reynolds. 'The axe has been used as both a slashing tool and as a blunt weapon,' he continued.

'Any signs the victim made any attempt to fight back?'

'Yes, old fruit. Looks as though he may have tried to defend himself but we'll only know for sure after we get the body to the lab and examine any content trapped in his finger nails. There are also injuries to his hands and arms.'

'Any idea about the exact time of death, Silas?' Roscoe inquired.

'Can't be too certain at the moment, but sometime last night, judging by the appearance of the blood.'

'This could be crucial for us. Any chance you could be more specific?' Roscoe asked.

'Full rigor mortis is just setting in now. So, along with the analysis of the body temperature, I'd make a guess as to the time of death being between 7 and 10 p.m. But that's only a rough guide, old fruit.'

Sunita put her notebook away. 'Dr Reynolds, it looks as though the killer must have gone crazy. Is it possible to give an estimate as to how long the attack went on for?'

'No, Sergeant. I'm afraid it isn't. But in view of the number of wounds and knowledge that the victim fought back, I think we can safely assume it would have lasted a good few minutes. Whoever it was wore gloves. There are no signs of dabs anywhere.'

'And the sound of the assault was probably masked by the loud music?' she asked.

'Was there loud music being played?' Reynolds replied. 'I wasn't aware of that.'

Roscoe nodded. 'Yes. Haven't you seen this smashed sound equipment?' He stepped aside, allowing the pathologist a moment to gaze at the wrecked hi-fi system.

'Someone's made a good job of that,' Reynolds remarked.

Roscoe continued, 'Silas, a man's helping us at Queensbridge nick. There's a history in the building of noise complaints. This poor fellow on the living-room floor, whom we believe to be the leaseholder, Miles Kenworth, was a fan of loud music.'

'I'm trying to picture what might have happened,' said Sunita, sounding as though she was speaking her thoughts out loud. 'Since the door is damaged, we must assume the killer or killers stormed through the door carrying the axe. Mr Kenworth was taken by surprise and tried to fight back, but he was overwhelmed by the force of the attack.'

'Yes, that would fit the facts,' said the pathologist. 'Once we've removed the weapon, we'll take it away with the body and should have more information within a few days.'

After Reynolds returned his attention to the body, Roscoe led his sergeant back into the entrance hall.

'Change of plan, Sergeant,' he said. 'I've decided I'm going to go straight to Queensbridge nick to interview this guy, Harris. I want you to chat to Aimee Granville-Cole. Her flat's just along the corridor and around the corner.'

He reached into the pocket of his coat and withdrew a crumpled piece of paper.

'Here's the statement she gave Khalid early this morning. Have a chat with her and see if you can elicit any more. Her evidence is going to be vital if we're going to put away the maniac who committed this appalling murder.'

Chapter 5

Sunita Roy had to knock several times on the door of Flat 3 before it opened. Then, yawning and rubbing her eyes, Aimee Granville-Cole inspected her warrant card and invited her in.

'You got me out of bed,' she moaned as she led the sergeant into her bright, airy living room which had paintings of Scottish mountain scenes on two of the walls.

'I'm sorry about this,' said Sunita, 'but this has been an horrendous murder and we want to find the culprit as quickly as possible.'

'I've already given a statement to your DC Khalid,' Aimee continued as she slumped down onto a sumptuous grey settee like a sulky teenager. 'I'm sure I won't be able to tell you anything more.'

'I think my boss is worried we might overlook something,' said Sunita, sitting on a dining chair so she could face the woman. 'You say in your statement you heard someone knocking and calling, "Come out, Miles" and "Open the bloody door."'

Aimee nodded. 'Yes. Jake Harris. He lives above Miles.'

'How did you hear this when the music was playing?'

'Well, as you can see, my flat's only a short distance from Miles's flat. It shows you how angry that man Jake must have been for me to be able to hear him. I heard him charge downstairs like a... I don't know, like a Viking warrior.'

'So you watched as he kicked the door in?' Sunita asked.

'I was horrified. I recognised him as the man from Flat 7 upstairs. I sometimes chat to his girlfriend, Hannah, who lives with him.'

'What time was it when you saw him breaking in?'

'Sometime after ten.'

'Can you be any more specific?'

'Oh, hold on. I'd started watching the news. So it must have been about three minutes past ten.'

'Your statement says he was carrying a cricket bat.'

'Yes, that's right. And he didn't have the look of a man set to score runs on the cricket field either.'

'You couldn't see his face but you knew he was angry because of the banging and shouting.'

Aimee nodded. 'I was shocked by how shameless he was, breaking down a fellow resident's front door. Then I heard him smashing up Miles's sound system. I mean, I know we've all been suffering from our noisy neighbour, but to charge inside, smash up his gear and then split his head open with an axe? It's the actions of a madman.'

Sunita, who had been taking notes, put her small book down on the nearby table. 'The police don't know for certain that Jake attacked Miles with an axe,' she said. 'We're keeping an open mind at this stage.'

'No?' said Aimee. 'Then who else could have done it?'

'Listen,' said Sunita. 'You didn't actually see him using an axe as a weapon, did you?'

'No, but he was standing over the body when we went into the flat. Maybe the axe belonged to Miles.'

'Do you know what Miles does for work?'

'Well, he wasn't a lumberjack, if that's what you're thinking. No, until recently he'd been working as what they call a lighting rigger, putting up lights for major shows and concerts at places like Earls Court and the O2. But he was trying to move into events management or talent management or something. That's what Miles told me anyway.'

Sunita wondered whether Miles would have owned an axe as part of his toolkit as a rigger. If that was the case, he could have been smitten by his own axe. The idea was forming in her mind that the killer – possibly Jake Harris – had seen the axe among Miles's belongings and taken the opportunity to use it as a weapon.

'Aimee, you say in your statement that you knew your neighbour Jake Harris was hot-tempered. How did you know that?'

Aimee drew her legs up onto the settee and wrapped her arms round them. 'I've heard him arguing with his girlfriend, Hannah, on a couple of occasions while they were searching for their door key. Once he was calling her a bitch. Another time he was shouting, "You're wrong and you just can't admit it," then he swore at her. I've also heard him slamming doors and I've been told he's been in court for assault.'

'Any idea which court?'

'I think it was Worcester magistrates.'

Sunita picked up her pen and began writing notes again. 'You also say in your statement that Hannah came down the stairs and the pair of you entered the flat. What time would that have been?'

'Just a few minutes later. Certainly no later than ten minutes past ten.'

'You saw Jake Harris actually standing over Miles's body?'

'Yes,' said Aimee. 'He ordered us not to come into the flat. He obviously didn't want us to see what he'd done. But I suppose Hannah was concerned about him. I was just curious to see what had happened. I'd seen the man breaking in and heard smashing. I'd decided he was capable of doing anything. When we reached the lounge, there he was – looking proud of himself, staring down at his murderous handiwork.'

'You don't think Miles might have been dead already and that Jake was just a witness, like you and Hannah?'

'No. He broke in with murderous intentions. When Miles confronted him, Jake obviously went mad and killed him. It's the only thing that makes sense.'

* * *

Sunita was contemplating what Aimee had told her as she left the woman's flat and walked along the corridor that led to the main doors.

She was about to step outside and read the messages that had been left alongside three bouquets of flowers outside the entrance when she noticed a short, neatly dressed man lingering by the foot of the stairs.

'Are you– are you police?' he asked.

'Yes,' she replied.

'I spoke to a detective last night, DC Khalid.'

'Last night? You mean early this morning.'

'That's right,' said the dark-haired Asian man.

'Sorry, you're a resident, are you?' she asked.

'That's right. Ali Aziz. I'm in Flat 8 upstairs. It's just that something's been on my mind.'

'Perhaps we should go and talk in your flat,' she suggested.

Aziz led the sergeant up the stairs to his home, adjacent to the flat shared by Jake Harris and Hannah Taylor.

He led her into his gloomy hallway and shut the door.

'Let me get this right,' said Sunita. 'You've already given a statement to us about the death of Miles Kenworth?'

'Yes. Mr Khalid talked to me for a long time. You see, I think I was one of the only people in the building who used to talk to him. We both moved in about the same time a few months ago. Well, after Mr Khalid left, I got to thinking about this terrible murder and whether there was anything else I could think of that might help police. Then I remembered that, last evening, I was moving some furniture into my place.'

'What time was this?'

'Must have been around seven thirty. The music stopped briefly for a time. I thought he was changing the track or something.'

'So what's the significance of this?'

'Well, I'm just thinking that I wedged the main door open for about ten minutes.'

'Till twenty to eight?'

'Something like that. I'd bought some new tables and chairs. It occurred to me, after I heard about what happened to Miles, someone without permission might have been able to gain entry to the building around this time.'

'That's very helpful, Ali. Thank you for mentioning that. It's a possibility, isn't it? You didn't see anyone going in – such as a stranger?'

'No.'

'You say you knew Miles fairly well. Did you know about his private life? Did he have a girlfriend, for example?'

Ali paused to think. 'Miles had just broken up with a long-term girlfriend. I don't know her name, but she works as a riding instructor at some local stables.'

'Any idea where she might live?' asked Sunita.

'Oh, now you've got me,' he replied. 'I think it's somewhere on the other side of Queensbridge. Something he told me made me think she lived there. That's about all I know, except that he came from a wealthy family.'

'Did he?'

'Yes, have you heard of Culverdon Hall?'

'Yes, vaguely.'

'He was the black sheep of the family. Apparently, his mother died and his father stopped having anything to do with him.'

'That's sad.'

Sunita drew back the door and stepped onto the landing. She handed him a small card.

'Here's my direct line. Please feel free to call me if anything else occurs to you,' she said.

'Oh, there's one more thing I should probably mention,' said Ali as she began walking down the stairs. 'After Miles broke up with his girlfriend, he told me the woman's family were absolutely furious with him. They'd only recently got engaged, you see, and they'd been planning a big wedding.'

Chapter 6

'You're going to have to help us a lot more than you've done so far,' the chief inspector insisted as he stared at the burly transport manager sitting across the table from him.

'I've told you everything I know,' Jake Harris replied. 'I came with you willingly because I didn't have anything to hide and you'd every right to talk to me about why I was in Miles's flat. But I've given my explanation and I think you should let me go home now.'

The thirty-year-old leaned back in his chair in the interview room at Queensbridge police station and yawned. He peered hopefully into the faces of Roscoe and DC Khalid. He looked bedraggled. He was still wearing the same casual clothes he'd worn the previous evening.

Khalid, a serious-minded detective, folded his arms. 'We can't let you go until we've worked out who's telling the truth about how you came to be in Mr Kenworth's flat.'

'Yes,' agreed Roscoe. 'Your account differs widely from the one given to us by one of the residents. You're still happy to proceed without a solicitor?'

Harris nodded.

'Very well. Mr Harris, you say you went down to Mr Kenworth's flat simply to ask him politely if he'd mind turning his music down. You found the door had been forced and, becoming concerned for his welfare, you went inside, found the damaged hi-fi equipment and discovered Mr Kenworth dead in his living room.'

'That's right,' said Harris before giving a yawn. He had been awake in his cell for most of the night.

'Our witness, on the other hand, maintains she saw you outside the flat with a cricket bat. She says you broke into the flat by booting the door in,' Roscoe continued. 'The music stopped almost at once and she heard something being smashed. She tells us she herself then entered, along with your partner Miss Taylor, and found you hovering over the body.'

'It's Aimee you're talking about, isn't it? She's got that wrong,' said Harris. 'I'm a professional man. I'm a transport manager responsible for a fleet of lorries. I'm not the kind of person who breaks down people's doors.'

Roscoe shook his head. He stood up and collected a transparent bag containing a cricket bat from the back of the room. He placed it on the table.

'For the purposes of the DIR, I'm showing Mr Harris exhibit A,' he said, 'an English willow bat made by Humphreys and Littlejohn. Do you accept that this is your bat, Mr Harris?'

The suspect stared down at the wooden bat. The makers' name was clearly visible.

'It's not mine,' he said. 'I don't play cricket.'

Roscoe tutted. 'We've been told you used to keep wicket for Shawley Green Cricket Club.'

'That was a long time ago. What I mean is I don't play now. So why would I have a bat?'

'Our witness is adamant that she saw you brandishing a bat. Our forensic people have examined it carefully and found some dents which suggest it was used to damage the music equipment. There are also microscopic fragments of black plastic embedded in the bat. And, of course, it was on the floor beside you when the witness and your partner entered the living room.'

'Maybe it belonged to Miles,' he insisted.

Khalid sneered. 'What?' he said. 'Are you suggesting he might have smashed up his own equipment?'

'Maybe he was high on drugs,' Harris suggested.

Roscoe leaned back on his chair as Khalid raised his voice. 'Maybe he damaged his own front door, Mr Harris, and then maybe went inside and attacked himself with the axe,' said the constable.

Harris stared out of the barred window into the police vehicle yard outside.

'Look, I'm an innocent party in all this,' he said. 'It was just coincidence that I was there after someone had broken in and attacked Miles. I was as shocked as anybody else at finding him in that state. There's no way I'd have smashed his head in like that.'

The chief inspector opened a folder containing several sheets of paper. He placed them on the desk one at a time, like a bank cashier counting out notes.

'We've found your antecedents, Mr Harris,' he said. 'It doesn't make very comfortable reading. In May 2010, when you were seventeen, you were given a two-hundred-hour community order by Worcester magistrates for common assault on a man you'd been out drinking with.

'Three years later, you were up before the Queensbridge bench and received a twelve-month community order for an affray outside a pub.'

Harris nodded. 'Yes, it was a stupid row over a woman.'

'And then seven years ago, you were given a suspended prison sentence and fined £550 for common assault on your then girlfriend.'

'Yes,' said Harris. 'It's all to do with drink. But I've given up alcohol now and you'll see that I've not been in trouble for seven years. My probation officer blames youthful exuberance.'

Khalid glared into the suspect's eyes. 'You say youthful exuberance. We say proven violent streak.'

He shook his head vigorously. 'That's not fair. I really am a changed man – since I met Hannah – and I've been keeping a clean sheet. My boss says he might put me in charge of a second depot soon.'

Roscoe shook his head. 'You agree that this list is an accurate record of your past offences?'

'Yes.'

'All right. At the least, you're looking at a charge of causing criminal damage. We're going to keep you here at the station for a little while longer while we discuss what action we're going to take.'

Roscoe strode to the door, opened it and called a uniformed constable, who then escorted Harris, complaining bitterly, back to his cell in the basement.

'Early next week, Khalid, I want you to become a leading expert on axes and hatchets,' the chief inspector said.

'We've got to find out whether the weapon that ended Miles Kenworth's life belonged to him or whether it was brought to Flat 1 by someone else. Contact the makers. See if you can find out where and when it was purchased. Ask Dr Ling in forensics if it's got a serial number or product number.'

Alice Ling was the senior forensic scientist, based at police headquarters.

'Right, sir. No problem.'

'So what do you think of our edgy suspect, Khalid?' asked the chief inspector.

'Well, we know he's told us lies,' said the constable. 'The statement from the neighbour, Aimee, is much more compelling evidence than his. His partner, Hannah Taylor, supports his story that he only went downstairs to have a polite word with Kenworth. But when we showed her the bat, I was watching her face. I'm certain she recognised it, although she kept denying it belonged to Harris.'

'So you think he's lying?'

'Yes,' said Khalid.

'If he is lying, why?' said Roscoe. 'Is it simply because he doesn't want us to nail him for causing damage to property?'

'No, sir. I think it's more than that,' said Khalid. 'I'm inclined to believe he broke in, rampaged through the flat and was in such a temper he murdered Kenworth in cold blood.'

Chapter 7

It was a mild, cloudy afternoon when the chief inspector arrived at his home on the outskirts of Queensbridge in his navy-blue BMW. He parked in the garage next to his 1930s detached home, The Willows, and stepped onto the gravel drive.

He was delighted to find his twenty-five-year-old son, George, standing by the open front door, ready to greet him.

'This is an unexpected surprise, George,' he exclaimed after the pair entered the hall.

'I'm just back for one night,' explained George, who worked as a constable in Warwick. 'Amanda's gone to see her parents, so I thought I'd drop by.'

'It's great to see you,' said his father. 'Your mother should be back soon. Shall we have some tea?'

After making them both tea, the pair sat down together in the dual-aspect living room.

'We're buying a flat in Warwick,' George announced with a smile as he turned the volume down on the television.

Roscoe placed his cup of tea on a side table before walking to the patio doors at the far end of the room and gazing out into the back garden.

'You've found a suitable place already?' he asked without averting his gaze from the garden.

'Yes. It's got two beds. It's not far from Warwick Racecourse.'

'Oh, so not far from DS Roy's place,' he said, turning round to face his son. 'And you're sure you can afford it?'

'Yes, we can just afford it on our combined income. Oh Dad, it'll be such a relief to get out of my lodgings.'

He sat beside his son on the settee and sipped some tea. 'So when do you think you'll move in?'

'Oh, it could be some time yet. Our offer's only just been accepted and the whole process could take weeks. Anyway, how have you been getting on, Dad?'

'Oh, much the same. You heard about the death in Fishpond Lane last night, did you?'

George nodded. 'Only that there'd been a suspicious death.'

'It's murder, George, but the media team are only just revealing details to the press today.'

'I expect it might be in the papers then,' said George. 'Listen, I've got some other news. I told Mum on the phone this morning. Amanda and I are getting married next month.'

A broad smile crept across the chief inspector's face.

'Well, that's wonderful news.'

'We went together to see Peter Hughes,' said George.

'The rector over at Norton Prior?'

'Yes, Dad. We both wanted a church wedding, but the only building we both like is St John the Martyr. We're entitled to hold it there because you and Mum once lived in the parish for more than six months.'

'Can I hear a car? I think your mother's home.'

He stood up and peered through the blinds. Helen Roscoe's blue Fiesta was pulling into the drive. He opened the front door for her and kissed her on the cheek as she hurried inside.

'We've been so busy today, darling,' she said, pausing in front of a mirror to straighten her long, blonde hair. 'We couldn't have managed without Mel.'

Right on cue, their lively daughter Melody, who was a year younger than her brother, came in from the car. As their mother headed into the kitchen, she joined the men in the living room.

'Dad, I found out something today that might interest you,' she said after sitting down next to her brother. 'You know the man who died in Fishpond Lane?'

'Yes, that's a case I'm dealing with,' said her father solemnly as he stepped into the middle of the room and leaned against the open-brick fireplace.

'Well, earlier on I was chatting to one of my friends from the riding school. One of the instructors has gone AWOL. Ursula Grey. My friend thinks she's the dead man's girlfriend or ex-girlfriend. She hasn't been seen

28

around the stables the whole day and they've had to cancel all her lessons.'

Her father turned one of the dining chairs round and sat down.

'This is Green Meadow Riding School in Inkberrow?' he asked.

She nodded. 'Yes, Dad.'

'I don't suppose you know where she lives, do you?'

'I think it might be Glebe Gardens or Glebe Drive.'

'In Queensbridge?'

'Yes.'

'Thank you. I'll get someone to look into that.'

* * *

Later that evening, as he was relaxing with his family watching television, the chief inspector received a call from Sunita Roy.

'Sir, I'm sorry to disturb you,' she began as he stepped out into the hall to take the call. 'I've discovered that Miles Kenworth is from a well-to-do family. His full name is the Honourable Miles Cedric Kenworth and he's the younger son of Lord Culverdon.'

'Good God! That's the family that owns Culverdon Hall near Stratford-on-Avon. How on earth did Miles end up in a one-bed flat in Fishpond Lane? I've heard the phrase "how the mighty have fallen". In his case, it's more like "crash-landed".'

'One of the witnesses says he fell out with his father. Sir, I thought I should go over to Culverdon Hall tomorrow and talk to the family.'

'That's a very good idea. I think I'll break my rule about Sunday being a family day and join you. We need to find out all we can about Miles Kenworth. There's a good chance we'll be able to catch the whole family at home.'

Chapter 8

Lavinia Faulkner stepped slowly down the sweeping cantilevered staircase in a light-blue dressing gown and suede Gucci-monogrammed slippers.

'Sarah, is my father up yet?' she asked the housekeeper, who was passing through the vaulted hallway, carrying a jug of milk and packets of cereal.

'I haven't seen Lord Culverdon this morning, ma'am,' Sarah replied as she continued her journey into the dining room. 'Would you be wanting a cooked breakfast?'

'Yes, please, Sarah,' Lavinia continued in a husky, smoker's voice. 'Have you seen the weather forecast for today?'

'Light rain but some sunshine,' Sarah replied as she hurried on.

Lavinia, whose blonde hair was styled in a mid-length, wavy bob, walked into the light, airy dining room which had high ceilings and two sash windows flanked by blue curtains.

'Good morning, Rupert,' she called to her husband, who was drinking coffee at the far end of the long mahogany table. 'Couldn't you sleep?'

'Slept well. Only just got up,' he replied. 'Have you thought any more about the funeral?'

'Oh, for God's sake, Rupert. My poor brother was only found dead two days ago. Give us time to grieve before we have to think about that.'

'I didn't mean to be indelicate,' Rupert replied in an educated voice. He was more than six feet tall when standing. He had a bony face with a long jaw and piercing blue eyes.

Lavinia sat down in a cream-coloured, upholstered chair opposite him.

'It's just that arrangements will eventually have to be made,' he said.

She frowned. 'I know, but a funeral's the last thing on my mind. In any case, Daddy's been told it may be a while before we can hold one. The coroner won't release the body at least until after a post-mortem and even then it's unlikely to happen quickly.'

She glanced at her watch as her father entered the room. Lord Culverdon smiled broadly.

'Good morning to you both,' he said, stroking his grey beard. 'Did you both manage to get any sleep?'

'Not much,' said Lavinia. 'Daddy, I'm going to go to the kitchen and see what's happened to Sarah.'

After she had swept out of the room, her father poured himself an orange juice at a side table and chose a chair close to his daughter's.

'Still can't get the terrible news about Miles out of my mind, you know, Rupert?'

His son-in-law nodded. 'I know. Such a horrendous way to die. Do you think the police will find the culprit quickly?'

'Who knows?' said Lord Culverdon as he sipped his cold drink beneath an oil painting of a dapple-grey horse in woodland which hung above the fireplace. 'You see, Rupert? This is what happens if you abandon your family and go off the rails.'

'I'm not sure he actually went off the rails, sir,' said Rupert. 'I think he just got tired of the pressures of life on the estate.'

Lord Culverdon tutted. 'He was a bloody rebel,' he said in a deep, cultured voice. 'Had too much mollycoddling when he was young and grew up refusing to take any responsibility. Still I don't want to speak ill of him at this time.'

'Can't understand why he ever moved into that apartment in Queensbridge,' Rupert continued.

'He told me he fancied the simple life. After his mother's death and his nervous breakdown, he ventured out on a different path in life in an effort to find happiness. He always said he'd found it. He was doing a job he claimed he loved, working with minor celebrities—'

'Mainly pop singers, wasn't it?'

'I think so. He said he was happy. But what concerned me was that he never seemed to find a woman to settle down with.'

Rupert took another sip of coffee. 'There was that woman from the riding school.'

'Ursula? Yes, I thought they might have tied the knot at some point, but in the end that fizzled out. I don't know why.'

'Who do you think could possibly have murdered him?'

Lord Culverdon shook his head. 'No idea. But he mixed with a rum lot of people. Any one of them could have done it. You know, it'll be to my eternal shame that we couldn't get him to remain here as part of the family. He'd had a good education. I set him up in a good job at a bank in the City, and look what happens. He just throws it all away.'

'That was more than ten years ago.'

'I know. But a day doesn't go by when I don't think: what if?'

Footsteps could be heard in the hall. Lavinia was returning.

'It's all right. Breakfast is on its way,' she said, as she resumed her seat beside her father.

Moments later, Sarah the housekeeper pushed a trolley into the room and began serving three steaming hot breakfasts.

* * *

A light drizzle was falling as the chief inspector left his home, ready for a fifteen-mile journey to Warwick.

Sunita Roy was waiting outside her flat in the town's Crompton Gardens when he drew up at 10.15 a.m. She smiled as she climbed into his car.

'How do you always manage to look like a burst of summer sunshine first thing in the morning, Sergeant? I looked a wreck when I got up an hour ago and still don't feel too lively.'

'I think I'm a morning person. I'm always inclined to be more active at the start of the day.'

As they set off on the road to Culverdon Hall, seven miles away, he regaled his sergeant with a colourful account of how he once, as a young detective in his twenties, had to go to the stately home to arrest one of the gardeners.

'I'll never forget,' said Roscoe. 'His name was McGinty and he was caught growing cannabis in one of His Lordship's potting sheds. Of course, it's a magnificent place, you know. It's a Grade II-listed Palladian country mansion and its landscaped deer park stretches across something like a hundred and eighty acres.'

It was nearly a quarter to eleven when the two detectives, after travelling for two miles along narrow country lanes, reached a Victorian gatehouse and then the black metal entrance gates to the estate.

Their car swept past oak and elm trees which stood at intervals along the narrow drive. Here and there, they spotted groups of deer grazing beneath the trees.

'What a fantastic house,' Sunita remarked as they approached the hall.

'Yes,' said Roscoe. 'If I remember rightly, they've got thirty bedrooms and six bathrooms. There's a lake, tennis courts, a swimming pool and a stable block. The main house was remodelled in the 1930s by the tenth Viscount Culverdon.'

'The cost of the upkeep must be phenomenal,' she said.

'It would be if they hadn't come to an arrangement with the National Trust a few years ago. Part of the main building and the formal gardens are open to the public, but the family continue to reside in the east wing.'

'What do we know of the family?' she asked as they approached a gravel turning circle with an ornamental fountain outside the hall's main entrance.

'Not much,' said Roscoe. 'I know the good lord can't be short of a bob or two. He's spent his life working in the City as an investment banker and he's chairman of a host of companies. Lady Culverdon died about fifteen years ago and the eldest son went missing about two years ago. Do you remember? It was in all the papers at the time.'

'Was he on holiday somewhere when it happened?'

'That's right. Tragic accident while out hiking. Missing, presumed dead. I believe there's a married daughter still around who lives here at the hall, along with His Lordship.'

The pair stepped out of the car and began walking towards the main doors, which were flanked by Doric pillars. A sign saying 'Private Residence' directed them along a concrete path to the left, which was shielded by hedges. They followed it round to the side of the house.

Finally, they came to an oak door, which was partly open.

A mellow male voice came from nowhere. 'Can I help you?'

They spun round to be confronted by a man who looked the epitome of an English country gentleman. Two liver and white cocker spaniels accompanied him.

'Heart of England CID,' said the chief inspector, slipping his warrant card from his pocket. 'DCI Roscoe. This is DS Roy. Is Lord Culverdon about?'

'Oh, I can guess what this is about,' said the man, peering over his black-framed glasses. 'I'm Charles Laxton, Lord Culverdon's estate manager. You'd better follow me. They're in the morning room.'

Laxton tied the two spaniels to a metal railing and then led the detectives inside.

While they crossed the black-and-white tiled floor, Roscoe said quietly, 'Mr Laxton, please don't go far away. We'll need to talk to you in a minute as well.'

Laxton said nothing. He simply nodded before leading them into the morning room, where the sixty-two-year-old head of the house was sitting on a red chesterfield club chair. He was chatting to his daughter.

Laxton announced, 'The police are here,' before departing.

Lord Culverdon glanced round at his visitors while remaining in his chair. Lavinia stared across the table at them.

'Please come in,' Lord Culverdon boomed. 'And whom do we have the pleasure of addressing?'

Roscoe stepped forward into the room until the peer could see him. 'I'm DCI Roscoe from Heart of England Police, sir,' he said with a friendly smile. 'This is DS Roy.'

Sunita moved forward to stand beside her boss. 'We're deeply sorry to call at a time like this,' she said.

'We'll do all we can to help you,' Lavinia promised in a low voice as she walked towards them and invited them to sit on a chesterfield settee.

'Yes, well, what do you want to know?' said Lord Culverdon.

'Well, could we begin by asking when you last saw your son, Miles, or when you last spoke to him?' Roscoe asked.

'I haven't seen him for about two years,' Lord Culverdon replied.

Sunita wasn't focused on the conversation. She was watching through the window as a man in a shooting jacket and flat cap helped two spaniels into a green Land Rover Discovery, jumped behind the wheel and raced away down the drive. It was the man they had asked to wait for them, Charles Laxton.

Chapter 9

Lord Culverdon stretched himself out on his chair and yawned.

'To be totally honest, I've only seen the boy about three times in the last thirteen years,' he said. 'He didn't want to have anything further to do with the family.'

Roscoe leaned forward. 'Was this because of a family row, sir?'

'You could say that. He went to pieces fifteen years ago when Lady Culverdon died. Had a breakdown and didn't want the job I found him in the City. He changed. After a few months, he said he couldn't stand living here anymore and wanted to find a different life.'

'Is that when he went to live in Fishpond Lane?'

He shook his head. 'No. Although I only spoke to him a few times, I received regular reports from people who kept in touch with him or saw him around. He went through a number of addresses—'

The sergeant broke in to ask, 'He always managed to pay his way, sir?'

'Yes, he never owed anyone money, as far as I know. He started working as a member of a lighting crew, helping to put on pop concerts. Then I heard he moved into events promotion and talent management. He was always crazy about music – not classical, the noisy modern music played with guitars and drums.'

Lavinia, who had been listening to the conversation, interrupted them. 'He was a bit of a musician himself. He could play both the piano and the guitar very well,' she said.

'Sorry,' said Sunita, 'are you—'

'I'm Lavinia Faulkner, Miles's sister,' she explained.

Roscoe gazed across at Lord Culverdon. 'So, just to be clear, you saw your son two years ago, sir?' he asked.

'That's correct, Chief Inspector,' he said. 'It must have been about the time of his brother Arthur's tragic accident. He just phoned to ask what we knew and catch up with family news. Lavinia spent more time talking to him than me.'

'So how would you describe your relationship with Miles?'

'Well, it had completely broken down. And he only had himself to blame. He was a bloody rebel.'

Lavinia yelled, 'That's very unfair, Daddy. He was just a little mixed up.'

'No, he was a bloody rebel.'

'And, Lavinia, what about you?' asked Roscoe. 'When did you last see your brother Miles?'

'I saw a little more of him than Daddy,' she said. 'I once went round to his flat in Fishpond Lane. That was about two months ago – shortly after he moved in.'

Sunita turned her eyes first towards Lord Culverdon and then to Lavinia. 'Do either of you have any idea who might have done this terrible thing to Miles?' she asked.

'No, not at all,' said the peer.

'Did your son own an axe or did you ever see him with one?' she said.

'We do a lot of wood cutting on the estate as you can imagine. We've got several hundred trees, but I've never seen Miles with an axe or in fact seen him so much as snap off a branch,' said Lord Culverdon.

Lavinia removed her iPhone from her Gucci handbag and began tapping out a text message to somebody. Sunita considered it the height of rudeness.

The chief inspector gave the matter no attention. He was keen to ask Lord Culverdon a few more questions. 'Sergeant, if you've finished for the moment, I'd like to ask you, sir, how your wife and first son came to die,' he said. 'I'm sorry if the question brings back unhappy memories.'

'That's all right,' he replied. 'Cordelia died from a heart attack at the age of forty-five and then there was Arthur's unexpected death in Spain. You could say we've been dogged by tragedy.'

'Very sad,' said Roscoe. 'I'm most terribly sorry to hear what you've been through.'

'Me too,' whispered his sergeant. In a louder voice, she asked, 'By the way, Mrs Faulkner, I understand you're married. Is that correct?'

Lavinia nodded. 'Yes. My husband is Rupert Faulkner.'

'Is he around at the moment?'

'He's down in the stables. I've just sent him a text message. He'll be up in a minute. I know he'd be pleased to talk to you.'

'Now, this is important,' said Roscoe. 'Can I ask you, sir, where you were on Friday?'

Lord Culverdon stroked his beard. 'Let me think. I was at the House of Lords in the morning. After lunch, I chaired a directors' meeting in Lombard Street before going to the National Liberal Club for a light tea. I got home here at about ten o'clock.'

'That's fine,' he said. Inwardly, he was surprised at the speed with which the peer summarised his day – like a speech he'd been rehearsing for his parliamentary chums.

Turning to Lavinia, he asked her the same question.

'I was here on the estate most of the day,' she replied.

'Lavinia has always been the most trusted and responsible member of this family,' Lord Culverdon remarked. 'The running of the estate nowadays is mainly down to her and her husband, while I spend a great deal of time in London.'

'On Friday, I spent most of the day in the estate office,' Lavinia explained. 'I was supervising staff who were pruning the fruit trees and hedge-laying.'

'And in the evening?' Roscoe asked.

'I went to visit some friends and was back here by nine thirty.'

'Thank you,' said Roscoe. 'Perhaps you could give me the names of your friends and their address later. Your husband wasn't with you on Friday night then?'

'Um, no.'

Sunita interrupted. 'Do you know where he was that evening?'

She shrugged. 'I think he was here most of the day. You'd have to ask him. He'll be here in a minute.'

Sunita shuffled round uneasily in her seat. Unlike the chief inspector, she was unaccustomed to interviewing members of an upper-class family.

'We were shown into the room by your estate manager,' Sunita said. 'We wanted a quick word with him, but I noticed him driving away a short while ago.'

Lavinia looked as comfortable as a prestige job recruit who'd arrived unprepared for an interview.

'I'm sorry. He probably had an urgent appointment. Could you come back to see him later?'

The chief inspector said they would try to contact him later in the week.

'We could show you round the house and orangery if you came back another time,' said her father. 'I'm busy this morning. I've arranged to go riding.'

'Very kind, sir,' said Roscoe. 'But from now on we're going to be heavily tied up, investigating your son's untimely death.'

'Of course,' Lord Culverdon said with a smile.

Roscoe glanced at Lavinia. 'Mrs Faulkner, could you kindly ask Charles Laxton to phone us on this number when he's got a moment?' he said, handing over his card.

'No problem,' she replied.

'Do either of you have a photograph of Miles, by any chance?' the chief inspector asked.

'I'll fetch one for you in a minute,' said Lavinia.

'Sir, I was wondering if I could ask another question?' Sunita asked the chief inspector.

'Please, go ahead,' said her boss.

'Thank you. Mrs Faulkner, I wanted to ask if you had any knowledge of your brother's girlfriends.'

'I knew a little about his personal life,' Lavinia replied. 'But brothers can be so secretive. I know there was Ursula. I met her once at a pop concert two years ago. They'd only been going out together for a short time at that stage.'

'Were there other women?'

'Who knows?'

'Do you know why the relationship with Ursula ended?' asked Sunita. 'I mean, if they'd been close for around two years, as we've been led to believe, there must have been a good reason.'

Lavinia shrugged her shoulders. 'Maybe he just grew tired of her. That sometimes happens.'

Sunita looked directly into her eyes. 'I've been told the woman concerned was devastated.'

Lavinia shook her head. 'I've no idea,' she said.

'Do you know Ursula's family at all?'

'No. Ursula told me herself that she lived in Queensbridge. But I've no knowledge of where her family are. All I know is that her father runs a security firm.'

'Ursula and your brother had become engaged and had been planning a big wedding,' said Sunita. 'We're told her family were livid when he broke it off.'

'I can quite understand if they were annoyed with him. After a two-year relationship, a wedding proposal and an engagement, I'd have been incandescent with rage,' said Lavinia.

Chapter 10

The two detectives followed Lavinia Faulkner along the corridor and into a vast room with a small sign on the door saying 'Library'.

Most of the walls were stacked from floor to ceiling with books. Each bay of shelves had a classical writer's name painted on the cornice above.

However, two large sash windows at the far end ensured it was a light, airy room.

The pair chose to sit on one of several green leather settees and were at once joined by Lavinia's husband.

'I had no idea you were here,' said Rupert, taking a seat in one of the matching armchairs. 'I was just seeing to the horses. It's most desperately sad about poor old Miles.'

'This is DCI Roscoe from Heart of England CID,' Lavinia explained as she stood by the door. 'And his sergeant – I'm sorry, I've forgotten your name.'

'DS Roy,' said Sunita.

'They've already spoken to Daddy,' Lavinia added. 'So I'll leave you to it.'

'Thanks for all your help, Mrs Faulkner,' said Roscoe as she left the room, promising to find them a photograph of her dead brother.

'We don't need to take up much of your time,' the chief inspector said. 'Just needed to ask a few questions. When did you last see your brother-in-law, Miles?'

'That's a difficult one,' replied Rupert, who was brushing some dust off his khaki waistcoat. 'I used to bump into him occasionally. I think the last time would have been just after Christmas. I was driving into Queensbridge and recognised the car in front as his silver Nissan Qashqai.'

'Did you catch up and speak to him?'

'I haven't spoken to him for years. He wasn't among my circle of friends. Don't get me wrong. I had nothing against the guy. He was a pleasant enough chap. It's just that he'd caused a bit of upset in the family and I didn't want to annoy Lavinia or His Lordship by becoming too pally with him.'

There was a tap on the door, which caused Rupert to spin round.

'Yes? What is it, Sarah?' he asked as the smartly dressed housekeeper appeared in the doorway.

'Sorry to interrupt, sir, but Mrs Faulkner asked me to come up and see if anyone wanted some tea?'

Rupert turned to his guests. 'Of course,' he said. 'Would either of you like tea? Or perhaps some coffee?'

'Not for me,' said Roscoe. He glanced at his sergeant, who shook her head.

'That's very considerate, but we must be going in a moment,' she said.

As the housekeeper left, Sunita asked Rupert, 'Are there any other full-time staff members?'

'There's Hilary in the estate office and Mr McGrath who cares for the horses. Otherwise, no – just Sarah. Oh, and there are a couple of cleaners who come in for a few hours every day.'

At that moment, Lavinia stepped into the room, holding a photograph of Miles.

'Will this do?' she asked.

Roscoe gazed at the colour image of a tall, handsome man in his mid-thirties, smiling as he stood beside a silver car.

'This will be fine. Thank you,' he said.

As Lavinia nodded and left the room, he drew a small black notebook from an inside pocket and turned his attention to Rupert again.

'Could we ask where you were on Friday, sir?'

Rupert glanced down at the polished oak floor.

'I was at a community theatre in Stratford, rehearsing for an amateur production of *Julius Caesar*,' he said. 'One of my first ventures as a thespian.'

'Is that the Avon Players?' asked Roscoe.

'Yes. We're lucky enough to perform in Shakespeare's home town. I'm playing Brutus.'

'The guy who plunged the knife into Caesar?'

'Precisely. It's getting quite nerve-racking now. We've only got three weeks to go before opening.'

Roscoe frowned.

'We'd need to vouch for you being there on Friday,' Roscoe continued. 'So we will need details of one of your fellow performers, sir.'

'Why don't you speak to Craig Armitage? He's the stage manager and was around for most of the evening.'

'Where exactly are you staging this production?'

'Stratford East Memorial Hall.'

'Well, if you'd like to give me this man's phone number, I'll have a word with him. I might come along to the opening. I'm quite a fan of Shakespeare.'

Rupert read out the phone number. Roscoe jotted it down in his notebook, beside the man's name.

Sunita had been watching Rupert's face throughout the discussion.

'I was just wondering if I could ask something,' she said. 'Sorry that it's rather personal, but could I ask how long you've been married, and how you came to meet Mrs Faulkner?'

'Yes, of course. We met on a cruise in the Mediterranean about three and a half years ago and were married six months later. I'm pleased to say we hit it off straight away. We had a lot of common interests – including polo, croquet, shooting and classic car events. But the one thing that really brought us together was our mutual love of horses.'

'So you both live here at the house with Lord Culverdon?'

'That's right. We tend to monopolize the rear of the east wing, whereas His Lordship resides in the front.'

Sunita nodded. 'Do you work on the estate, sir?'

'As little as possible,' he replied. 'No, I'm joking. I help tend to the horses. We've got six at the moment. I also get involved from time to time in work around the estate – building hedges, tree felling. That sort of thing.'

Roscoe glanced across at his sergeant. They both nodded.

'Thank you, Mr Faulkner,' he said. 'I think we've got all we need for the moment.'

* * *

'So what did you make of the Kenworth family?' asked the chief inspector as he drove them back down the driveway.

'Lord Culverdon and Mr Faulkner were pleasant enough,' she replied. 'They were both helpful, but I found Lavinia a bit of a cold fish.'

'You're far too polite about them,' said Roscoe with a smile that could have lit up a darkened street. 'I find folk from our upper classes, like them, to be rather pompous and patronizing. Give me an ordinary fellow who works hard and remains true to his roots over our landed classes any day.'

Sunita smiled back. 'I've got to say I was surprised the atmosphere was rather upbeat. I'd have expected a greater show of grief at the loss of their youngest family member.'

'These people don't like to give any sign of weakness to the likes of us. They grieve inwardly and show a stiff upper lip to the outside world. Of course, you've probably heard of the so-called curse of the Culverdons?'

'No, sir. What's that?'

'There's a legend that one of the first Viscount Culverdons upset an old woman by dismissing her from his employment. She ended up in prison, accused of bad debt and witchcraft. While awaiting trial, she stopped eating and wasted away. Then, on her deathbed, she placed a curse on the nobleman's sons and their descendants. For centuries many of the men from the family were destined to die before they reached forty.'

Sunita laughed. 'That's all nonsense, isn't it?'

'I suppose so. Nonetheless, over the generations, there've been many early deaths on the male side of the family through alcoholism, suicide and motoring accidents.'

Sunita laughed again. 'I think that's more to do with the riotous lifestyles that young men from these noble families tend to engage in rather than some medieval myth.'

As they turned out of the narrow country lane and headed onto the main Warwick road, Sunita had a suspicion that solving the mystery of Miles Kenworth's murder was going to prove more challenging than they had first thought.

'Despite His Lordship's hostility towards his son, I'm sure that, deep down, he must be upset at his loss – especially since the death happened in such a brutal way,' she said. 'I can't imagine His Lordship or any member of his family having any reason to harm a hair on his head.'

'I'm inclined to agree,' he said. 'It's important now to try and focus on Miles Kenworth's social and work life. It's so crucial in these cases to try to understand fully the life of the victim before you can understand the circumstances that led to the murder.'

Chapter 11

The chief inspector put on his dressing gown and stepped over to the window. He drew back the light-brown curtains and gazed out at the primroses, mauve crocuses and snowdrops now thriving in the back garden. It was a scene of rural serenity, he thought.

But moments later, he glanced at his watch and realised that it was half past eight – time he should be leaving the house. He must have forgotten to set the alarm.

'Any news about the riding instructor?' he asked his daughter Mel, after dressing and coming downstairs.

'She's told Martha she'll be coming back to work tomorrow,' said Mel as she sat down at the table and sipped from a mug of hot tea.

'Good. I might send someone round there,' he said. 'Have I got the right address? Green Meadow Riding School, Meadow Lane?'

'That's right.'

The chief inspector's hopes of a quiet day evaporated within minutes of his arriving in CID.

No sooner had he hung up his coat and switched on his computer than he received a call from Chief Superintendent Nicola Norris, requesting to see him.

He had once had a friendly relationship with his superior, but these days he dreaded visiting her office. Since tighter budgetary limits had been imposed from above, she took a greater interest in his activities – an attitude which, in his eyes, sometimes constituted interference.

He suspected she sought every opportunity to find fault with his style of operating, although he refused to endorse the nickname 'Niggler Norris', which colleagues sometimes used behind her back.

He climbed the stairs to the second floor and straightened his yellow tie before knocking on her door. His confidence began to seep away like sand in an egg timer.

'Come in!' she exclaimed.

Norris, a stern-faced woman with neatly combed, mid-length grey hair, was sitting in her wheelchair. She was studying some photographs of police award ceremonies on the left-hand wall. She always reminded him of his former headmistress at junior school. They were both women capable of instilling fear into the stoutest of hearts.

'Have you seen this photograph, Gavin? It's Sean Munro receiving his bravery award yesterday.'

Roscoe stared at the framed picture. His mind at once leaped back to the horrific moment, three years before, when his son's friend Sean had been shot tackling an escaped serial killer.

'Terrible business, ma'am,' he said. 'I'll never forget what that boy did.'

'Cost him his career in frontline policing,' she said.

'I'm afraid it did.'

'Anyway,' said Norris, propelling her wheelchair across the beige carpet towards her desk, 'how are things shaping up in CID?'

'Pretty good, ma'am. Of course, we're at least one senior staff member down. Tom Vickers is sorely missed.'

She shrugged. 'I haven't heard recently how he's getting on over in Summerstoke. Have you?'

'Not recently, but I imagine he's enjoying having charge of his own team.'

She moved her wheelchair until it was positioned behind her desk.

'Now look, Gavin,' she said. 'The assistant constable is keen to know what's happening about the axe murder. Did you see the Sunday papers? Look.'

She spread some newspapers out. One tabloid headline proclaimed, 'Peer's son in axe murder,' while another banner headline read, 'Axe murder victim in noise row.'

'It's very early days, ma'am,' he said, taking a seat. 'DS Roy and I were with Lord Culverdon yesterday morning. Although we were only alerted about the death of Miles Kenworth late on Friday, we've set up an incident room and the team are making reasonable progress.'

'Good,' she said. 'Any suspects in mind?'

'The team are focused on the victim's private life, ma'am. He loved loud music and we've been speaking to one of his neighbours, Jake Harris, whom we strongly suspect of being involved. We had to release him on Saturday, but he's on police bail and he's been requested to report to Queensbridge police once a week. He's been ordered to keep away from Waverley Court and stay at his brother's address, but he remains a person of interest.'

'That's encouraging,' she added.

* * *

As the chief inspector returned to his office, he immediately regretted mentioning the suspect Jake Harris to the chief superintendent.

He believed Harris may well have stormed into Flat 1 at Waverley Court with murderous intent. But he was not convinced he carried out the horrific act himself. Perhaps someone else got there before him, as Harris claimed.

Sunita Roy was waiting outside his first-floor room when he returned. 'Could I have a quick word, sir?' she asked.

'Yes, come on in,' he replied, ushering her in and closing the door.

'First of all, I wanted to thank you for letting me have next Wednesday off to visit Leicester.'

'Well, it's not very convenient right now. I can't deny that. But you so rarely take time off. I am hardly in any position to refuse.'

'Thank you,' she said as she drew up a chair. 'The other thing is I think we should stop treating Jake Harris as a suspect.'

'Why do you say that?' he replied.

'Well, there's the timing,' she said. 'The witness Aimee says she saw Harris break into Flat 1 at three minutes past ten. She and Harris's partner, Hannah, witnessed him stooping over the body no later than ten minutes past. Hannah gave the time in her statement as eight minutes past ten.'

'So what's the point you're making, Sergeant?' Roscoe asked as he sat down in his black executive chair.

'Well, that means Harris would have had a total of around five or six minutes to kick in the door, smash the sound system, find an axe inside the place, overpower Miles Kenworth and inflict countless wounds. Doesn't sound likely, does it, sir?'

'No, not in that time frame. You're right,' he replied. 'I'd already been thinking along those lines. So you believe the axe would have been inside the flat before Harris arrived?'

'It looks that way. Aimee only remembers seeing him with a bat, so I think we've got to assume that either the axe was already there as part of Miles's equipment or someone other than Harris brought it in. On top of that, who brazenly carries an axe into somebody's home? They'd have to walk along the street with it. There's then a high chance of being observed.'

'But they could have used some kind of container – such as a bag,' her boss pointed out.

'That's true. But I think everything points to the weapon being owned by Miles.'

She slipped her notebook from her jacket pocket and glanced at one of its pages before continuing.

'I've had some other thoughts, sir,' she said.

'Go on,' he said. 'As you know, I encourage members of my team to come up with their own ideas.'

'The whole manner of the axe attack seems strange,' she said. 'In order to use a heavy weapon like that, you probably need some element of surprise.'

'What do you mean – coming up behind them, for example?'

'Yes, or creeping up on them when they're asleep. If Miles had seen his attacker coming towards him with the weapon, he could have taken defensive action – you know, grabbing a chair, a small table or a cushion to ward off the blows.'

He nodded. 'Yes. That makes sense.'

'Then the third issue concerns how the killer gained entry,' she said. 'Did Miles let the killer in and then succumb to a surprise attack? Or did someone have a key?'

'As it's a ground floor place, the killer could have come in through the window,' said Roscoe. 'As you found yourself, the window handle had been left in the open position. The window had simply been pushed to – possibly by the killer when they left. I'll have to call Dr Ling in forensics about that and see if there's any news about DNA or dabs.'

'If the killer didn't enter through the window, there's also the question of how the killer would have got through the main door,' she said. 'Did they speak to Miles on the intercom and get him to buzz them in? Or did he or she follow someone else in?'

Roscoe leaned across his desk towards her. 'I was going through some of the statements last night. There's this guy Ali Aziz you spoke to. He says the main door was left wide open for ten minutes. I suppose it's possible the killer took advantage of the entrance being open.'

'Yes, sir.'

At that moment, there was a knock and DC Khalid put his head round the door.

'Sir, I've got some interesting information about the axe,' he said.

'Well, come in. Let's hear what you've got,' said the chief inspector enthusiastically.

Khalid was smiling as he took a seat beside his sergeant. He looked like a man who had just scored a goal for his football team.

'I've been in touch with the axe company Better Age, who are based in Derby,' he said. 'They don't make them – they just sell them. They're wholesalers.'

He glanced at a sheet of paper in his hand. 'Dr Reynolds' assistant, David, gave me the twelve-digit serial number which is on the axe and, from that, the company were able to tell me it was among a batch sold to a builders' merchants, Homelove Building Supplies.'

Roscoe leaned back on his chair. 'Don't tell me. Let me guess. They've got branches all over Britain and there's no way of telling where it was bought or who bought it?'

Khalid smiled. 'It's not quite as bad as that, sir,' he said. 'There are just two branches in the whole of the West Midlands. One's in West Coventry and one's in North Birmingham. Since the murder happened in Queensbridge, I thought I'd start by visiting the Coventry branch.'

'You may even get CCTV of the customer who bought it,' said Roscoe. 'And if you find the customer who bought it, there's a good chance we've also found the killer.'

Chapter 12

Sunita Roy peered through her living-room blinds into the street outside. It was a cold, cloudy Tuesday morning.

A neighbour opposite who worked in Birmingham city centre was climbing into his car, ready to set off for the railway station.

In the distance, a bin lorry roared along a nearby street while a chirpy post girl hurried along the pavement, swinging a bag full of letters and parcels and greeting strangers with a smile.

Sunita showered and dressed, tucked into her light breakfast and set off for the office.

As soon as she arrived in CID, she found her colleague, Detective Constable Brett Dawson, had just fetched coffees and teas for her and the team.

'Here you are, Sarge,' he said, passing her a cardboard cup. 'Nice cup of tea without milk.'

'Thanks, Brett. Are you enjoying it a bit more in CID now?' she asked.

'Definitely,' said Dawson, who was tall and slim with spiky blond hair.

'And everything's going well socially?'

'Yeah. Everything's great. Emma and I are going to watch Coventry play Cardiff round the pub tonight.'

'Is Emma the paramedic?'

'That's the one. Anyway, what have you got there, Sarge?'

She was examining a small black book.

'It's Miles's diary,' she replied.

'I bet all the secrets of his life are recorded there,' said Dawson, as he sat down and took a sip of coffee. 'All the revelations about his celebrity pals from the music world, his wealthy friends, his exotic women. I bet the secret behind this murder is hidden away in that book, waiting to jump out.'

'No,' she said. 'It's actually a bit of a let-down. He may have led an interesting life, coming from an aristocratic background and working in the music business. But he doesn't recreate much of that excitement in his diary. It's mainly birthdays, dentist and doctor appointments, and dates for car servicing. All I've discovered is the firm he worked for is called Talent Master, which is an entertainment agency based in Birmingham. He's got a solicitor called David Walker and there's a mysterious person referred to simply as *V* that's he's met up with on three occasions.'

'The solicitor could be really helpful,' said Dawson. 'He might know whether Miles made a will.'

She shook her head. 'His secretary says he's on a skiing holiday. How are you getting on with the CCTV?'

Dawson shrugged. 'There weren't as many cameras as I was expecting,' he admitted. 'There's only one at the top of Fishpond Lane and that's not working at present. The one outside Waverley Court is a dummy. Disks are available from three cameras: one on the outskirts of Queensbridge, at the start of Evesham Road; one outside The Woodman pub in Mill Road; and one outside the Mill Road Nail Bar.'

'You've got all three disks?'

'I'm still waiting to hear back from The Woodman but I've got the other two and I've made a start on going through them.'

'Remember, Dr Reynolds reckons the death was likely to have occurred after 7 p.m.,' she said. 'So we should be looking for cars and pedestrians between 7 p.m. and 10 p.m.'

An hour passed in which the pair worked steadily at their desks without saying much. Then Sunita stood up and walked across to Dawson's desk.

'Any progress, Brett?' she asked.

He shook his head. 'I've found plenty of vehicles travelling along Mill Road, either in the direction of town or going towards Evesham. But not many turning into or out of Fishpond Lane.'

'What's that car on your screen right now?' she asked.

'It's a Nissan Qashqai.'

'Didn't Miles Kenworth have one of those?'

'Yes, but his is silver. This one's black.'

She stepped across to his monitor and zoomed in on the car.

'I can see you're right,' she said. 'Do we have details of cars owned by the residents of Waverley Court?'

'Yes.'

'Seen any of them on camera?'

'Only Miles's car, which is outside his flat, and a Picanto and a Citroen. The Picanto belongs to Aimee Granville-Cole. She arrived back from her job in Birmingham at 7.55 p.m. The Citroen belongs to Uzma Sadiq from Flat 14, who came back at about 7.35 p.m.'

* * *

Later that morning, the chief inspector sent the pair to interview Miles Kenworth's former girlfriend, Ursula Grey. They set off in Sunita's car for a twenty-mile journey through the wilds of the Worcestershire countryside and approached the village of Inkberrow shortly before eleven o'clock.

The chief inspector had decided not to attend himself because of his daughter's connection with the stables.

'I don't want to compromise the investigation,' he had told his sergeant.

The detectives passed the parish church and several thatched cottages before finding Meadow Lane and arriving in the potholed car park next to the riding school.

'I hope you're wearing sound shoes, Brett,' said the sergeant as they stepped out of her car. It had just stopped raining and the ground was caked in mud.

Dawson, who was four years younger than his thirty-year-old sergeant, peered down at his black leather walking shoes.

'Don't worry, Sarge,' he said with a grin as he began negotiating his way across the car park. 'If the worst comes to the worst, I'll just have to break all the rules tonight and give them a clean.'

The constable, who was not considered the sharpest member of the CID team, followed his sergeant through a farm gate. They then found themselves in a concrete courtyard surrounded by a set of red-brick buildings.

Two teenage girls were sitting astride a pair of piebald cob horses. A blonde woman in a blue jacket, jodhpurs and riding boots was bending down by the first horse, adjusting the rider's stirrups.

'Can I help you?' she asked, without glancing up.

'Heart of England CID,' said Sunita. 'We're looking for Miss Grey.'

'That's me,' the woman said. 'I can guess why you're here. Hold on, girls. I'll fetch Martha.'

After arranging for her colleague to take the girls out hacking, she led the two detectives into the tack room.

'We're really sorry to bother you at a time of sadness,' Sunita began as she showed Ursula Grey her identification. 'We just need to ask you a few questions. We won't take up too much of your time. We understood you recently took some time off work.'

Miss Grey looked drained and full of sleep. She put Sunita in mind of a sickly hospital patient with hollow eyes.

'Only the weekend and yesterday,' she said. 'I really wasn't up to it. Anyway what do you want to know?'

'We understand Miles Kenworth was your boyfriend. Can I ask exactly how long you knew him?'

She looked around at the saddles, bridles, stirrups and other equipment on show in the centre of the room.

'I first ran into him at a concert in the O2 Academy in Birmingham. He was struggling up the stairs with some equipment and I offered to help.'

'That was very thoughtful of you,' said Dawson, who was standing next to his sergeant.

'I suppose so,' she said. 'We got chatting and I let it slip that I was single. He asked me out and we found we had a lot in common. We became very close.'

'How long were you together?' asked Sunita.

'A couple of years.'

'I gather your relationship ended recently,' said the sergeant.

'Yes,' she admitted as a sad smile flickered across her face. 'I was devastated.'

'I'm sorry,' said Sunita.

'It's still very raw,' Miss Grey continued. 'It was around the middle of last month. Out of the blue, while I was on my way to work, he phoned me up and said he had suddenly become very busy and couldn't see me that week.

'When I asked why, he said he was tired of his life in Queensbridge and was planning to move away. I asked when I could see him again and he was silent for a moment. Then he said, "I think it would be good if we didn't see each other for a while." He said he needed a break.'

'How terribly hurtful,' said Sunita.

She nodded. 'Yes.'

'And he didn't give you any proper reason as to why he wanted a break?'

'No. He just said he felt he was in a bit of a rut and that his life needed to take off in a different direction. It didn't really make any sense to me. We got engaged last year and we were due to be married this year. We'd already booked the reception. My family are seething. I was with them over the weekend. My brother and father are still incensed about the way I was treated.'

'It must have been shattering to hear he'd been murdered,' said Dawson. 'I mean, on top of what happened between the two of you.'

'Yes. It was a terrible shock. I can't believe that anyone would do that to Miles – with an axe,' she said.

Sunita folded her arms. 'You clearly don't believe your boyfriend's claim about being in a rut. What do you think was the real reason he ended your relationship?'

'I was thinking about it for days afterwards. I've really no idea, although I wondered if he meant that he wanted a reconciliation with his family.'

'After all this time?' said Sunita. 'I find that difficult to believe. My DCI and I were at Culverdon Hall on Sunday and it was clear, despite their sorrow at his loss, that a reconciliation hadn't been on the horizon.'

'Well, it was just one possible explanation for what Miles meant.'

'Do you think he'd started another relationship and wanted to be free for that reason?' Sunita asked.

'I've really no idea. I'd have thought one of my friends would have told me if they'd seen Miles with anyone else.'

'What was Mr Kenworth like as a person?' asked Dawson.

Miss Grey looked at the ground as though an answer might have been written on the red quarry tiles.

Then, seconds later, as she raised her eyes again, they could see tears were beginning to form.

'He was educated, kind, funny, affectionate,' she said in a voice barely above a whisper. 'He could also be rebellious, stubborn, a real maverick. But I loved him. I'd still been hoping to make things up with him – despite the cruel things he'd said. Now it's all too late.'

Sunita nodded sympathetically. 'Miles was thirty-five. I was wondering if he'd ever been married?'

'Yes, briefly, when he was nineteen. Miles met a girl who was the same age at college and they got hitched, but they were too young. It only lasted a year and they got divorced.'

'What interests me,' said Dawson, 'is he had skills as an electrician. Bit strange, coming from his background, I'd have thought.'

'Miles was a complex character,' she replied. 'He was fascinated by electrics at school and was shown how to wire a plug and run cables by a handyman at the hall. After that, he went on a college course.'

'By the way,' said Dawson, 'can we ask where you were on Friday evening?'

'I went shopping in Queensbridge, watched a bit of television and then had an early night.'

Sunita stroked her chin. 'Do you have any thoughts on who might have wanted to murder Miles?' she asked.

'No. He was the sweetest guy.'

'Sorry to ask you this,' Sunita continued. 'But do you know whether, among his tools, Miles owned an axe?'

'I wondered about that terrible weapon when I read about the murder in the press and saw it on television,' she said. 'I never saw him with an axe. But that doesn't mean he didn't own one. He might have had one without my knowledge. He had a lot of tools for his work and I never really saw any of them.'

Dawson interrupted to say, 'Miss Grey, were you ever with Mr Kenworth in his flat when he was playing music on his sound system?'

'No, he was generally on his own. I know he was music mad, but we didn't really share the same tastes. He was more into heavy metal.'

'Were you aware he wasn't popular in Waverley Court because he insisted on playing his music at a high volume?' Sunita asked.

'I told him countless times to keep it down. But, as I just said, he was stubborn and what Miles wanted to do, Miles did.'

'We understand he worked for Talent Master Entertainment Agency. Is that right?'

'Yes. At one time, he was with High End Events in London,' said Miss Grey. 'He'd always been involved in lighting and sound, but he was gradually moving more into talent and events management. He joined Talent Master a couple of years back.'

'Would you know their address?' the sergeant asked.

'Yes. I'll write it down for you.'

'You don't know where he might have kept his mobile phone, do you? It's just that it wasn't in the flat or in his car outside.'

'Maybe he'd lost it. He'd lost two before.'

'Did Miles have a lot of friends?' asked Dawson.

'Not really. He spent most of his time with me over the past two years – horse riding, going to occasional concerts, going out for food. We spent a bit of time at my place in Glebe Gardens. He didn't really have time for friends, apart from Terry and John, whom he worked with.'

Sunita looked at her with a solemn expression. 'We're really trying to work out how a man with no enemies ended up suffering such a tragic death,' she said.

'I'm as perplexed as anyone,' said Miss Grey. 'None of it makes any sense. I've been going through what happened in my head time after time. I keep coming back to the same question: who on earth would want to murder him?'

Chapter 13

After removing his peaked cap and washing his hands at the kitchen sink, Logan Price cooked and ate a microwave meal. Then he ran upstairs to the bedroom he shared with his wife, Stephanie.

He was just slipping out of his work overalls and deciding what to wear for the evening, when his mobile phone rang. He could see who was calling.

'Funeral directors. Can I help?' he asked.

'You weren't running funerals when I spoke to you two hours ago,' said his workmate, Vivian Tyler, with a laugh.

'No? Well, can I interest you in our "Bury One, Get One Free" offer?' asked Price.

'Stop playing around, Logan. What pub do you want to go to?'

Logan Price was a tall, muscular man with short, ginger hair. 'Do you fancy The Coach and Horses in Norton Prior?' he said. 'They've got a really good range of real ale.'

'Nah, one of us would have to drive if we went over there,' said Tyler. 'I don't mind The Woodman.'

'We go there all the time,' moaned Price. 'I reckon we should try The Crown and Sceptre for a change. It were all right last time we went there.'

'All right, mate. I'll see you in half an hour.'

Just before eight o'clock, Price left his one-bedroom house in Mill Road, Queensbridge and walked to the bar where he had arranged to meet his friend.

The Crown and Sceptre was in the heart of the market town. Once a busy commercial hotel, it suffered from a fading elegance.

This evening the venue was virtually empty. A bearded, stocky man was seated at a corner table, huddled over a pint of lager. A cheerful barman was trying to whistle a tune behind the counter while wiping pint glasses with a tea towel. There was no sign of his friend.

'On your own tonight, Logan?' asked the barman as he lay down his towel.

'My mate should be here in a minute,' he replied, stretching out his tattooed arm and holding out a ten-pound note.

'How's the missus?'

'Fine. She's away at the moment.'

'What can I get you?'

'Pint of QB, please.'

After paying for his glass of QB Bitter, a medium-strength beer produced by the Queensbridge Brewery Company, he found a table in the centre of the bar and sat down.

No sooner had he done so than Vivian Tyler arrived with a beaming smile.

'Sorry, mate,' he said. 'The phone rang just as I was leaving.'

'No problem,' said Price. 'What would you like?'

'Pint of Strongbow, please, mate. Is your missus still away?' asked Tyler, a slightly built man with a youthful face and a receding hairline.

'Yeah. Still at her mother's.'

'Depression's a bloody terrible thing.'

'Tell me about it. She had a bad spell a year ago and I thought she'd got over it, but on Saturday she got hysterical over nothing.'

'What? You said the wrong thing, mate?'

'I sometimes don't know what to say. She sent me a text to say she might be back tonight. She's due in work.

They let her have a few days off, but they say they need her tomorrow. How's your missus?'

'Same as ever, mate,' said Tyler. 'If the kids are behaving well, she's happy.'

As the evening drew on, more customers arrived – a group of sports fans and several young couples. After two hours and four rounds of drinks, it was Price's turn to go to the bar again.

As he queued at the counter, he noticed the bearded man in the corner returning from the men's toilets. He lurched his way, drunkenly, back to his seat, knocking over a vase of flowers as he did so. More than a dozen daffodils tumbled to the floor.

'Oy, pick that up,' ordered the barman, rushing across the room.

Price strained to hear the man's response. It sounded like, 'Sorry, mate.'

'Oh, leave it to me,' snapped the barman. 'Just watch what you're doing.'

'All right. There's no need to go on about it. I said I was sorry.'

The barman returned to the counter and began serving again. After a few minutes, he poured a fresh pint of bitter for Price and a pint of cider for Tyler.

'Someone's in a bad mood, aren't they?' said Price, pointing at the man in the corner.

The barman nodded. 'He's the guy arrested at the weekend over that business at Waverley Court,' he said. 'Jake Harris.'

'Really?' said Price.

'Yes. Bloody troublemaker, he is. We nearly had to throw him out the other day.' After taking Price's twenty-pound note and handing back his change, the barman added, 'According to him, he just went to ask the guy to turn his music down in the flat below and found him dead. The cops pulled him in, but then they let him go.'

'Bloody hell. That were a horrific murder, mate,' said Price. 'And it weren't too far from my gaff. Just up the road and round the corner.'

'Bloody shocking,' the barman agreed as Price picked up the two drinks and carried them back to his table.

'What was all that about with the vase?' asked Tyler. 'That barman really lost his cool with that guy.'

Price nodded. 'Yeah. Barman says he's called Jake Harris. He were pulled in for that killing in Waverley Court.'

Perhaps he emitted these final words more loudly than he'd intended. Perhaps the effects of his drinking were beginning to take their toll.

Harris had been watching the pair from his table. He drew himself out of his chair and meandered drunkenly across to them.

'Don't bloody talk about me behind me back,' said Harris.

'What's that, mate?' said Price.

Harris bent down over their table, his breath reeking of alcohol.

'I heard you say Waverley Court. Don't try and deny it,' he continued. 'I ain't got nothing to do with what happened on Friday. Got it? Not that it's any of your business.'

The barman hurried over as Harris began waving his fist at the two friends. He tried to restrain the aggressive man. 'Come on,' he said. 'We don't want no trouble here.'

'It's all right. There won't be no trouble,' said Tyler.

Harris broke free of the barman's grip and punched Tyler on the jaw. Tyler struck back with a blow to his attacker's head and they were soon trading blows. Price tried to separate them and got struck on the nose for his trouble.

'Come on. Break it up,' yelled the barman.

Two burly men wearing red Liverpool shirts stormed across the room. Together with the barman, they managed to eject Harris from the pub.

The trio stood for a few moments outside, watching Harris stagger away up the high street like a wounded animal. When they were certain he had left the scene permanently, they returned inside.

'You both all right?' the barman asked as he approached Price and Tyler.

'Just a scratch,' Tyler replied as he picked up his pint of cider. 'I'm sure I'll survive.'

'Yeah, we're all right,' said Price, who was holding a paper handkerchief by his injured nose to stem the bleeding.

'That guy's got a serious drink problem,' the barman continued. 'But we've watched him walk off up the road and I don't think he'll be back. I tell you what though, you should both take care when you head home – you know, keep an eye out. Just in case.'

* * *

'Is that you, Logan?' The voice was soft and plaintive. It was coming from the bedroom.

'Well, it's not the bloody man in the moon,' Price replied. He closed the front door and climbed the stairs.

'Feeling any better, love?' he asked as he entered the bedroom. His wife, Stephanie, was lying on top of the bed in a slinky white negligee.

'Not really, but the boss wants me back at the shop, doesn't he? God, you stink of drink. Don't come near me.'

Price sat down on the edge of the bed. 'Look, I've only had a few drinks with Vivian Tyler. All right?'

'That two-faced weasel. And what have you done to your nose?'

'There was a fight. This drunk guy got aggressive and hit us both,' he replied.

'You know I'm not feeling good, but, behind my back, you go out and get into a drunken pub brawl.'

'Oh, for God's sake,' he yelled. 'It wasn't like that, you stupid woman. Some bloke who lives round the corner in

Waverley Court was causing trouble. We just helped kick him out.'

'Well, I don't want you sleeping next to me, especially with you smelling like a brewery. You'd better sleep downstairs tonight.'

Chapter 14

Omar Khalid drove slowly along the bustling city street in West Coventry, frantically looking for the builders' merchants called Homelove.

'Where the hell is this place?' the conscientious detective constable murmured to himself as he passed a shop selling fitted kitchens and another bathroom supplies.

Eventually, after a row of trees loomed up on the left, he spotted a blue sign saying 'Homelove Building Supplies'.

He took a parking space outside the glazed front doors, went inside and asked for the manager.

A stout, balding man stepped out of a back room and approached him.

'I'm the manager, Colin Smith,' he said with a concerned expression. 'Can I help?'

'DC Khalid, Heart of England CID,' said the detective. 'We're making inquiries about an axe with a sixteen-inch handle. It was imported by Better Age of Derby and they've told us it was part of a consignment sent here.'

'Have you got the serial number?' asked Colin.

'Yes,' said Khalid. He read out the number from his notebook and Colin wrote it down on the back of a blank invoice.

'Do you know when we're meant to have received this batch?'

'October.'

'Well, I'll have a look on the computer. Can you hold on?'

Khalid watched as Colin returned to his office. Through a window behind the counter, he could see the manager sitting behind a computer screen, pressing various keys.

After nearly five minutes, he was back.

'Yes, you're right. It was one of sixty axes with a sixteen-inch handle that we bought for our stores in Birmingham and Coventry. They're splitting axes. Is that right?'

'I don't know. What's a splitting axe?'

'For cutting wood. It's just got a bit more weight in the head.'

'Has it? Can you tell from the serial number at which branch it was bought and who bought it?'

'Now you're asking, mate,' said Colin. 'You haven't got the receipt, I suppose?'

'No.'

'Hang on.'

He returned to the back room and tapped away at his keyboard again before reappearing at the counter clutching a printout.

'You're in luck, mate. It was bought online from us on 20 November by someone called Gordon MacLeod.'

'Any more details than that?' Khalid asked.

'Yes, let's see. I can tell you he paid the princely sum of thirty-one pounds ninety-nine pence. His address is 4 Manor Close, Shawley Green. Do you want the postcode?'

'No. It's all right. I think I know where that is. All right. Thanks very much.'

* * *

The chief inspector was excited when Khalid called in to report on the quick progress he had made. But he was also cautious.

'Be very careful when approaching this guy,' Roscoe insisted. 'He could be the guy who carried out the attack on Miles Kenworth or he may have lent the axe to someone. Alternatively, a relative or friend might have taken it. So we've got to play this carefully.'

He paused before adding, 'Nonetheless, if it turns out to be the killer himself, he could be a desperate man and might attack you.'

Khalid followed the Warwick bypass and, just before midday, arrived in the picturesque village of Shawley Green, which lies between Queensbridge and Stratford-upon-Avon.

He had been there at least once before – to visit the clubhouse run by the Warwick and Queensbridge Company of Archers at a time when a series of crossbow murders created fear throughout the Midlands.

Checks on the national computer simply revealed MacLeod had been born in Scotland in 1957 and had no previous convictions, apart from motoring offences.

The man's home was a four-bedroom detached house nestling in a quiet, tree-lined close of around twelve properties.

As he stepped out of his car, Khalid glanced up at the red-brick house.

'So this is the home of the mad axe murderer,' he told himself while walking past the neat front lawn. 'Such a tranquil spot. You can hear the birds singing and the wind rustling in the trees. Surely that guy in the builders' merchants must have picked out the wrong customer?'

After receiving no reply at the house, he learned from neighbours that the MacLeods owned the Orchard Lane Farm Shop, a short distance away on the main road, and were probably there.

It was nearly lunchtime by the time he reached the premises, a large timber-fronted, single-storey building with a car park at the side.

He found a space for his car and walked across to the entrance, where a huge sign declared, 'Know your farmer, know your food.' He noticed two CCTV cameras fixed above the doors.

As he stepped inside, he found there were separate sections for dairy produce; meat, fish and game; beers and wines; vegetables; jams and chutneys; and a variety of other products.

But where was the check-out? And where were Mr and Mrs MacLeod?

Then an assistant from the meat counter in white overalls and a striped apron came to his rescue.

'You look lost, sir,' he pointed out with a smile.

'I'm looking for Mr MacLeod,' the detective explained, showing his police identification.

'The boss? He'll most likely be in the office. If you'd like to follow me.'

He was led through the cafe to a corridor towards the rear of the building. The shop assistant knocked on a door marked 'Office' and, to Khalid's relief, a middle-aged man was inside, working studiously at a desk.

'Mr MacLeod, someone from the police for you,' the young butcher explained before leaving.

'I'm DC Khalid from Heart of England CID,' said Khalid. 'Sorry to bother you.'

'It's nay bother,' said the man, who stood up and walked round the desk. MacLeod was a rather dour man, who wore glasses and was balding. He gave a weak smile.

'How can I help you, DC Khalid?'

'It's about an axe you bought from a firm called Homelove Building Supplies.'

MacLeod nodded. 'Aye, that would have been in November.'

'Well, you may not be aware of this, sir, but it's featured in a murder investigation.'

The shop owner looked aghast. 'What? You dinnae mean that business that's been on the television – the murder in Fishpond Lane?'

'That's right.'

'Oh my God! Are you sure it's the one I bought, officer?'

'Well, I checked the serial number with Homelove earlier today.'

'I'll just check our storeroom if you don't mind,' said MacLeod, pushing past the detective. He went to the door of a larger room next door containing logs.

'I bought the axe because some of the logs we were getting from one of the farms needed to be cut down.'

He unlocked the door with a key from his pocket, turned on the light switch and stepped across to the far side of the windowless room. He reached up inside a wall cupboard.

'Good God!' he exclaimed. 'It's not here. I could have sworn it was here the other day.'

Very nicely done, thought Khalid. Is this man a brilliant actor, pretending in front of a policeman that his weapon has mysteriously vanished? MacLeod didn't have the look of a killer about him. But then who does? Or maybe MacLeod was expressing genuine surprise, he thought.

'Is this door normally kept locked?' asked Khalid.

'Most of the time.'

'How many keys are there?'

'Two. I keep one on my key ring and the other is always locked away in my desk in case my one should get lost.'

Khalid watched as the store owner raced down the corridor to his office, unlocked his desk and searched it.

'It's all right,' he called. 'The other key is here.'

Panting and perspiring, he rejoined the detective outside the storeroom door.

'Are you in the habit of lending the key to staff?' asked Khalid.

MacLeod nodded. 'From time to time.'

'So I suppose there's two possibilities,' the detective continued. 'Either someone who borrowed your key took the axe or, more likely, someone wandering around in the back of your shop noticed it was unlocked and saw an opportunity.'

'Aye. That does sound more likely.'

'Can you remember who you've lent the key to?'

'Let me think. My wife, Grace; Nick, the manager; and three of the check-out girls. But unfortunately, there have been occasions over the past few months when I've gone to the door and found it unlocked. Some of the girls are a bit slack sometimes.'

'All right, sir,' said Khalid, who had written these details down in a notebook. 'I'll have to call my DCI straight away. It's vital we find out how an axe delivered to your shop came to be involved in our murder case.'

Chapter 15

The village of Shawley Green was eerily quiet as Gavin Roscoe came to the end of his brief early morning car journey from his home in Queensbridge. The streetlights were losing their glow and daylight was approaching.

He had passed Orchard Lane Farm Shop so many times in the past on his way to Stratford and never stopped. He had never paid the retail outlet much attention.

Now it was crucial to their investigation that he got to know everything there was to know about the business and its staff. It might lead them to the killer's door.

It was half past six when he drew into the car park. Two police cars in the Heart of England livery of blue and yellow drew up on the road outside as he walked towards the shop entrance.

A young, uniformed policeman approached him.

'DCI Roscoe?' he asked. 'Morning. Apparently, we're going to be holding interviews with staff?'

'That's right. I haven't informed them yet of our plans, so there might be a few tantrums. Thought it might be helpful to have you guys around.'

'No problem,' said the officer as he returned to his vehicle.

A slim, dark-haired woman, DC Wendy Hopkirk, made her way towards them.

'Morning,' said Roscoe.

'Good morning, sir. Have you tried the door yet?' she asked.

'Not yet, but a light's just gone on, which is a good sign.'

They were joined moments later by DC Khalid.

'Right,' said Roscoe. 'Just to fill you both in, Dr Ling called me at home last night. Her team have been right through the farm shop's woodstore, where the axe was kept. The whole place has been dusted for dabs and she's going to let me know more later. Are you both ready?'

They nodded and followed him towards the main doors. He pressed a bell on the right of the entrance.

A middle-aged man that Khalid pointed out as being the owner waddled towards them.

He shouted through the glazed doors, 'We don't open till eight.'

Then the chief inspector showed his warrant card through the glass and Mr MacLeod spotted the police uniforms.

'What's this all about?' he demanded after unbolting and unlocking the two doors.

'DCI Roscoe,' said the chief inspector as Khalid joined him in the doorway. 'You'll remember my colleague here from yesterday. I'm afraid we need to speak to all your staff about this axe.'

The shop owner wrung his hands.

'Oh, this is nae good for our business,' he said. 'We're about to open in just over half an hour.'

'We came early in order to get as many interviews as possible out of the way before your customers arrive,' said Roscoe.

'Not all the staff are here,' MacLeod replied. 'I'm sure you won't be able to complete your work in just half an hour.'

'Well, I'm afraid you won't be able to open up until our work's done.'

'Do you have the right?' he asked as two anxious staff members appeared behind him.

'This is a murder investigation, sir,' Roscoe added as the owner reluctantly stood aside and let the police in.

The chief inspector quickly established that already on the premises and available to be interviewed were Mr and Mrs MacLeod; Nicholas Halfpenny, the manager; checkout girls Danielle, Alex and Kate; a butcher's assistant; a cheese counter assistant; and two cafe staff.

Three other employees were due to start work at 10 a.m. Two more were on holiday. One was sick. Two part-time workers had the day off.

Roscoe chose to interview the MacLeods himself, along with their manager. The remaining staff interviews would be conducted by Khalid and Hopkirk, with instructions to obtain the addresses of the absent staff and contact them at their homes later.

After showing Roscoe where the axe had been kept, Gordon MacLeod invited him to take a seat in his office. They were joined by his wife Grace, who was a few years younger than her husband. Her grey hair was drawn back in a bun. Her face suggested an honest, conscientious businesswoman.

'Mrs MacLeod, I've got a statement from your husband already, so I mainly need to speak to you,' said Roscoe. 'Do you recall when you last saw the axe?'

'I know it was here the first week of February, wasn't it, love?' she said with a glance towards her husband. 'That's when we had those logs delivered from Culverdon Hall, just down the road.'

'Aye.'

'But I've no memory of seeing it since.'

'Do staff members frequently use this corridor – either to visit the office or the woodstore?' Roscoe asked.

'Aye,' said Mr MacLeod. 'They all do. The same corridor serves the toilets.'

'Is it usual for customers to wander through here?'

'From time to time. Sometimes they ask at the check-out to use the toilet.'

Roscoe frowned. 'How often do you get a customer request to use the toilet?'

'Two or three times a week. Maybe more,' said Mrs MacLeod.

'It would be helpful, Mrs MacLeod, if you could ask those staff to think back about these requests. I also need a list of all your customers.'

'The main problem here is staff who forget to lock the woodstore,' said Mrs MacLeod. Her husband winced as her words tumbled out. 'I'm afraid our manager, Nick, is one of the worst offenders.'

The MacLeods agreed to let the chief inspector use their office as an interview room, hoping this would hasten proceedings. Then the pair headed to the check-outs, with a request that Nicholas Halfpenny should make his way to see the chief inspector.

Minutes later, a tall, excitable man in his early thirties stormed towards him along the corridor.

'This is a bloody liberty,' shouted the newcomer, who had thick, wavy, blond hair.

'Who are you exactly, sir?' asked Roscoe, who was standing in the doorway.

'I'm the manager, Nick. We've got hundreds of customers wanting to shop and your people are turning them all away. A woman's just phoned me from outside to say that she's travelled twenty-five miles from Worcester to find us shut.'

Roscoe shrugged. 'I'm very sorry about the disruption to your business, but we have an investigation to run,' he said.

'That's all very well,' Halfpenny continued. 'But it's obvious no one working here has got the slightest connection with the terrible murder that happened in Queensbridge. Someone without authority has obviously sneaked in and stolen the axe. I'm sure none of our staff will know who. You're wasting everybody's time, Chief Inspector, including your own.'

'Well, you've said your piece,' said Roscoe. 'But it's occurred to me that, whoever took it, can't have just waltzed out of here in broad daylight carrying this weapon. They must have been carrying a bag, a box, some kind of container, otherwise it would have been too obvious. I've noticed you provide customers with branded jute bags for £3.50 each. Isn't it possible one of these might have been used to conceal it?'

'Well, of course, that's possible,' the manager snapped.

'We'll have to look at the CCTV footage over the past two weeks, if you don't mind, sir,' he said before lowering his voice. 'Another thing. I've been told by the MacLeods that some staff members sometimes forget to lock the woodstore after they've been there. Your obvious annoyance wouldn't be a sign of your personal guilt in that regard, would it?'

'You've got some cheek,' said the manager. 'No, I bloody wasn't in the habit of forgetting to lock the door.'

'That's not what I've been told.'

'I hope you and your team get a move on this morning,' said Halfpenny. 'You've absolutely no idea how bloody inconvenient this is.'

'The situation isn't terribly convenient for the family and friends who have lost a loved one either, sir.'

Chapter 16

The chief inspector never felt at ease while visiting Dr Silas Reynolds' laboratory in the Kings Heath suburb of Birmingham.

Whenever he walked through the main door of the building, he was reminded of school chemistry classes. The smell of solvent vapours or bleach was never far away.

However, he recognised that, to the middle-aged pathologist, this corner of the world was like a second home. It was a sanctuary where he revelled in examining, cutting, testing and conferring with colleagues.

Roscoe was forced to overlook his reservations that Wednesday morning, if he were to find out more about the final moments of Miles Kenworth.

The pathologist was in the examination room, about to dissect a body, when the detective poked his head round the door.

'Morning, Silas,' he said.

'Morning, Gavin,' came the reply. 'I'll just put this fellow away and I'll be right with you.'

After a few minutes, Reynolds joined the chief inspector in the main room of the department, where the policeman was sitting on a stool.

'So you want to hear about our Mr Kenworth?' he began. 'Well, the guy's suffered a total of seventeen slash, stab and cut wounds as well as contused lacerations to the scalp, face and neck. Superficial abrasions and bruises are apparent on the hands.'

'A really sustained attack then?' said Roscoe.

'Yes, old fruit. Poor Mr Kenworth did his best to defend himself but the attacker showered him with pepper spray.'

'Good God. So he overpowered him by spraying him in the face?'

'Exactly.'

'Silas, what about the post-mortem?'

'It was held here last night. The cause of death was extensive brain contusion after fragmentation of the neurocranium,' he said. 'Prior to death, despite being incapacitated by the spray, Mr Kenworth put up a spirited defence, scratching his attacker, and the killer's clothing would also have been splattered with blood. We're testing microscopic blood samples and cells from beneath the victim's fingernails which should produce results.'

'That's all very encouraging,' said Roscoe.

'We took a swab of the handle, the blade and the butt of the axe for testing,' said Reynolds. 'Unfortunately, the blood on the axe only matched the victim's DNA. There were no dabs found on the axe because, as I told you the attacker must have worn gloves.

'Following the trails of blood, it seems likely he was sprayed near the window and then assaulted because there's a blood stain on the floor there. He almost certainly put up a brave struggle. Then the final act of murder appears to have taken place on the rug involving a severe degree of force. It was clearly a pre-planned attack.'

'What about the victim's stomach contents?' asked Roscoe.

'The victim had been drinking heavily,' said Reynolds. 'Mr Kenworth had consumed a fair amount of whisky ante-mortem. The body contained 120 milligrams of alcohol for every 100 millilitres of blood. He was almost one-and-a-half times over the legal drink-drive limit of 80 milligrams.'

Roscoe nodded. 'I noticed the empty whisky bottle beside the body.'

Reynolds clambered onto a stool.

'We wondered why there was no blood in the hallway since the obvious point of entry was through the main door to the flat,' said the pathologist. 'But we took on board DS Roy's observations about the window and have now concluded that she's right – the killer must have come in through the ground-floor window. Almost certainly as soon as Mr Kenworth opened it, the intruder would have blasted pepper spray into his eyes. I found traces of the chemicals used to produce pepper spray on the victim's clothing and on surfaces around the window.'

'So the effects of Miles Kenworth being sprayed in the face would be what?' said Roscoe. 'A burning sensation in the eyes, nose and mouth and being temporarily blinded?'

'That's right,' said Reynolds. 'It can also impede breathing.'

The chief inspector paused. He was engrossed in thought.

'Do you have a clearer idea of the time of death, Silas?'

'My assistant, David, took a rectal temperature of the victim at 11.45 p.m. when he arrived at the flat. This gave a temperature of 95.5 degrees Fahrenheit. He took the temperature of the air in the room at the same time and I can now confirm we've calculated that death occurred at around four hours earlier – 7.45 p.m.'

'It's beginning to look to me as though either the window was open when the killer arrived – unlikely since it was a cold night – or, more likely, the victim invited him in.'

'Has Dr Ling told you the good news?'

'I haven't spoken to her since yesterday morning.'

'Some of the chemicals from the spray will probably have been passed onto the killer's clothing or transferred to his clothing from surfaces around the window. If that's happened, they can remain on the clothing for a relatively long time. You can't wash them away with water. Only bleach might remove them.

'So, if you make an arrest and the suspect's clothing shows any trace of the same spray, you've got your man.'

* * *

Later that day, while on his way home, the chief inspector needed to stop and buy some fuel for his car. He drew into a filling station at Studley, four miles from his home, and got out.

He noticed a green Land Rover Discovery coming to a halt at the neighbouring pump. As the driver got out in a shooting jacket and flat cap, he remembered where he had seen the man before – at Culverdon Hall.

After replacing the nozzle in his holster, Roscoe walked round the pump and confronted the driver.

'Mr Laxton,' he called. 'You're just the man I wanted to see.'

Charles Laxton seemed embarrassed. 'Oh, hello. DCI Roscoe, isn't it?'

Three days earlier, the forty-two-year-old estate manager had raced off like a startled rabbit within minutes of the detectives saying they wished to speak to him. This time the chief inspector was determined to give him a grilling.

'Yes,' he said. 'After we've both paid, I'd be grateful if you'd pull over in the parking area there so we can have a chat. And if you speed away this time, I'm afraid I'd treat the matter extremely seriously.'

A few minutes later, the chief inspector got out of his car and stepped round to Laxton's open window.

'We were rather annoyed by the way you drove off on Sunday after we'd specifically told you we needed to speak to you,' he began.

Laxton raised his eyes. 'I'm very sorry, Chief Inspector,' he said. 'It went completely out of my mind and the dogs were getting overexcited.'

'I need to ask you where you were last Friday evening, sir?' Roscoe continued.

'My wife had arranged some time ago to meet some friends for a girls' night out in Stratford,' he said, 'so, a few days ago, I looked up an old pal of mine and we arranged to meet at the Plough Inn at Hartston for a drink.'

'Were you there all evening?'

'Yes.'

'From what time?'

'From around eight o'clock.'

Roscoe frowned. 'What's the name of your drinking partner?'

'Roland Duffy.'

'I'll need an address and phone number.'

'Upper Oaks Farm, Brook Lane, Hartston. Here's his mobile number.'

Roscoe jotted the information down before asking, 'How long have you worked for Lord Culverdon?'

Laxton glanced across the brightly lit filling station where homebound motorists were now queuing for the pumps.

'I suppose it must be six years now,' he replied.

'Where were you before that?'

'I was working on a country estate in Scotland. I prefer the quieter life down here and my wife likes it better living in the Midlands as well.'

'How well did you know Miles Kenworth?'

'Hardly knew the guy. Met him once a few years ago and I can tell you I wasn't very impressed.'

'Oh? Why's that?'

'I could see how much he'd hurt his relatives by turning his back on them and on all the responsibilities that go with being born into a high-class family.'

'Do you have any thoughts on who might have attacked Miles Kenworth?' he asked.

'The family's spoken of little else since Friday. We can't think of anyone who might have wished him such terrible harm.'

Chapter 17

Sunita Roy opened her eyes and gazed round her room in the dim light of dawn. She could hear a buzzing coming from the bedside table. Was it her phone?

She switched on the lamp and realised at once her boss was calling.

'Good morning,' the chief inspector began. 'Not phoning too early, am I?'

'I don't know. What time is it?'

'Nearly seven,' he replied. 'I thought you'd be up and about by now. Listen, not much of interest came out of our interviews at the farm shop in Shawley. We've found a couple of customers with records for theft who've been picked up on the shop's CCTV and Dawson's checking them out. I've also discovered the shop does a lot of business with Culverdon Hall and some of Our Lordship's family shop there.

'Anyway, I want you to go over there today and speak to a woman called Stephanie Price. According to the shop owner, Gordon MacLeod, she's been off work for a few days, but she's coming back this morning. She sometimes works on the check-outs and also has a role in making deliveries.'

'I'll go over there at about nine o'clock, sir.'

'Good. While you're there, keep your eyes and ears open, Sergeant. The manager resented us being there, which is a little suspicious, and a lot of the staff were disgruntled. See what you can pick up.'

Sunita set off for Shawley Green on a journey along mainly country lanes and reached the village in good time.

On arriving at the farm shop, she learned Stephanie was out on her rounds.

But minutes later, a white van with 'Orchard Lane Farm Shop' on the side headed towards a rear garage.

Sunita watched as a cheerful woman with black, wavy hair, approached.

'Do you need to speak to me?' asked Stephanie as Sunita produced her warrant card.

'Yes, is there somewhere quiet? It's about the murder of Miles Kenworth.'

'I don't think I can help much,' said Stephanie. 'But there's a bench at the edge of the car park.'

'Perfect,' Sunita replied as she followed the woman outside. 'You know the axe used in the murder was stolen from here, don't you?'

'Yes, I heard about that yesterday.'

Stephanie, dressed in a cardigan and slacks that seemed rather tight, was softly spoken with lily-white skin and a face that many would consider attractive.

She led the detective to the wooden bench beneath some oak trees, where they sat down.

Then she made an admission that took the sergeant by surprise. 'You know I knew him, don't you?' she said.

'Miles? I didn't realise,' said Sunita. 'How did you know him?'

'He used to come here a lot. He loved organic food. Plus he grew up at Culverdon Hall, down the road. Oh God, I can't believe he's gone. He was such a wonderful guy.'

Sunita frowned. 'Is there anything you can tell me that might help find the person who killed him?'

'I know he wasn't getting on very well at work. His boss strung him along for months. He let him believe he could become a partner in the business. Then, the other week, he told Miles it just wasn't going to happen. That upset him. But I can't imagine that would have had anything to do with his death.'

'How long had you known him?'

'Well, I'd seen him around as I was growing up. My dad did some work for the Kenworths and once or twice he pointed him out to me in the street as the youngest member of the family. I've been for a drink with him a couple of times.'

'What work did your father do for them?'

'He was a solicitor in commercial litigation. I was amazed when Miles first came over here about a year ago. He said he'd only just discovered the place. I used to help him find certain groceries he wanted.'

All this talk about a man that had died so recently and so shockingly seemed to be unsettling Stephanie. She fiddled nervously with a lock of her hair.

'Sorry. Can you give me a moment?' she asked. She stood up, walked towards the trees and gazed down at the grass. Then she returned to the bench, shaking her head.

'Thinking of what happened… it's so upsetting,' she said.

'Shall we leave it there?' Sunita suggested. 'Perhaps I could give you a call in a day or two?'

'No. I want to help you. What else would you like to know?'

Sunita leaned back on the bench. 'When did you last see Mr Kenworth?'

'At the start of the month.'

'You sound as though you knew him fairly well.'

Stephanie appeared shocked. 'No, not really.'

'I'm sorry,' said Sunita. 'I must have confused your sympathy for the deceased with something stronger, something more personal.'

'Don't get me wrong. He was a nice guy, but I'm married.'

Sunita felt embarrassed. For a moment, she had sensed close feelings for the deceased. Perhaps it was simply grief for the tragic loss of a friend.

The detective realised she had not yet brought Stephanie round to the main purpose of her visit.

'I need to ask you about the woodstore,' said Sunita. 'Have you seen anyone loitering outside the room? Can you think of anyone who might have gone in and taken the axe?'

'Well, customers and staff are often in that area because the toilets are at the end of the corridor,' said Stephanie. 'Frankly, I've no idea who might have taken it. But, if you've got more questions, I'd be happy to try to help. I want you to catch the murderer and get justice for Miles.'

Chapter 18

The arrival of spring seemed to have been unexpectedly delayed as landscape gardeners Logan Price and Vivian Tyler set off from Queensbridge on their eight-mile journey to Stratford.

Temperatures had been falling for the past few days and now scattered rain showers were forecast as their blue van approached Shawley Green.

Price's mobile rang and their plans changed in an instant. Since he was driving, he handed the phone to his colleague, who saw the ominous word 'Boss' burst onto the screen. He hit the 'Answer' key with some trepidation.

'That's Vivian, isn't it?' asked the employer.

'Yes. Logan's driving.'

'Vivian, that job today's been scrapped. The owner wants us to make a start next week. I explained you were on the way, but he didn't seem to want to listen. Twiddle your thumbs for a while till I find you another job for today.' Then he rang off.

'You'd better pull over,' said Tyler. 'The job's been scrapped.'

'What?' said Price. 'You're joking. After loading up with that digger and all the tools?'

'Never mind. At least we've got some time off. We're not far from that farm shop where your missus works. We could call in there and get a spot of breakfast.'

Price drove into the car park and they parked the van. Then they strolled to the shop entrance and made their way to the cafe.

'Hello, Jess,' said Tyler, as he greeted a slim, red-haired woman bustling about behind the counter. 'Any chance of some grub?'

Ten minutes later, they were tucking into a breakfast.

The only other customers, a man and a woman, were sitting at the far side of the room.

'It's all very well these fancy foods but they come with fancy prices,' moaned Tyler. 'Do you know this little lot cost nearly sixteen quid?'

Price smiled. 'It's all right, mate. I'll chip in.'

'So I suppose you know your way round here a bit, don't you?' said Tyler. 'Since your missus works here?'

'Yeah. She thought she were in line for the manager's job, but they brought in some prat that she doesn't get on with, called Nick.'

Tyler put his cutlery down on his plate. 'Do you know where the gents is?'

'Yeah, come out of here. Go past the cheese, and you'll see a corridor on the left. It's down there. Go past the office and the storeroom. You can't miss it.'

'Thanks, mate,' said Tyler as he got up and walked off.

While he was away, a young mother with a crying baby in a buggy entered the cafe and approached the counter, asking if the assistant could warm up her baby's bottle.

'Sorry, madam. You can't bring your baby's buggy in here,' said the assistant.

'Why is that?' asked the blonde woman.

'New regulations,' came the reply.

Price leaped up from his table and marched to the counter.

'That's ridiculous,' he said. 'Can't you see her little 'un needs a feed? What's the matter with you people?'

The cafe assistant apologised profusely before the angry man returned to his table. He was still fuming when Tyler returned.

'It's bloody not good enough,' he said loudly as the disgruntled mother left with her baby.

Then Nick Halfpenny burst into the cafe. He had a quick word with the canteen assistant, Jessica, before turning his attention to the two men.

'What in God's name do you mean making all this din at a quarter to nine in the morning?' he demanded.

'Who the hell are you?' asked Price.

'I'm the manager, that's who,' said Halfpenny.

'The poor woman who just left wasn't able to feed her starving baby because of some stupid new rule,' said Price. 'Why couldn't she bring her buggy in here?'

'Customers can leave their buggies outside,' he replied. 'We're very sorry but we've just had the place refurbished and these new buggies are too wide for the tables.'

'That's ridiculous,' said Price. 'You should put the needs of customers first – especially when you're charging sky-high prices.'

'That's right,' said Tyler.

'I've heard enough,' said Halfpenny. 'You can finish your breakfast and leave. And don't bother coming back again.'

'Don't worry, mate,' said Price. 'We won't.'

* * *

Laughing and joking, Sunita Roy and Samir Banerjee climbed the hotel steps that evening and made their way through the double glass doors.

'I'd like to sit over there by the window,' said Sunita as soon as they reached the restaurant entrance. She pointed across the vast room to a table for two nestling beside a drinks trolley.

Shortly afterwards the manager of the restaurant on the northern outskirts of Coventry arrived and granted Sunita's wish for the window table, which afforded views of a lake and golf course. As they pored over the menu beneath the dimmed lighting, Sunita gazed into his dark eyes.

'Do you remember when we last came here?' she asked.

'Of course,' he said, slightly embarrassed. 'It was almost exactly three years ago.'

'Yes,' she said, reaching across and clutching his hand.

'So much is changing since we were here last,' he said.

A young, blond waiter came and took their orders – salmon for Sunita and seabass for Samir, together with two ice-cold orange juices.

'Sam, I've been dying to tell you about Leicester,' she said excitedly. 'Tulika and I have been left a lot of money – several hundred thousand pounds each.'

'Oh my God,' said Samir, who just managed to avoid spitting his mouthful of orange juice over his cream-coloured suit. 'How wonderful that is. And it's split between you and your sister?'

'Yes. My dear uncle was a lovely man, but a bit eccentric. He fell out with my parents for some reason – I never found out why – and against expectations and our family traditions, he left everything to the two of us. So we owe it to our Uncle Ramit to invest the money wisely. The solicitor we met was a right old fuddy-duddy who obviously didn't approve of two unmarried girls being left the proceeds of such a sizable estate.'

'How lucky you both are,' said Samir.

'I know. It means I could pay off my mortgage and still have plenty of money spare to invest. Or I could sell the flat and buy a house. I also want to help my parents, who have been very good to me. What do you think?'

'Sunita, I've got very little knowledge of these things,' he replied.

Their conversation about Sunita's inheritance resumed after they had finished their main course.

'I've got something to tell you that should help you,' said Samir. 'I have a friend who's very good with investments. He's telling me how successful he is at making money for people.'

Sunita shrugged. 'Tell me more about him.'

'Well, he's twenty-seven and comes from Tamworth. His name's Indrani Sarkar.'

'How do you know him?'

'He was having a problem with his PC, which I was able to fix easily. It was no fantastic achievement, but he seemed to think I'm the world's greatest computer technician. Ever since, he's always calling me if he's got a problem and he's recommended me to all his friends. He's got an investment advice company, Safe Bastion Wealth Management, and he's the managing director. He knows how to make money for himself and for his friends and acquaintances. I think you should meet him and your sister might be interested in talking to him as well.'

'It sounds interesting,' said Sunita.

'You're not sounding very enthusiastic. Perhaps I shouldn't have mentioned it,' he said.

'No, thank you for telling me. It's just that—'

'What's the matter?'

'Well, you hear about these charlatans who rip people off. I'm not saying your good friend is like that, but I'm sure I ought to be wary.'

'Oh, absolutely, Sunita. Buyer beware. Of course, we read about these cases, but I can assure you he is a very honest, reliable person. I've known him for more than five years.'

'Well, I suppose there can be no harm in meeting him. I haven't got the money yet, of course, but, in a few weeks' time, I'm going to receive this amazing windfall and then I'll have to decide very quickly what to do with it. I don't want to lose interest on the money.'

Samir nodded. 'Would you and Tulika be free one evening next week to meet my friend?'

'I won't involve my sister for the moment. She's got very fixed views on things. She's very independent and likes to take her own decisions. But I'd like to meet this guy.'

'How about next Monday evening?'

'That sounds perfect.'

'I'll have a word with him and try and arrange things.'

Chapter 19

The headquarters of Talent Master Entertainment Agency turned out to be a huge red-brick building in the Birmingham suburb of Moseley.

Omar Khalid's sat nav led him along the traffic-clogged Queensbridge Road before directing him down a side street.

There was a small, off-road car park at the front. He parked between a pink Jeep and a beautifully restored E-Type Jaguar and stepped out. For a moment, he shivered in the cold morning air.

He had barely travelled three miles from his home in Acocks Green, but the temperature seemed to have plunged several degrees. He reached for his blue parka coat and slipped it on before negotiating his way round parked vehicles and reaching the main door.

'I'm looking for Mike Clayton,' he announced to a young blonde woman, sitting inside at a desk marked 'Reception'.

'Can I take your name, sir?'

'DC Khalid, Heart of England Police.'

'OK,' said the woman. She pressed a button on her phone and a man's voice responded.

'Mr Clayton, there's an officer of the law to see you,' she said.

After replacing the handset, she turned to Khalid. 'Mr Clayton says, if you'd like to go up to the first floor, he'll meet you there.'

After finding the lift, the detective was whisked to the floor above where a tall, bearded man with dark hair and a cheerful expression greeted him.

Clayton looked as bright as a Hawaiian sunrise in an orange shirt and crisp white suit.

'Sorry to call at a sad time,' said Khalid. 'Just need to ask a few questions concerning Miles Kenworth.'

'Of course. No problem. I'm Mike Clayton, managing director. Would you like to follow me? By the way, would you like a tea or coffee?'

'A black coffee would go down well,' he replied.

Clayton, whose Birmingham accent reminded Khalid of the chief inspector's voice, poked his head inside a nearby door.

'Claire, could you sort out two coffees – one white, one black?' he asked.

'Of course, Mr Clayton,' said a young female voice.

Turning to his guest, Clayton asked, 'Are you a music fan?'

'I listen to a bit of rock.'

'Are you familiar with the group called the Trojan Knights?'

'Don't think I've heard of them.'

Clayton led the detective into a bright, spacious room which resembled a living room rather than an office. There

88

were three luxurious leather sofas, a large desk, a grand piano and a sound system playing a slow ballad in the background.

Sitting on one of the sofas was a pretty teenager with pink hair and sunglasses in a long black dress and black leather boots.

'This is Tammy, the lead singer,' Clayton explained. Then he paused. 'I'm sorry, I didn't catch your name. Is it Khalid?'

'That's right,' said the detective.

'Tammy,' Clayton continued, 'this is a detective, Mr Khalid from Heart of England Police. Tammy and I have just finished our business and she's leaving in a moment.'

Tammy stood up and faced Clayton. 'So I'll come and see you on Thursday then,' she said, waving sweetly to Khalid.

'Yes, ten o'clock. Try to be prompt,' he said while escorting her out of the room.

'She's great,' he muttered on his return. 'Now, how can I help? What would you like to know about Miles Kenworth?'

'How long had you known him, sir?' asked Khalid as a woman served them both coffees.

'Altogether around ten years,' he replied. 'Miles was always fanatical about music. He was the go-to guy for any problems with light boards, mixing boards, microphones, amps and PA systems.'

Khalid took out a notebook. 'We've heard he'd made a move into events management.'

'Yes. He was very highly educated, of course – went to a public school in Shropshire, like his brother – and he was very professional during the two years he worked in the office as an events coordinator. He had the cachet that comes with being the son of a peer of the realm.'

'I sense there's a "but" coming,' said Khalid as he sipped his coffee.

'Yes. The bottom line is that he wanted my job, and, with the best will in the world, there was no way I was going to let him march in and take over from me. So, as you can imagine, there was some friction in the office.'

'Really?' said Khalid. 'So you fell out with him?'

'I wouldn't say that. We still got along all right, even though it's been hard because of the economic uncertainty. He was a very laid-back guy. Nothing much troubled him, so it was hard to dislike him. I'd just say he wasn't entirely happy playing along as my number two.'

Khalid was writing furiously in his book. 'So was he depressed?'

'No. Not at all. Quite the opposite – what with his new girlfriend and everything. He was in quite a bubbly mood all last week.'

'Did you just say he had a new girlfriend?' Khalid asked while drinking more of his coffee.

'Yes. He was besotted with her. He previously went around with a horsey type called Ursula. But this new woman seemed to have knocked his socks off.'

'What was her name?'

'Don't ask me. I only saw her the once last month. He brought her along to a rock concert we organised in the city.'

'What did she look like?'

'Now you've got me. I only saw her briefly at the start of the show. She wore a cowboy hat and a facemask.'

Khalid put down his pen. 'Were you in the office yourself all last week?'

'Off and on. I had to go over to Walsall to meet up with members of the Trojan Knights.'

'How about Friday?'

'I had to go over to the Resorts World Arena over at the NEC and I was there till eight o'clock.'

'Anyone vouch for that?'

'Yes, of course. Ask the Arena manager or any of his staff. I was there on business for several hours.'

'As far as you know, sir, apart from his thwarted ambitions in the events business, was anything troubling Mr Kenworth?'

'Like I say, he was a very laid-back guy. Nothing much troubled him.'

Chapter 20

The chief inspector watched from his doorway as his sergeant pinned photographs of all 'persons of interest' to the whiteboard near the coffee machine.

The gallery consisted of six faces. It began on the left with the scowling, bearded face of Jake Harris. It ended on the right with Charles Laxton, stern and business-like in his black-framed glasses.

'I see you've included a woman,' he remarked as Sunita scribbled names beneath each one.

'Yes, sir. Ursula Grey.'

He shook his head and tutted. 'In the realms of murder, we know women can be just as cruel and barbaric as men,' he said. 'But, in this case, all the signs are that the killer was a man. It takes a bit of muscle to wield an axe, you know.'

'Well, I thought I'd better include her,' said Sunita. 'She's obviously bitter about the way she's been treated. Her family were livid with Kenworth. If not her, maybe someone acted on her behalf.'

He shrugged. 'Unlikely. Anyway we'd better round everyone up,' he said. 'We said midday and it's nearly that now.'

Within the next few minutes, members of the CID team gathered in the area around the whiteboard. They sat themselves on chairs or desks as Sunita Roy added finishing touches to the display.

The moment Dawson arrived, he took a seat beside fellow constable Wendy Hopkirk and noticed several of the male suspects up on the board had facial hair.

'Not so much a bunch of suspects. More like a "Best beard of Britain" contest,' he joked.

'Have you got to sit so close to me?' Hopkirk complained.

The chief inspector clapped his hands and called his team to order.

'We've got some updates I wanted to share with you all,' he announced. 'Rupert Faulkner's alibi for last Friday evening checks out. The stage manager of his am-dram group has confirmed they were rehearsing Act 1, Scene 3 of *Julius Caesar* and Faulkner was there for the whole of Friday evening.

'But Charles Laxton's alibi has fallen through. The estate manager is meant to have spent the evening at The Plough pub in Hartston.'

'They do the best fish and chips in West Warwickshire,' remarked Dawson.

'It's all right, Brett,' said Roscoe drily. 'If I want to swot up on the county's cuisine, I'll reach for my *Michelin Guide*. If I can proceed, we've spoken to his drinking pal, Mr Duffy. He says they only met up in the pub at nine o'clock. So Laxton would have had time to enter through the window at Flat 1, attack Kenworth, go and clean himself up and still make it over for his drinking session.'

There were several murmurs among the team on hearing this.

'But what possible motive could Laxton have for killing Kenworth?' asked Dawson.

'I'll come to that in a moment,' said Roscoe. 'I'll let our sergeant give us a rundown on the other faces.'

Sunita nodded. 'Thank you, sir. Jake Harris is the guy found at the murder scene. There's still a thought that, maybe, he was responsible and simply ran out of time to escape. But there was no blood on his hands or clothes. If we accept the evidence of Aimee, the neighbour, it's unlikely he'd have had time to carry out the murder.

'Ursula Grey is the next mugshot. It's thought unlikely she'd be strong enough to wield an axe. It's possible a man acted on her behalf, although her father and two brothers have alibis.'

The chief inspector peered at the set of expectant faces.

'Her younger brother, Tony, was at a Young Farmers' social event,' he explained, 'while her older brother, Richard, was visiting family in Nottingham. Ursula's father, Claude, was at the Jolly Waggoners in Stratford the whole evening, according to the manager. Now we've just added Mike Clayton, Mr Kenworth's boss, to the board.'

'I'm glad he's up there,' remarked DC Khalid, who had arrived back from Moseley shortly before the briefing began. 'I sensed some ill feeling when I visited Mr Clayton just now.'

Sunita turned to Khalid. 'Clayton told you he was at the Resorts World Arena till eight o'clock, didn't he?' she said. 'But what do the staff there say about that?'

'I haven't had a chance to speak to them yet,' he admitted. 'But I managed to speak to a couple of Clayton's staff in the car park. They claimed the directors of the company had been talking about giving Clayton's job to Kenworth.'

'Really?' said Roscoe. 'That's interesting. See if you can get any more on that. Anyway, we finally come to Mr Laxton again. Now Dr Ling revealed to me a few days ago that there were traces of cocaine on Mr Kenworth's coffee table at the flat. Then this morning the incident room had an anonymous call to say Laxton has been in the habit, on occasion, of providing cocaine to his well-heeled chums. Of course, we need to check this out. In particular, we need to know if he ever supplied Miles Kenworth.'

* * *

A faint light shone down the stairwell as Logan Price turned his key in his front door and stepped into the hallway.

He glanced into the living room. No. His wife, Stephanie, hadn't waited up for him. He couldn't recall the last time she had.

After pouring himself a glass of water to take with him to the bedroom, he mounted the stairs and heard Stephanie's agitated voice calling.

'Can't you be a bit quieter? You've probably woken the whole street up,' she said. 'Did you know it's nearly half past one?'

'Since when were it a crime to go out on a Friday night?' he demanded.

'Suppose you've been with that Vivian again.'

'Yes. Just went back to his gaff to eat our kebabs and have a coffee.'

Stephanie appeared to have been asleep. She was sitting up on the far side of the bed in a pink nightdress. A table lamp glowed white beside her.

'You've got a nerve,' she said.

'How do you mean?'

'I've heard all about it. You went for breakfast at the shop and got slung out. How do you think that makes me feel?'

She slipped out of bed, picked up her hairbrush and threw it at him. More by chance than careful targeting, it struck him on the nose.

'Hey, that bloody hurt,' he shouted. 'There was a woman with a baby and your stuck-up manager wouldn't let her bring her buggy into the cafe.'

'Yes, it's fire regulations. Not only that. People sometimes can't get to a table because of pushchairs.'

'I were just having breakfast, which I'd paid for, when that Nick charged in, effing and blinding.'

She strode round the bed and glared at him.

'How do you think it makes me feel when everybody where I work is talking about us? Saying how Stephanie's husband lost his rag and had to be ordered out? You made me a laughing stock.

'Nick called me into the office. He said, "I've just had your husband in here. He was behaving like an idiot, arguing with me when I tried to explain to this woman that she couldn't bring her buggy into the cafe." He said you were rude and he told you to leave.'

She picked up a potted plant from the window ledge and hurled it at him. The pot smashed. The bamboo plant and earth landed on the carpet by the door. Then she picked up an upholstered footstool and struck her husband over the head with it.

'You've gone bloody mad,' he said, grabbing the stool from her and thrusting it back. She lost her footing and tumbled backwards onto the bed.

'I never know what to expect when I get home here,' he screamed. 'Your manager were behaving like a total prat.'

'I don't care. He's the bloody manager. Now everyone at work knows what a complete asshole I've got as a husband.'

She scooped up a quilt and a pillow which had been left on a pink velvet chair and hurled them at him.

'You can take your bloody bedding and go downstairs with it,' she cried. 'And you can move out at the weekend.'

She waved a book above her head in a threatening manner.

'First thing Monday I've got an appointment to see the solicitors. You're going to have to move out and I'm going to take you for every penny you've got. You're no husband to me anymore and I don't want anything more to do with you.'

Logan Price flew across the room and pushed her up against the bedroom door, crushing her neck with his right arm.

'I've stuck with you loyally for seven years, despite your cheating and your lying,' he yelled. 'I'm not going to let you throw this marriage away. If you go to the law, I'll fight you every step.'

Chapter 21

Stephanie Price could barely remember the last time she had been in such a foul mood.

As she negotiated her work van along the winding country lanes of West Warwickshire on Monday morning, thoughts of her car crash of a marriage and the impending divorce had been swirling round in her mind.

What concerned her most was whether her husband of seven years would ultimately take a reasonable approach and cooperate with the legal moves.

He seemed to have grown increasingly prepared to use violence against her. She simply had to escape from his coercive and controlling behaviour.

But it seemed likely he would dig his heels in and make the whole process as onerous as he could. If she succeeded in getting him to leave, would he help her with living costs or would she be forced to downsize and find a home that better suited a single person's income?

Her morning had started badly. After visiting her solicitor in Queensbridge High Street, the van had proved difficult to start and now it was raining. Further scattered showers were forecast for the rest of the day, she recalled, as she drove to Hartston Mill Farm in the village of Hartston and spent twenty minutes loading some logs into the back of the vehicle.

The only uplifting moment during the whole morning came while travelling to Lower Wood Farm, near Stratford.

She passed a field containing freshly born lambs beside their mothers. The idyllic scene caused her to smile. Then she rounded a bend and reached the farm entrance, where she was due to collect her second batch of winter logs.

After a brief drive along a stony track, she reached the red-brick, Victorian farmhouse at half past eleven and cut the engine. The air was still apart from the occasional bleating of sheep on the hill.

She would have expected the farmer, Mark Webster, to have come rushing out of the nearby concrete yard, carrying armfuls of logs. But nothing and no one stirred.

She gazed across at the barn beyond and the trees at the foot of the hill. A blue car was parked on a patch of grass beside an old mower, two tractors and a bicycle. There was no sign of jolly, rotund Mr Webster or his bubbly young wife.

Her attention was drawn to a white sheet of paper, pinned to the front door of the six-bedroom farmhouse.

She strolled across until she was close enough to read it.

> *Sorry, Steph. Taking ewe to the vet's. Logs behind machinery shed.*

She at once moved her van into the muddy yard, which was surrounded by single-storey sheds and stables, and began loading bundles of logs into the back.

Once all the logs had been loaded, Stephanie searched for the van keys in her pocket.

But some faint sounds caught her attention. She detected a muffled laugh, followed by moaning and groaning. The noise seemed to be coming from the dilapidated, timber-built barn, more than twenty metres away.

Her curiosity awakened, she left the van and strolled across. It was then she realised she had seen the blue car before. If she was not mistaken, it belonged to her friend Vicky Jones, a part-time assistant at the farm shop. She peered through the car windows. She was right. It was definitely Vicky's car. Two cute toy ducks were hanging from the rear-view mirror.

So was Vicky inside the barn? She heaved the door open and peered into the dark, musty space. Her eyes took a few seconds to focus.

Shafts of sunlight were streaming in through the open gable door and through gaps in the timber cladding onto the hayloft above.

Then her attention was drawn to the light-brown form of a man's naked back and posterior rising and falling at regular intervals among the hay. His movements were accompanied by the sound of heavy panting.

For a moment, her eyes remained absorbed by this frenzied activity close to the wooden loft ladder. Then, to her further surprise, she noticed some clothing draped haphazardly across hay bales on the barn floor. A purple top, dark trousers, white knickers and a bra. They were clearly Vicky's. But beside them were far more intriguing items of clothing: an olive-green waistcoat and matching pair of plus-fours together with a cloth cap. By a quirk of fate, she knew at once to whom they belonged.

'Opportunities like this don't come round that often in life,' she murmured to herself.

As she gazed up, an idea was forming in Stephanie's mind. She took her mobile phone from her jacket pocket and took several pictures of the bawdy scene being played out before her eyes like a porn movie.

The couple's actions continued unabated for several more minutes as she pressed the shutter button. At one point, Vicky sat up, her bare breasts swaying in the dust-filled beams of light.

Their ears seemed oblivious to the sound of the clicking camera as they reached the heights of passion.

Then Stephanie gasped as the man ceased his actions, raised himself up and crawled towards the ladder.

Fearing she would be seen and recognised, Stephanie took one more photograph of the crouching man and hurried out through the door, which she had left partly open.

Perhaps this final camera shot had constituted a step too far. Perhaps the man had heard the click of the camera. Or perhaps he had seen her figure slip from the shadows and dart through the doorway.

However it happened, the couple must have sensed they were not alone and rushed down the ladder to fetch their clothes.

Overhearing their garbled conversation, Stephanie panicked. Instead of returning to her car, she fled in the other direction.

She ran towards the pair of parked tractors and hid behind them.

Moments later, the couple, still buttoning up their clothes, darted out of the barn.

'I tell you there was definitely someone here,' the man was saying as Vicky, her blonde hair blowing in the breeze, unlocked her car. He ran to the side of the barn that was closest to the farmhouse and looked about.

Then he dashed to the other corner of the barn, a few metres from where Stephanie was crouching. She stayed stock-still as he peered out towards the fields and woods. She could hear every footstep. She could hear him breathing and swearing to himself.

'There's no one here. You're imagining it,' said Vicky as he walked back towards her and clutched her hands.

'Maybe you're right,' he said.

Again Stephanie snapped away with her camera as the couple, now reassured that they were alone, embraced and kissed before climbing into the car.

'Sorry,' said the man while settling into his seat. 'I was sure we'd closed the barn door. I must have been mistaken.'

'Maybe it came open on its own,' Vicky suggested.

'Yes. Maybe.'

Then, amid the sound of clanking gears, Vicky turned the car round and the vehicle sped away, up the farm track and out into the country lane.

Stephanie waited until she was sure they had gone. Then she viewed her phone's photo gallery while emerging from her hiding place.

She was delighted to find that, although some of the barn images were dark and of poor quality, several clearly showed the lascivious couple together. Several showed the man's naked, arched body. And several more showed their divested garments lying like a shameful secret among the hay.

She was equally pleased to see the sharp images taken in broad daylight of the couple with their faces turned towards the camera.

As she drove away from the farm, she smiled to herself. She was certain no one would have any difficulty identifying the brazen couple who had been making love in the cold morning air.

Chapter 22

As dusk approached that Monday evening, Sunita Roy drove into the North Warwickshire market town of Sedgeworth.

Her sat nav took her to Sidney Road, a narrow, one-way street of terraced houses with small front gardens on the southern side of town.

Her boyfriend had been watching through the downstairs window for her arrival and threw open the door to greet her.

'Is your friend here?' she asked.

He nodded. 'He's in the living room. Shall I take your coat?'

He helped her slip out of her beige woollen coat and hung it at the bottom of the stairs.

'Come on,' he said. 'I'll introduce you.'

Indrani Sarkar, a short, stocky man, rose from his seat on a grey, upholstered sofa and shook her hand. Then he gave her a smile like a ray of sunshine streaming across a cloudy sky.

'Such a pleasure to meet you, Miss Roy,' he said. 'Have you come directly from work?'

'Yes,' she said. 'It only took half an hour.'

She sat down in an armchair beside the brick fireplace while Samir joined his friend on the sofa.

'So I hear you're an investment manager?' she said, leaning back on her seat.

'Yes,' he said. 'You're welcome to have one of our brochures.'

He rose and handed her a shiny blue folder containing a brochure, a leaflet about interest rates and a business card. She glanced at it before placing it on the arm of the chair.

'Sunita, this is your lucky day,' he said, as he resumed his seat. 'You're probably familiar with the pathetic interest rates currently achievable on the high street. They're disgraceful, aren't they? Well, how do interest rates of between six and twelve per cent a month sound? Impressive, eh?'

'I must say that does sound good,' she admitted.

He twiddled with the end of his black moustache.

'You probably saw my new Ferrari sports car outside,' he remarked.

'The yellow car?'

He nodded. 'That's the one,' he said. 'I also have my own yacht at Folkestone and a villa in Calais. It's all possible, Sunita. You don't have to live a hand-to-mouth existence in this country. The openings are available for anyone with the gumption to take them. That's all it needs, Sunita. Gumption. Have you got gumption, Sunita?'

She giggled. 'I'm not sure.'

Samir interrupted to say, 'If you look through his brochure, Sunita, you'll see that a lot of celebrities have made money through investing in Indrani's scheme – sports people, actors and business people.'

'Yes, Sunita,' said Sarkar. 'All our success stories are in the brochure.'

She found his sales talk slightly irritating, but was intrigued by the revelations about his personal success. Samir was right. He seemed to have a knack of making money for both himself and for others.

'I understand you're a very fortunate young lady and that you've come into some money,' Sarkar continued. 'That's wonderful, but you have to be wise. A fool and their money – you no doubt know the expression.'

She nodded.

'Your money will be completely safe with my company. Guaranteed. All investment companies like ours are regulated these days. We provide short-term, bridging loans for companies that need finance urgently and cannot obtain it through the normal channels, for whatever reason. They're charged a high rate of interest for the privilege of obtaining these loans from us. As a result, we're able to pay our investors up to twelve per cent a month, Sunita. Everything is strictly confidential so that our niche area of funding doesn't attract much competition.

'Our investment fund was set up two years ago and you can only participate in it through personal invitation from myself. So this is a fantastic opportunity for you. Now how much money were you thinking of investing, Sunita?'

She felt uncomfortable. Mr Das in Leicester had informed her and her sister that an interim payment – representing around a third of the final expected payout – would be sent to their bank accounts within a few days. The figure he mentioned was a substantial sum in Sunita's eyes and she was slightly nervous even to speak about it.

But after a brief pause, she decided to disclose part of the amount which she wished to invest initially.

'Something like £300,000,' she said.

Sarkar was unfazed.

'That's fine, Sunita,' he said. 'We can promise you a very secure investment for that.'

'I'm not sure I want to invest all the money in one place,' Sunita remarked. 'Isn't it wise to spread your investments? That's what I was always told.'

'Who told you that?' he demanded.

'Well, my parents, for one thing.'

'And how successful are your parents?'

'Well, they're comfortably off. They own a guesthouse.'

'Do you want to be like them and comfortably off or do you want to be rich?' he continued. 'That's what you have to ask yourself, Sunita. I'm in the fortunate position of never having to worry about money again. And you could be too.'

He stepped across the room and picked up the folder from the arm of the chair. He opened it and showed her an application form, tucked inside the brochure.

'All you have to do is fill in your details,' he explained with a grin. 'Then, when you're ready to proceed, simply send it to me with a cheque for the correct amount or pay the money directly into our bank. Whichever you prefer.'

Sarkar spent the next half hour speaking glowingly of his firm and trying to get Sunita to complete the form there and then.

'You can send the money as soon as you receive it,' he said. 'Oh and by the way, I understand from Samir that your sister Tulika is also looking for somewhere to invest. Could I have her phone number? I'd hate it if she should miss out on this fantastic chance.'

'I'll have a word with her and see if she wants to become involved,' said Sunita. 'But she's a very independent lady and I think it unlikely.'

Sunita contended that she needed time to read the brochure and consider the proposition before completing the form.

But Sarkar warned her she might be sorry if she turned her back on the chance of a lifetime and failed to accept his invitation.

Samir supported his friend. 'Sunita, I think you should fill in the form now and send Indrani your money as soon as it comes through.'

'Do you?' she asked.

'Yes. Indrani isn't allowing all members of the general public to take advantage of his fund. It's strictly done on a friendship basis. He knows me very well and now he knows you.'

'That's right,' said the financial adviser. 'You're a preferential client. But I'm afraid my wonderful offer isn't open-ended. It can't be. So the sooner you sign up, Sunita, the better.'

Sunita had some doubts in her mind. Wouldn't it be better to read through the brochure first? But Sarkar sounded so convincing and her boyfriend of four years was sure the investment was safe.

'I'm sorry. I just want to run this past one of my police colleagues before I put pen to paper,' she said.

Chapter 23

Perspiring heavily after unloading all the logs at the farm shop and then visiting several other farms, Stephanie Price set off on one final journey of the day to the centre of Shawley Green.

She parked her van outside one of the semi-detached houses that curled round the far edge of the old village green and pushed open the wooden gate.

Clutching a large manilla envelope, she ran up the tarmacked path just after four o'clock and pressed the doorbell. Then she waited.

'Come on, Bella,' she muttered. 'I know you're in.'

After pressing the bell a second time, her older sister Isabelle finally drew back the door.

'I thought you were coming to see me tomorrow,' said the householder, who, unlike Stephanie, was overweight with short, auburn hair.

'I was passing, so I thought I'd drop by,' said Stephanie, brushing past her. She hurried through the dark hallway and took a seat at the kitchen table.

'How have you been getting on?' Isabelle asked, heading straight for the kettle and filling it with water.

'I've thrown Logan out,' she replied. 'I've decided I'm going to start a new life and I've found exactly the way to fund it.'

The older woman took two mugs from a Welsh dresser and placed a teabag in each. 'Sounds all very dramatic, Steph. You told me you'd finished with Logan anyway. You've been sleeping apart for months, haven't you?'

'Yes, and I'm finally calling it a day now. About a week ago, he was involved in a brawl in The Crown and Sceptre, and the other night he nearly strangled me.'

'Oh my God,' said her sister.

'Yes. He had me up against the bedroom door and really hurt my neck, pressing his arm against me.'

'You must be a bit concerned about going back to your house,' said Isabelle, whose eyebrows rose and fell continually while she spoke. 'Do you want to stay here with me for a while?'

'No. It's all right. Logan doesn't always come home. I think he might be staying round at his mother's. He'll gradually accept it's over between us.'

'That explains why I saw his van round here the other day,' said Isabelle, pouring out the tea and adding milk.

Stephanie glanced up. 'Where did you see it?'

'In Highfield Road. He must have been on the way to see his mother after work. So you've got some clever scheme to make some money, have you?'

'Yes,' Stephanie said, as her sister handed her one of the mugs of tea. 'I've been worried that, while the divorce is going through, Logan won't give me a penny. I'm not sure I could manage on just the wages I get from the shop. But then, today, a bit of luck fell my way.'

'Good to see Lady Luck's smiling on someone,' said Isabelle as she sipped from her mug. 'I've been having a terrible time at work. So what's happened?'

'I don't want to say too much. Let's just say I've caught someone in a compromising situation and I've got pictures. I know this guy's got money. I'm sure he'd do anything to prevent his wife seeing them, so I'm going to make an anonymous call to him.'

'Oh, Stephanie,' said her sister. 'Are you sure about this? I mean, you could get into trouble – you know, with the police. It's blackmail.'

'How could I?' asked Stephanie, sipping her tea. 'You're the only one that knows. I'm not telling anyone else.'

Isabelle sat down, looking pensive. She seemed as comfortable as an Eskimo in a heatwave.

'Where are the pictures? On your phone? I think you should delete them,' she said after a long pause. 'No good can come from this.'

'Bella,' said Stephanie, 'I've just told you. No one else knows except you and no one else is going to know. And if the guy gives me enough money, no one will EVER find out.'

'Who is this guy and who's the woman?'

'It's no one you know.'

'It's not old man MacLeod at the shop, is it?'

'No. I'm not going to tell you.'

'At least tell me who the woman is.'

'I don't think I ought to at this stage.'

'She's not a kid, is she?'

'She's someone I vaguely know who's in her twenties.'

'How much are you going to be looking for?'

'I thought £50,000 would be a reasonable amount to ask for after a romp in the hay, don't you? He obviously doesn't want his wife to know. I think that's a fair sum for me to delete the pictures and keep my mouth shut.'

Isabelle tutted. 'Maybe he won't play ball. Maybe he's planning to leave his wife anyway and was about to break the news to her.'

Stephanie shrugged. 'I must admit that's the only flaw in my scheme. But hey! Nothing ventured, eh?'

Isabelle was still thinking. She drank some more tea.

'How do you propose to contact him? You're not going round to where he lives, surely?'

'No, no. I'll find his phone number.'

'How do you plan to get that?'

'From the shop. They take emails and phone numbers of customers. They should have his mobile on the system.'

'You cunning little vixen.'

'I've got to learn to stand on my own feet now, Bella. I need to get Logan out of my life. Every day he becomes more and more violent. I've been thinking about it for a long time. I've seen a solicitor.'

'Have you told Logan?'

'Yes.'

'Don't suppose he's very happy about it.'

'He's furious, but life moves on. It can be really tough out there, you know? Look what happened to poor Miles.'

'I know. Dreadful,' Isabelle agreed.

* * *

As she had expected, it proved relatively easy for Stephanie to obtain the man's mobile phone number from the farm shop's computer system early the next morning.

She was alone on the check-out till for the first hour and it took just five minutes for her to find the information.

Over the rest of the day, she carefully planned her strategy. She decided to make contact with her target by phone and withhold the number so the call could not be traced. She had to remain anonymous.

At home that afternoon, after making herself a cup of tea, she called a friend who worked for a phone company. She explained she wanted an untraceable prepaid mobile phone.

'I'll have one ready for you tomorrow,' he assured her.

'Perfect,' replied Stephanie, who had decided to transfer all the compromising pictures onto this new burner phone.

Then she sat down at her dining table with her laptop and set up a temporary email account with bogus personal details so that she could send a few of the pictures to the man – to prove she had the incriminating material and wasn't making the whole thing up. That process took her nearly an hour.

She decided, once she received the money she was demanding, she would simply hand the prepaid phone over to him.

The next morning, she collected the prepaid mobile, returned home and sat down at her dining room table. Then she readied herself to make the call.

'If he answers, I may have to make up a name,' she told herself. 'It's very unlikely he'll recognise me from my voice. I'm just going to tell him I've got some pictures that he'd be very interested in. Here goes.'

She dialled the man's number.

Somebody answered. It sounded like a man's voice but there was some static on the line.

'Hello,' said Stephanie in her mellow voice.

'Who's this?' he demanded.

'You don't know me but I know what you've been up to.'

'What on earth do you mean? Hang on a minute. I'd better take this call outside.'

There was a muffled background conversation before he spoke to her again a few seconds later.

'Are you still there?' he asked.

'Yes, I'm still here. I was just saying I know what you've been up to. I saw you with Vicky Jones at Lower Wood Farm yesterday.'

'I've not been to Lower Wood Farm.'

'I saw the two of you in the barn. I've got pictures. They're probably not the kind of pictures your wife would want to see. Or your employer. Or the local newspaper.'

There was a pause. Stephanie imagined the shock of her disclosure had hit home.

'I understand what you're saying,' said the man.

'If you give me an email address, I can send some of them over – you know, to give you a flavour of what we're talking about. Or I could put some in the post.'

'No, don't do that,' he said abruptly. She noticed he had raised his voice; the latter suggestion had caused him alarm.

'Perhaps we can come to some arrangement,' he said. 'But first of all I need to know that you're genuine. What's your name by the way?'

'You can call me Jackie,' Stephanie replied.

'Listen, Jackie. I'm sure we can come to an understanding over this. How did you get my number, by the way?'

'Let's just say I have my means.'

'All right. You're not going to tell me. You must be someone that knows Vicky as well as myself.'

'You're straying away from the main topic,' she said. 'Give me your email address and I'll send you some of the pictures I've got.'

'Are you going to send them straight away?'

'Yes.'

'How did you get hold of these pictures anyway?'

'Let's just say it was a lucky break. I came into the barn to see what was going on.'

'Do you work at the farm?'

'No.'

'Does anyone else have these pictures?'

'No.'

'How do I know you're telling the truth?'

'You'll just have to trust me.'

'Trust you? Trust someone who...? Oh all right. Look, send me this email. Then call me back after ten minutes.' He then hung up.

Stephanie emailed him three images. One portrayed him crawling towards the ladder in the hayloft. One showed his clothes strewn across a hay bale. One depicted him and Vicky kissing passionately in the open air.

Ten minutes passed. She phoned his number again.

'All right,' he told her. 'What exactly do you want?'

'I want £50,000 in fifty-pound notes. For that you can have my phone with all the pictures on. I'm going to wipe all other information off the phone.'

There was silence for a moment. Then the man said, 'I can't get all that money together straight away. It'll take time.'

'How much time do you need?'

'A day or so.'

'All right. How about tomorrow evening?' she asked.

'How can I get this money to you?'

Stephanie said, 'You know the farm shop at Shawley Green?'

'Yes. The Orchard Lane Farm Shop.'

'That's it,' she said. 'I'll be there at eight o'clock tomorrow evening.'

'That's after the shop closes.'

'That's right. Just make sure you bring the money in a carrier bag. I'll bring my phone and we'll do the exchange.'

'How will I recognise you, Jackie?'

'You won't. I'll come and find you. Do you know the bench on the grass area next to the car park?'

'Is it the one that's close to some trees?'

'The very same. Sit down on that bench at eight o'clock and I'll come over to find you. And there's something else I need to tell you. Don't go to the police or those pictures will go straight out on social media.'

Chapter 24

'They still can't make up their minds,' said Helen Roscoe as she poured her husband a second cup of tea.

He looked up from reading his newspaper. 'Who can't?' he asked as he finished eating his cooked breakfast.

'George and Amanda,' she replied. 'You haven't been listening to a word I've been saying, have you?'

'Of course, I have,' he insisted. 'You've seen snowdrops in the back garden.'

'It was two minutes ago I told you that. I've begun discussing the wedding plans.'

'I thought they were going to hold it at St John the Martyr. They haven't dropped that idea, have they?'

She took a chair on the opposite side of the kitchen table.

'No. It's the reception that's causing a problem. They thought of holding it at Culverdon Hall, but it's quite expensive. So they're toying with the Coach and Horses.'

'Brian's pub's got a large enough function room. I'd have thought that would be ideal.'

'It's either that or the church hall in Oxford Lane.'

'Oh, it would be a shame to hold it there. There isn't room to swing a cat.'

'Or a grasshopper, as George would say,' she remarked.

'In any case, it's only half a mile from the church to The Coach and Horses,' he continued. 'It would make things a lot easier for the guests.'

The faint sound of throbbing music interrupted their conversation. Mel, with a pair of headphones strapped to her head, poked her head round the door.

'Just off now,' she said, nodding her head in time to a rap music track.

'Hold on!' said her mother. 'Have you got your sandwiches?'

'Yes, Mum. Oh hi, Dad. Didn't see you there. Everything all right? Haven't seen you in days.'

'Been working long hours,' her father said. 'Off to the riding stables?'

'Yes. I'm helping out with a group of novice riders,' she said while detaching her headphones and turning the music off.

'Have you seen anything of Ursula?' he asked, pushing his empty plate aside.

'Yes. She hasn't said much to me,' she replied. 'But one of the other instructors was chatting to me the other day. She said Ursula keeps going through Miles's Facebook page.'

'Rather a morbid thing to do when the guy's dead,' said Roscoe.

'Yes. I suppose it is. Apparently she's been looking to see if he had another girlfriend, but hasn't found anything yet.'

'Interesting,' said her father, slurping his tea. 'Let me know if you get to hear anything else, won't you?'

* * *

An hour later, after arriving at the CID office, the chief inspector called Omar Khalid into his room.

The young detective appeared slightly dishevelled. His curly black hair was mussed and his shirt creased.

'Everything all right, Khalid?' he asked.

'To be honest, sir, I've been doing a lot of overtime. Just need to catch up on my sleep.'

Roscoe nodded. 'Make sure you do,' he said. 'How did you get on at the NEC?'

'I spoke to the manager at the Arena, someone in the ticket office and a guy at the Explorer Lounge. They all remember seeing Mike Clayton on the Friday evening.'

Roscoe smiled. 'I remember in your report you described Clayton as flamboyant. He's clearly the kind of guy people remember.'

'Yes, sir. They all confirmed he was there on the Friday night.'

'So I guess that rules him out as a suspect.'

'Yes.'

Their conversation was interrupted by a knock. Sunita Roy's cheerful face appeared in the doorway.

'Sir, are you busy?' she asked.

'No. Khalid's just going. Come straight in, Sergeant. We'll talk later, Khalid.'

The constable held the door open for his sergeant as he left.

'We've finished going through all the CCTV,' she informed him as she took a seat. 'There's only one positive result from the hours we've spent trawling through all the footage. We've found Charles Laxton's car entering Fishpond Lane at a quarter past seven on the evening of the murder.'

'Laxton's car?'

'Yes. His green Land Rover Discovery.'

Roscoe leaned forward in his chair. 'That's brilliant,' he said. 'I've been suspicious of that guy since we first met him. Do you remember? He evaded us at the hall. He's clearly got something to hide.'

'As well as an alibi that doesn't hold together,' added Sunita.

'That's right. We've got a lot more questions for him. A quarter past seven, you say?'

She nodded. 'Yes, sir.'

'Don't you think that's a little early in the timescale? Everything seems to be pointing to the murder occurring closer to a quarter to eight.'

'If Laxton's the killer, maybe he was with Kenworth for half an hour?'

'Yes. Anyway it's a giant leap forward for us,' said Roscoe.

'Yes, sir. Dawson picked him up passing the Mill Road Nail Bar and turning into the top of the lane. The only trouble is there's no sign of his vehicle leaving by the same route. We've checked thoroughly.'

He shrugged. 'Maybe he drove off down the lane. It's not a cul-de-sac, is it?'

'No. Fishpond Lane leads to De Vere Road. He could have gone off that way. Perhaps we should see if there are any CCTV cameras in De Vere Road?'

'Don't worry about that for the moment. The main thing is we've got a suspect in the vicinity at around the time of the murder. So we'll need a search warrant for his home. Do you know where he lives?'

'Yes. He's renting a detached bungalow in Brook Lane, Hartston, but right now I imagine he'll be at the estate office, near Culverdon Hall.'

'We ought to go there straight away, the two of us,' he said. 'It looks very much as though Laxton may have been supplying Miles Kenworth with drugs. Perhaps Kenworth wasn't paying Laxton what he owed. Or perhaps there was some other dispute between them.

'Anyway we'll have to search him and his car for any substances, so we'd better invite some of our uniformed friends along and a forensics team. This is an important moment, Sergeant. Our first major breakthrough in the case.'

Chapter 25

The Culverdon Hall estate office was based in a small, detached house a quarter of a mile from the main house. But it was hidden away behind trees on the opposite side of the main road.

The chief inspector, accompanied by his sergeant, was convinced they might never have found it at all but for a small sign they spotted among the bushes.

He stopped his car by the side of the road. He and his sergeant chatted together for a few minutes until two cars in the Heart of England Police livery arrived. Then they drove in convoy down a narrow lane, shrouded on both sides by high hedges.

The red-brick office building was surrounded by a series of outbuildings – giving the impression they had once formed a thriving farm.

Charles Laxton's Land Rover Discovery was among vehicles parked beside the two front windows.

Roscoe led his sergeant and four constables to the main door and pressed the bell.

After nearly a minute, a middle-aged lady with grey hair and glasses appeared on the doorstep, looking bewildered.

'Can I help?' she asked.

After showing his warrant card and explaining their purpose, they watched as she retreated into a large, plain hallway and knocked on a side door.

Laxton emerged, casually dressed and looking slovenly.

'Perhaps he saves his best look for the weekend,' Sunita mused.

'Morning, Chief Inspector. What's all this about?' he asked with a cheery expression as he reached the doorway.

'Sorry, sir. We need to ask you more questions.'

His smile faded. 'Oh for heaven's sake,' he said.

'Your car's been picked up on camera driving into Fishpond Lane round about the time of Mr Kenworth's murder.'

'Has it? Well, I can explain. But I'm at work at the moment. My staff are around and it's all very embarrassing to have you people here. Could you come back later?'

Sunita interrupted. 'In view of your failure to liaise with us last time, I think you know what our answer to that's going to be.'

The chief inspector continued, 'Mr Laxton, you have a choice. You can either come with us now to police headquarters of your own free will and have a chat or we can arrest you and take you away for questioning.'

'Doesn't sound like much of a choice. All right. I'll come with you. I'll just get my coat.'

He walked back towards his office. Sunita decided he was a man you couldn't even trust to feed a friend's pet rabbit. She turned to the constable standing behind her.

'Better get after him and see he doesn't try to make off,' she said.

The officer followed Laxton into his room. A few minutes later, they both appeared. The estate manager was holding his khaki shooting jacket.

'There's absolutely no need for this intrusion,' he insisted. 'I never gave permission for this policeman to enter my office.'

Roscoe sighed. He was becoming exasperated by Laxton's attitude.

'We need your car keys as well, sir,' he said.

'Oh for God's sake,' Laxton replied, reaching into his trouser pocket. 'Here you are.' He dropped the keys on the ground beneath Roscoe's feet.

'Oh dear. I seem to have dropped them.'

'Right, that's enough,' said the chief inspector. 'Charles Laxton, I'm arresting you on suspicion of the murder of Miles Cedric Kenworth. Read him the caution, Sergeant.'

* * *

Three hours later, Charles Laxton was sitting in Interview Room One at St James Street, casting his eyes through the window at the car park and the children's playground on the other side of the street.

The chief inspector and his sergeant peered through the one-way glass from the office next door.

'You wouldn't think an educated man like that would be involved in drugs,' Sunita remarked.

'Sergeant, you've got a lot to learn,' said Roscoe. 'In my long years in the force, people who buy and sell drugs come from all walks of life. Come on. Let's go and see what he's got to say.'

A few moments later, the pair entered the room followed by Laxton's solicitor Salman Siddiqui, a short, plump man of fifty-five in a dark-grey suit. Roscoe sat down beside Sunita.

'I've spoken to my client and he simply cannot understand why he's here,' said Mr Siddiqui, as he and Laxton faced them across the table. 'Do you have evidence to suggest he's responsible for the murder of Miles Kenworth? My client says the whole matter is utterly preposterous.'

'Mr Siddiqui,' said Roscoe, pulling a black-and-white photograph from an envelope. 'First of all, I'm in charge of this interview – not you. I'm about to explain why we've decided to question him and he'll be given every opportunity to explain himself.'

He placed the picture in front of the estate manager.

'Now, Mr Laxton, is this your vehicle?'

The suspect peered at the image before acknowledging it was his Land Rover.

'For the purposes of the tape, Mr Laxton is nodding his head,' said Sunita.

Roscoe continued, 'You've been picked up on a CCTV camera, driving into Fishpond Lane in Queensbridge at around the time of Mr Kenworth's murder. So why did you lie to us and say you were at The Plough at Hartston from 8 p.m.?'

'Look, all right. I did drive over to Queensbridge.'

'What time did you arrive there?'

'I think it was something like half past eight.'

Sunita intervened to say, 'This still shows you turning into the lane from Mill Road at a quarter past seven.'

'Oh well, OK. It must have been then.'

'Where were you going?' asked Roscoe.

'I was going to see Miles. I've known him, off and on, for about five years.'

'So you called round at his flat in Waverley Court?'

'Yes, but I couldn't get a reply. He'd got his bloody music on loud. I tried phoning him, but his phone was off. So I gave up and went to The Plough.'

'Were Lord Culverdon and his family aware that you knew him?' asked Sunita.

'I don't really know. I suppose so.'

Roscoe leaned back in his chair. 'What was the basis of your friendship?' he asked.

'I was with Lavinia one day when we met up with Miles and I was introduced to him. We had a mutual interest in horses, conservation and he was very knowledgeable about sound systems.'

'I'm going to suggest to you that that's a load of hogwash. Your mutual interest was in drugs, wasn't it?'

Laxton turned red. He glanced at his solicitor, who whispered in his ear.

'I've been advised to make no comment,' he replied.

'While you've been waiting to be interviewed, our forensic people have been at work. They found some cannabis hidden in the central console of your vehicle.'

'That was for purely personal use,' he insisted.

'We've also found a small amount of cocaine in the kitchen of your bungalow.'

He glanced at Mr Siddiqui. 'No comment.'

'You were supplying Miles Kenworth with cocaine, weren't you?'

'No comment.'

'We found traces of cocaine on his coffee table. You visited him on 11 February because he'd reneged on a payment to you. As a result, you got into a dispute with him and attacked him.'

'That's a total lie,' said Laxton.

'He owed you money, didn't he?'

'No, of course not. Is this what this is all about? There's no way I was in any kind of dispute with Kenworth and I certainly wasn't supplying him with cocaine. The whole idea's ridiculous.'

'We've found his phone number on your mobile. Were you supplying him with cannabis?' Sunita inquired.

'All right. I won't deny I sometimes let Miles have a bit of weed, but that's as far as it went. I'm not a bloody drug dealer, I can assure you. I've got a reasonable job that pays well. I don't need to make any extra money from the drug world.'

Roscoe frowned. 'How do you account for the cocaine we found in your kitchen?'

'I know nothing about it. Perhaps it belonged to someone else. I certainly didn't know there was cocaine in the bungalow. You've got to believe me. All this could lead to me getting the sack from my job.'

Roscoe shrugged. 'You should have thought of that before, shouldn't you?' he said.

'Look,' Laxton continued, 'as far as Miles was concerned, I thought he was a great guy. I liked him a lot. I thought it was a shame he'd fallen out with his family, and I did my best to bring the two sides together. I think he thought that he could stand on his own two feet and, up to a point, he did. But he had a lot of demons. It's difficult being brought up in a well-to-do family and then turning your back on that way of life. But I have to tell you that, in the last few weeks of his life, I've never seen him happier.'

Sunita was intrigued by this revelation. 'How do you account for that, Mr Laxton?'

'He told me he'd met this amazing woman.'

'Any idea who she was?' asked Sunita. 'Or how he came to meet her?'

'He was very secretive about it, but he let her name slip by mistake. He just said something about being unable to stop thinking about Vani.'

'That sounds like a short form for Vanessa,' Roscoe remarked.

Sunita had her own theory. The name Vani was a name of Hindu or Sanskrit origin, derived from the name of the goddess Saraswati. It was a popular women's first name in India. But she kept that to herself for now.

'Mr Siddiqui,' said Roscoe, 'I've been minded to charge your client with possession of a class A drug. I'm not convinced by his denials. However, we want to make further inquiries. Should the CPS eventually decide to charge him, since this is a first offence, it may well be dealt with by way of a caution.

'He remains a person of interest to us as regards the murder of Mr Kenworth. However, for now, I'm going to release him on police bail.'

'You're bailing him?' said the lawyer.

'Yes. Otherwise, I fear he may vanish or refuse to cooperate in further proceedings. Conditions will be that he must surrender his passport and report to Stratford police station on certain dates.'

* * *

Following Charles Laxton's release, the chief inspector invited his sergeant and other members of the team for a drink.

But Sunita had had a tiring day and decided to head home. After making excuses, she hurried up to their first-floor office to collect her coat.

As soon as she reached her desk, she glanced at her phone and noticed someone had left her a message.

She pressed the playback button and the gentle voice of Stephanie Price flowed from the speaker.

Sunita had given the woman her direct line phone number and urged her to call if she thought of any further information that could be helpful.

'This is a message for DS Roy, who came to see me last week,' said the voice. 'This is Mrs Price. I need to speak to you urgently.'

Chapter 26

Eager to hear what Stephanie Price had to say, Sunita Roy tried repeatedly to reach the woman during Wednesday evening and Thursday morning.

But every time she dialled her phone, the call diverted to her answering service.

The sergeant even tried calling the farm shop, but failed to make contact with her there either and was obliged to leave a series of messages, urging Stephanie to phone her as soon as possible.

She was glad when six o'clock came and she prepared to leave the office.

Sunita was making her way down the stairs when she heard a cheerful voice in a Black Country accent say, 'Here's the girl of the moment.'

She was delighted to find her ex-boyfriend, DI Tom Vickers, waiting on the half-landing with a broad smile.

'Good to see you,' she said, beaming. 'What's it like to be a boss?'

Vickers, newly promoted to run the CID office in the Warwickshire town of Summerstoke, replied, 'It's bostin.'

Then, remembering she was unfamiliar with his Midlands slang, he quickly added, 'Smashing. Don't forget to let me know whenever you want a job.'

She laughed. 'I'm happy here. Tom, I might need your advice at some point. The DCI's current theory on the axe murder is that a guy working as a manager for the Kenworth family is behind it. I'd like to hear your thoughts sometime.'

'Why not now? I've just been called in to see Norris, but I'll only be a few minutes. Shall we have a drink in the Fleece?'

'Yes, sure. But I can't stay too long.'

Half an hour later, the pair were sitting in a corner of the CID pub, The Golden Fleece, amid the clamour of voices and clinking glasses. She was glad of his company as they discussed the Kenworth case like two long-lost friends reunited after a period of time.

'The problem with the guvnor is he gets fixated on a particular suspect and it's hard to shake him off,' Vickers admitted as he sipped his lager. 'Are there a lot of them?'

'We've got seven main suspects. Three relatives of Kenworth's ex-girlfriend; a guy caught beside the body; Kenworth's drug supplier; and his boss at work.'

'That's intriguing – the guy caught with the body,' he said.

'His presence there doesn't make sense,' she said. 'There were witnesses around. Looks like he just lost his temper because loud music was playing and got caught with the body by coincidence.'

'One hell of a coincidence. Tell you what. If you allow me access to the files, I'll have a look and let you know my thoughts.'

'Would you do that, Tom? That would be so helpful. I'm really determined to crack this case. I'm putting in for my inspector's exams soon and it would look so good if I could add this one to my CV.'

'By the way, I hear you may be buying a house,' said Vickers.

Sunita winced. 'Whoever told you that?'

'Oh, it was just something the guvnor said.'

'All that's happened is my uncle's died and left Tulika and me some money. Actually I was going to ask you about this. I've had a chat with a financial advisor and I wondered if you knew how I could check to make sure he's sound.'

'I'd be delighted to help,' said Vickers. 'There are so many sharks around these days and so many scams. What's the company called?'

She took a sip of her orange juice. 'Safe Bastion Wealth Management. The guy's name is Indrani Sarkar.'

'Are they regulated by the Financial Conduct Authority?'

'I've been told they are.'

'Look, one of my best mates, Gary, works for the fraud squad with City of London Police.'

'I'd be so grateful if you could make sure the guy is genuine.'

'OK. Leave it with me. I'll make sure you don't get into any trouble.'

* * *

Shawley Green was cloaked in darkness as Stephanie Price hurried along the main road later that same evening.

She walked into the farm shop car park, partly illuminated by the glow of two lamp posts, and made her way to the double garage behind the main building, where her van was kept. The area was partly shielded from the car park by a row of shrubs.

It was five minutes to eight. All being well, the man she'd seen in the hayloft would be arriving shortly with a carrier bag full of money. Money that would set her on the path to a new life.

As Stephanie reached the two linked garages, she put on a facemask. She didn't want the hayloft man to be able to identify her.

To her surprise, she found the white up-and-over door was unfastened and the padlock missing.

'I'm sure I locked it,' she murmured to herself. 'Maybe one of the MacLeods had to fetch something and forgot to secure it.' The lock on the second garage remained fastened.

She turned off the exterior light and stepped towards the bushes, where she eventually found the padlock.

She crouched down and smiled in satisfaction. From her vantage point close to the garages, she had an unobstructed view of the bench where, in a few minutes' time, she expected the man to arrive with her money.

Minutes passed. The only noise came from traffic on the main road. Then her attention was drawn to the sound of a car slowing down. Was its driver heading for the car park? No, he or she was merely stopping to read the opening times, listed on a painted board at the front. They pulled away soon afterwards.

It was now three minutes past eight. Perhaps the man was not coming. Perhaps he was calling her bluff.

Then she heard footsteps on the asphalt path. She stood up and looked around. A man in dark clothing was approaching through the gloom. Could this be the man with the money? Surely not. They'd arranged to meet by the bench, more than thirty metres away.

She turned the light on again for a better view.

She saw the man's face and gasped.

'What are you doing over here?' she demanded.

'Just wanted to look at you,' he replied.

'What do you mean?' Her heart was beating faster now. Her breathing quickened. She wished she'd stayed at home.

His eyes were crazed like those of a rabid dog. He was cursing her beneath his breath. He lurched towards her.

Unsure which way to turn, Stephanie raced inside the garage and tried to pull down the steel door, but he blocked her efforts. He put his foot in the way and, when she gave up struggling with it, he hauled the door up again and made his way inside.

She found herself trapped in the metre-wide gap between the van and the wall as he advanced menacingly towards her.

'I just wanted to see what you'd be like in the dying moments of life,' he declared while grabbing her neck and slamming her against the brick wall.

Stephanie was determined to break loose and seek help. She raised her right knee sharply, causing him pain in the groin. Then she tried to slip from his grasp but he was too swift.

He thrust her hard against the wall again with his gloved hands and, for several seconds, they grappled with each other in the corner. She punched him in the face and neck, and tried to grab his hair.

Then she saw him pull something heavy from his belt – a clawhammer.

In a frenzy, he began raining blows onto her head and her facemask slipped to the ground.

Such extreme force was used that, after several blows, she was unable to fight back and collapsed onto the garage floor in a pool of blood.

Chapter 27

Martyn Appleton smiled as the cup of steaming hot drink was placed on the table in front of him. He reached forward and took a sip.

'This is a lovely tea,' he announced.

'I get it from the farm shop across the road,' said the smiling guesthouse owner. 'They do a terrific range, but I prefer this particular blend.'

'I can see why,' said Appleton, a short, amiable man with dark hair.

'So what time's your interview with the insurance company tomorrow?' asked his hostess, sitting down on the other side of the table.

'Nine thirty,' he said.

'And what time will you be wanting your breakfast?'

'Could we say seven thirty? I need to get over there early. I won't know what the parking situation is like until I get there.'

'Oh, they're a big company. You shouldn't have any trouble getting into their car park.'

'Parking these days is such a worry,' he said.

'Yes. I only wish we'd more space outside here, but, as I warned you on the phone, we've only got the two spaces at the moment – till all the building work is finished.'

'It's lucky there's that huge car park at the farm shop opposite,' said Appleton.

'Yes. I'm sure your Audi will be quite safe over there. I've been telling our guests that they can park there at night and there've never been any problems.'

'I've just remembered… I've left an envelope with the company's brochure in the car. I think I ought to go and get it. I need to swot up on the firm and its history before my interview.'

The landlady smiled. 'You certainly are keen to get this job, aren't you, Mr Appleton?'

He nodded. 'Yes. It would mean a lot more money for me. I got married last year and we're saving for a house.'

Ten minutes later, Appleton left the Woodside Guesthouse. He crossed the Stratford Road and walked into the car park belonging to the Orchard Lane Farm Shop.

The site was deserted apart from his car and three other vehicles. It was shrouded by a line of trees on the edge closest to the road. On the far side lay open fields.

He strolled to his car and retrieved his brochure. But, as soon as he relocked it, he noticed a bright light shining out like a beacon from a building beside the shop. He stepped closer.

'Someone's working late,' he told himself.

Appleton was about to walk away, but a sudden thought occurred to him. He remained concerned about his car being parked on private land. If there was someone inside the garage, perhaps they could reassure him that it was safe to leave his car there. He only had the word of the guesthouse owner – and she was a relative stranger to him.

He walked towards the light until he reached the line of bushes in front of the garage and could see the front of a white van. He peered inside and then stopped in his tracks.

Beside the van lay a red trail on the concrete. He looked more closely. There was something on the floor at the rear of the van. Was it a bundle of clothing? Or was it someone lying there?

'Oh my God!' he said, clutching his face with his hands.

Whatever was lying there, beneath the gleaming light, was soaked in blood.

Suddenly a hooded figure dressed in black darted past him and sprinted off like a greyhound.

'Hold on a minute,' Appleton shouted.

The hooded figure – whom he assumed to be a man – careered out of the farm shop's main entrance and turned left. Then he stooped down on the grass verge where a bicycle was lying. He raised it by the handlebars, jumped into the saddle and cycled frantically away.

Frustrated at being unable to halt the fleeing figure, Appleton turned back to the garage and ventured inside. As he passed along the side of the vehicle, his worst fears were confirmed. A woman was lying on the ground. But he was uncertain whether she was dead or alive.

'Hello,' he said hesitantly. 'Can you hear me?'

Silence.

'Are you OK?'

Silence again.

He drew his mobile phone from his pocket and dialled 999.

'Ambulance service, please,' he told the emergency operator after returning to the path outside.

Within seconds, he was transferred to a female ambulance call handler, who asked, 'Is the patient breathing?'

Appleton was unsure what to say. Since entering the garage he'd been unable to think straight.

'I don't know,' he said. 'I've just found this woman lying on the floor of a garage. I don't know if she's breathing. Hold on.'

He walked back inside, taking care not to step on any blood. For several seconds, he stared at the woman, whose face and head were drenched in blood.

'Caller, are you still there?'

'Yes,' he said. 'I'm checking on her. I can't see her chest rising and falling. Oh my God, I don't think she is breathing. Can you send people quickly? I'm worried this poor woman's going to die.'

Chapter 28

Sunita Roy was relaxing on her sofa, reading a romantic novel when her handset began to vibrate and an image of the chief inspector's smiling face appeared on the screen.

'Don't know what he's got to smile about,' she whispered to herself before answering.

'Sergeant, have you heard what's happened?' he asked.

'No, sir.'

'A woman's been brutally attacked and she's not expected to live,' he said.

'That's terrible, sir. When was this?'

'About two hours ago,' he replied.

She glanced at her watch. It was just after ten o'clock.

'You're at home?' he asked.

'Yes. I've just had a call from the control room.'

Sunita put down her book. 'Whereabouts did this happen, sir?'

'Shawley Green. Behind the farm shop where the axe was taken.'

'Do you think there's a link to the Kenworth murder?'

'Too early to say, isn't it? I've sent Khalid down there, but I'd like you to go in the morning and link up with him. See what you can pick up. One of the first calls about it came from a guy called Appleton, who's staying at the guesthouse across the road. He'd left his car in the car park and went over to fetch something from it. He saw a light on behind the shop and found this woman in a bad way inside the garage.'

'Oh my God,' said Sunita. 'Inside the garage, you say? Do we know what she was attacked with?'

'Not yet. But it looks as though she was bludgeoned with some blunt weapon, like a club or hammer.'

'How is she, sir?'

'Well, she's still alive. I gather she's in intensive care on a ventilator. They don't expect her to make it through the night though. Oh, someone's just texted her name to me. It's Stephanie Price. Her name sounds familiar. I don't know why.'

Sunita was now pacing round her living room, taken aback by what she'd just heard. The shock was intense – like hearing a close friend had been violently swept out to sea.

'That's the woman I interviewed last week,' she said, struggling to digest the information. 'Don't you remember? The woman who works for the farm shop as a van driver. She left me a message, saying she needed to speak to me.'

'I remember you mentioning it,' he admitted.

'I tried hard to reach her.'

'Listen,' he said, 'while you're down in Shawley in the morning, I'm going over to Queensbridge General to see if Mrs Price is in any position to talk and maybe I'll get a chat with her husband and relatives.

'I'm sending Dawson and Hopkirk over to Mrs Price's house with a forensic team. We need to check the house for possible clues as to why she was at the farm shop out of hours.

'Oh, and one more thing. Charles Laxton's vanished. Someone at the estate office called, asking if he was still in custody. When we explained he'd been released, they said he'd failed to turn up for a meeting.'

* * *

Sunita slept fitfully that night. She was unable to dismiss from her mind thoughts of the amiable woman in her twenties with long, black hair – Stephanie Price. She had thought she would recover from her initial shock on hearing of the vicious attack. But the gruesome details had upset her more than she had imagined.

Eventually, by six o'clock, she gave up trying to sleep. She got up, showered and dressed, ate some toast and set off on the journey to Shawley Green.

She found police had cordoned off the entire farm shop and most of the car park when she arrived just before seven o'clock and parked her Peugeot.

The main focus of police activity was on the double garage, where she spotted Dr Ling, the senior forensic officer, talking to one of the CID team. Several scenes-of-crime officers were examining the path and bushes while a group of people were huddled outside the front entrance.

Eventually, she found her close colleague Omar Khalid, studying a sketch plan of the site. He looked up and smiled. Then he put his map away.

'Morning, Sarge,' he said. 'You're up early.'

'I wanted to get here as soon as I could,' she replied. 'Who are the people out the front?'

'That's Gordon MacLeod and his wife, Grace, the shop owners, and some of the staff. They're obviously very upset over the attack on Stephanie. They can't understand it. Nothing like this has ever happened round here before. It's just a sleepy village.'

'Have you asked about cameras?' said Sunita.

'Yes, the MacLeods are going to find us the disks.'

'Omar, the shop closes in the evening at 5.30 p.m., doesn't it?'

'That's right.'

'So what was Stephanie doing here at 8 p.m.?'

'No one knows. I asked the MacLeods and they haven't a clue. Her hours are nine to six,' said Khalid.

'Have we got a description of the man who fled by bicycle?'

'Not much, Sarge. Just dark clothing and a hood.'

'Not much help. You know I spoke to her last week, don't you?'

'Who? The dead woman?'

'Yes,' she said. 'Her husband's called Logan. Have you found out from the MacLeods about the victim's parents or relatives?'

'Yes. Her father's dead and her mother's in a care home. Not too *compos mentis*, I've been told. But she's got a sister called Isabelle King, who lives somewhere in Shawley Green.'

'A guy called Appleton was first to call us, wasn't he?'

Khalid nodded. 'Yes. He saw a man emerge from the garage but was unable to stop him getting on his bike and making off towards Stratford. He then tried CPR on her. Paramedics arrived and confirmed her heart was pumping.'

'That's a bit of good news,' she said. 'Have you spoken to Dr Ling?'

'Just briefly when they first arrived at eleven o'clock.'

'Shall we try and catch a word with her now?'

They walked along the path leading to the garages until they found Dr Ling, a solemn-faced woman in glasses wearing white overalls. She ended a conversation she was having with another forensic officer and greeted them both.

'Shall we move over here?' Sunita suggested, pointing to the centre of the car park. 'We don't want to get in anyone's way.'

'The key piece of evidence is a curved clawhammer which was left beside the woman's body,' said Dr Ling as they left the garage area. 'There's evidence of human tissue and hair on the striking face of the hammer.'

Sunita folded her arms. 'Any idea whether the weapon belonged to the shop or whether the attacker brought it with them?'

'I can help there, Sarge,' said Khalid. 'It was shown to Mr MacLeod and he's confirmed it belongs to him.'

'Yes,' said Dr Ling. 'MacLeod kept it in the garage, so it appears the attacker took it from inside somehow.'

'Maybe he forced the lock and broke in before Mrs Price arrived,' Khalid remarked.

Dr Ling nodded. 'That's possible. We haven't found any dabs so far, so our attacker may well have been wearing gloves. The only other clue is a partial footprint in the blood near the garage door.'

'That's interesting,' said Sunita.

'Don't get too excited,' said the doctor. 'We're not sure if it's enough to identify a boot or shoe from. But we'll give it a whirl.'

'Would you expect blood to have spread onto the attacker's clothing?' asked Sunita.

'Most definitely,' said Dr Ling. 'Whoever carried out this attack would have been splattered with blood. They'd have probably needed a change of clothes.'

As Dr Ling continued examining the garage with her scenes-of-crime colleagues, Sunita took Khalid aside.

'Omar, I've got a job for you,' she said. 'I happen to know there are lots of bushes and wooded areas along the Stratford Road. The attacker may have dumped his blood-strained clothing there. Worth taking some of the team with you. Meanwhile, I'm going to see if I can have a few words with this Mr Appleton.'

* * *

Sunita Roy crossed the road and gazed at the sprawling buildings which constituted the Woodside Guesthouse.

She followed a path to the main entrance and pressed the bell. It had only just turned 7.30 a.m. but she assured herself that someone would be around.

An auburn-haired, middle-aged woman answered the door with a blank expression.

'Sorry to call rather early,' said the sergeant. 'Is Mr Appleton about?' She displayed her warrant card. 'I'm from Heart of England CID.'

'Well, he's in a bit of a rush. He's got an important interview today, but I'll tell him you're here. You'd better come in.'

Sunita found herself in a bright hallway adorned with framed colour prints showing scenes from Shakespeare's plays.

A short, balding man made his way hesitantly down the stairs.

'You wanted to see me about last night?' he asked, straightening his tie.

She nodded. 'Yes, I'm DS Roy. I just need to ask a few questions.'

'Martyn Appleton,' he said, shaking her hand. 'This is a bit awkward. Can we talk here?'

'Yes. That's fine.'

'It's just I've got a job interview in an hour and a half.'

'This won't take long,' said Sunita.

'How is the lady, by the way?'

'Last I heard she was in a critical condition in intensive care.'

He shook his head. 'She was in a bad way last night. I hope she's going to be all right.'

'We'll have to see,' she replied.

Appleton explained as carefully as he could what he had seen at the garage, and Sunita wrote the details down in her notebook.

'What did the man you saw look like?' she asked.

'Well, he was taller than me, but then everybody's taller than me,' he said with a grin. 'He'd got a hood over his head and black clothing. I think he may have had boots on, but I'm not sure.'

'What kind of boots?'

'I'd call them black hiking boots. I was expecting him to get into a car but he just ran a short distance up the road, picked up a bicycle lying on the grass verge and made off on that.'

'Any description of the bike?'

'I'd say it had a dark frame – probably black. Just a standard bike. Not sure if it was a man's bike.'

'What sort of age would you say the man was?'

'I've no idea, but he was quite light on his feet. So not old. Maybe in his thirties or forties.'

'Did he say anything at all?'

'No.'

'Afterwards you realised the victim was a woman and carried out CPR. Is that right?'

'I'll be honest with you,' he said with a weak smile. 'I've never given any first aid before. But I was there. I was the man of the moment, so it had to be me. The call handler from the ambulance service was very good. She gave me instructions over the phone.'

'So you pumped away on her chest with both hands?'

'Yes. I must have done it for nearly ten minutes before the paramedics arrived.'

'Well done for that, Mr Appleton. You've obviously given the lady a fighting chance.'

'Do you really think so? I'd like to think I made a difference.'

'Yes, but I'm afraid to say it's a bit of a gloomy prognosis at the moment.'

Chapter 29

The chief inspector weaved his way through a maze of corridors at Queensbridge Hospital later the same morning.

Eventually, he found the intensive care ward on the first floor of the nineteenth-century building and queued at the reception desk.

'DCI Roscoe, Heart of England CID,' he explained to the young, blonde nurse once she became free. 'I was wondering how Stephanie Price is?'

'No change, sir. Still critical.'

'There's obviously no chance she'd be in a position to answer questions?'

'Absolutely none, I'm afraid. If you'd like to wait over there, I'll see if one of the doctors can speak to you.'

'Do you know if any relatives have turned up?'

'Just that lady over there,' she said, pointing to a woman in her late twenties, sitting on her own in the front of three rows of seats.

Roscoe settled into a chair next to the relative.

'I understand you're related to Stephanie Price,' he whispered while showing his identification.

'Yes. I'm her sister,' said the woman. 'Isabelle King.'

After introducing himself and shaking her hand, he said, 'Is there somewhere we can go and talk? It's a bit difficult here. The restaurant, perhaps?'

'I don't want to go far in case a doctor comes,' she insisted. 'But I don't mind if we have a chat just outside the ward.'

He led her through the ward exit doors to the corridor outside.

'This is better. A bit quieter,' said Roscoe. 'Before we go any further, I want to say how sorry I was to hear what happened to your sister.'

'Thank you. Everybody's been very kind. I'm absolutely devastated, as you can imagine. She was my little sister.'

He nodded. 'We understand she's twenty-six?'

'Yes. She's two years younger than me.'

'She's married, isn't she?'

'Yes, her husband's called Logan. Our father's dead and Mum's in a home. She's got dementia.'

'Sorry to hear that,' he said. 'I'd have expected the husband to be here.'

'So would I.'

'Is there any reason why he's not here?'

'All I can think of is he and Stephanie have just split up. He's living at his mother's in Shawley Green. So if anyone sent him a message at the house in Mill Road, he might not have got it. I can give you his phone number.'

After noting down Logan Price's mobile number in his book, the chief inspector asked, 'Do you know why your sister was at the farm shop last night?'

'She told me she was going to meet someone, but I don't know who it was.'

'Someone she knew?'

'Um, yes.'

'Why there?'

'I'm not sure.'

'Can you think of anyone who may have wished your sister harm?'

'No. Stephanie was popular with everyone.'

As they continued their conversation, a rattling noise behind them signalled a lift had arrived. The doors clanked open. A tall, burly man with short hair emerged.

'Hi, Isabelle,' he said. 'How's Stephanie?'

'Oh, it's you. She's just the same,' said Isabelle tersely. 'I suppose I'd better introduce you. Logan, this is Mr Roscoe from Heart of England Police.'

'Hello,' said the detective. 'Actually, it's DCI Roscoe. I'd like to have a brief chat with you about your wife in a moment.'

'Maybe later,' replied Price. 'I've only just found out what happened. I went round to me house and someone had left a note, taped to the front door. Look, I think I ought to make my presence known. It's just through here, isn't it?'

'Yes,' said Isabelle. 'Have a word with the girl at the desk. I'll come and see you in the waiting area.'

After Price had gone, she remarked, 'He's such a toerag.'

'How do you mean?' asked Roscoe.

'Perhaps I've spoken out of turn.'

'Well, you've said it now. Maybe you should explain.'

'He's a wife beater. He comes home drunk and then beats her up. She's been having a really rough time.'

'How long have they been married?'

'About seven years.'

'Any children?'

'No, thankfully. They've not been sleeping together for months.'

'Were they still living together?'

'No. They had a big bust-up a week ago and he moved back with his mother. Stephanie was seeing a solicitor about a divorce.'

'How did he take that news?'

'He was furious. He had her up against the bedroom door, crushing her throat with his arm. He called her a liar and a cheat, and would fight against any divorce. He didn't want them to sell the house.'

'Clearly a man of strong emotions. Perhaps you can give me his mother's address? And I'll also need an address and phone number for you.'

'No problem,' she said.

One of the double doors creaked open. Logan Price's face appeared.

'One of the doctors is here,' he announced before ducking back inside and allowing the door to close.

'Come on. Let's hear what the doctor's got to say,' said Roscoe, holding the door open for Isabelle.

A grey-haired, middle-aged doctor, who was speaking to Price, beckoned Isabelle and the detective over to where he was standing, at the far side of the reception desk.

'I'm Michael Adams, a surgeon from the neurology department,' he explained in a low voice. 'I'm awfully sorry to tell you that Mrs Price died at ten minutes past nine this morning.'

Isabelle broke down in tears. Price scowled and stared at the floor. Roscoe shook his head.

'Mrs Price had a number of head injuries, but the most serious caused an intracerebral haemorrhage,' Dr Adams continued. 'This kind of haemorrhage occurs when an artery in the brain bursts, causing bleeding in the brain tissue. Mrs Price was in theatre, and a colleague and I tried to act as quickly as we could to limit damage. But the bleeding was extensive and rapid. The brain was placed under intense pressure and it was deprived of oxygen.'

'I can assure you we did everything we could,' he added, 'but the injury was too severe. I can only repeat how sorry we are to bring you this devastating news.'

'I'm DCI Roscoe,' the chief inspector said quietly. 'Speaking on behalf of the police, we share your regret and promise to do everything in our power to catch the perpetrator. Dr Adams, this is a bleed on the brain we're talking about here?'

Dr Adams nodded. 'That's correct, Chief Inspector. Mrs Price had been bleeding profusely from one of several head wounds. She also had a fractured cheekbone and defensive wounds to her hands,' he said, then walked away.

Isabelle at first was too distraught to speak. Then she turned towards the detective.

'You make sure you catch the bastard who's done this to our Stephanie,' she said as she sobbed into her hands. 'That poor girl never hurt a fly. She should be here on earth like you and me, Mr Roscoe, full of the joys of life. Instead her bright spirit's been snuffed out by some murdering piece of vermin.'

Chapter 30

Winter was taking one more curtain call before the onset of spring as Sunita drove to the farm shop the next day. Temperatures had plunged overnight. Now they were barely above freezing point.

She got out from behind the wheel after finding a space in the car park and wrapped a scarf round her neck.

With her hands firmly in the pockets of her coat, she walked to the entrance and then followed signs to the owner's office.

Gordon MacLeod was bent over his desk, peering through his glasses at a document as she approached.

Three days earlier, she had turned down an opportunity to speak to the shop owner. Both MacLeod and his wife were too distraught. In any case, DC Khalid had obtained a statement from them at that time.

'Can I help ye?' he asked as she tapped on the door.

'Mr MacLeod,' she said, 'I'm DS Roy. We met briefly the other day.'

'Yes, I recall. We're still trying to get over the shock of what happened on Thursday night. Sit yourself down.'

She drew up an office chair. 'Have you any better idea now of how Mrs Price came to be in the garage at around eight o'clock?' she asked.

'Nae, we still can't understand it,' he replied. 'Her working day ends at six. Her van's strictly for farm shop deliveries. All I can think is maybe she'd been making personal use of it – you know, just returned from visiting a friend or relative in our van.'

'Or maybe she was about to set off somewhere?' Sunita suggested.

'Aye, that's conceivable,' he said. 'Whichever it was, it was against our policy. And if she hadn't been attacked and it had been brought to our notice, she'd have had questions to answer. As it is, we're upset at losing her and feel desperately sorry for her family. She was a conscientious, hard-working lassie. Did ye know she was studying accountancy part-time?'

'No, I didn't,' said Sunita. 'Mr MacLeod, there's another possibility. Mrs Price could have been planning to meet someone in the car park.'

'I hadn't thought of that,' he said. 'I don't know what the world's coming to, Miss Roy. A young lassie isn't safe on her own after dark anymore. There are these predatory males around, hunting for victims. We need more police, that's a fact, but can we afford it? The government say they're doing everything they can, but are they really?'

Sunita waited for him to end his short speech, which she suspected he had given before. Then she asked, 'How long had Mrs Price worked for you?'

'Must be more than five years,' he said.

'Did she have any enemies that you're aware of?'

'Nae. She got on with everyone.'

'Who normally had access to the two garages apart from her?'

'Only me and Grace, my wife. Do you know if she was robbed?' he asked.

'Her handbag was on the garage floor beside her when police and ambulance staff attended,' she replied. 'There didn't seem to be anything missing apart from her phone, and her clothing didn't seem to have been disturbed.'

'Just a meaningless attack,' MacLeod observed.

'One last thing. I know it's a tall order, but have you got any employees – or customers, come to that – who are of average height, in their thirties or forties and ride a bicycle?'

He shook his head. 'I can't think of anyone like that just now. But if you leave me your number, I'll have a think and if anything occurs to me, I'll give ye a bell.'

* * *

A light rain fell later that day as Sunita joined the chief inspector in the car park outside Queensbridge General Hospital.

They entered the Victorian building and followed signs for the mortuary.

'I've had a bit of good news, Sergeant,' he said. 'Dawson called to say Charles Laxton hasn't gone AWOL after all.

His car had broken down and he failed to let anyone know. Anyway, we need to focus on Stephanie Price. It's early days but it already looks like the husband did it.'

She nodded. 'I gather Logan Price has got form for violent offences.'

'He's been in trouble off and on for causing actual bodily harm. It's fair to say that he's never been convicted of causing GBH or murder, but he's got the right profile. The victim's sister described him quite openly as a wife batterer. Apparently he was furious with her for seeking a divorce.'

'I'm not sure about Logan being to blame in this case,' she said. 'If he'd been involved, the attack would most likely have happened at their home during a domestic row. It would have probably happened after he lost his temper with her over something. This doesn't come across as a typical domestic. Why travel four miles and beat her up at her workplace?'

Roscoe shook his head.

'You've not considered the full facts, Sergeant,' he said. 'Logan Price wasn't staying at the couple's home in Queensbridge. For a few days, he's been staying with his mother in Shawley Green – just a short distance from the farm shop. He'd only just been told she was seeking a divorce. Good God! He's probably been staking out the farm shop, waiting for his moment.'

'He's obviously got some cunning, that Logan,' he continued. 'Too open-and-shut if he'd lost his temper and killed her at their home. He'd have been a key suspect the next morning before I'd even got my coat on. As it is, this has all the hallmarks of a planned attack. He's found out she was visiting her garage after hours. He's waited until she's been off her guard, and then he's struck. Suggests to me it was planned and premeditated.'

She shook her head. 'I worry it might be too early to make these kinds of judgement, sir,' she said in a calculated way in order not to appear confrontational.

But her boss was in his element now. 'You know the statistics, don't you, Sergeant? It's a fact that nearly two thirds of all murder victims in Britain are killed by either their partner or ex-partner. This poor woman had just commenced divorce proceedings. Her husband was worried about being dragged through the courts and losing his home and possessions.'

They turned a corner and found themselves at the mortuary entrance. Two orderlies were pushing a trolley containing a corpse past the double swing doors. They waited before pushing their own way through.

After being greeted by the unwelcome smell of chemicals, they donned white gowns. They then made their way to the examination lab, where the body of Stephanie Price was lying on a stainless-steel slab beneath gleaming lights.

Dr Reynolds was bending over the corpse in his white overalls with a dome magnifier, peering across the dead woman's face like a grand inquisitor. His freshly cleaned chisels, knives, forceps and scissors stood lined up in pristine order along a nearby bench.

'Ah, Gavin and DS Roy. I'm glad you're here,' he said, standing upright and smiling towards them beneath the fluorescent lighting. 'The post-mortem's been completed this morning and the conclusion was she died from blunt force trauma. There were extensive fractures to the skull and a brain injury from which she'd have had no hope of recovering.'

Roscoe had been listening intently. 'Do you think the clawhammer found at the scene caused the injuries, Silas?'

'Undoubtedly. We've examined the tissue and hair samples collected from the face of the hammer and they're a match with the victim. She's also got a fractured right cheekbone and injuries to the knuckles on her right hand, where she's fought back against her assailant.

'This lady's put up quite a defence, but so far we've been unable to detect the DNA of the attacker from her fingernails. This is largely because the lady had fairly short nails. Did she carry out manual work?'

'She was a delivery driver for a farm shop,' Sunita explained.

'That makes sense. If she was lifting boxes and so forth, she wouldn't have wanted talons like Jennifer Lopez or Rihanna. Oh, I should mention that it appears from the shape of the indents, that the killer was standing directly in front of Mrs Price at the time of the onslaught. We can tell this from the shape of the circles and the arcs of circles formed on the skull.'

Sunita gazed into his eyes. 'I know her clothing wasn't disturbed, but were there any signs of sexual interference?'

'No. None,' he replied.

'And can you see any particular link between the attack carried out on her and the attack on Miles Kenworth? Any similarity of style or method?' asked Sunita.

The pathologist shook his head. 'No, other than that both victims sustained severe injuries to the skull. There's one more thing I ought to mention. This lady was in the early stages of pregnancy.'

Chapter 31

A soft rain patted against the upstairs window. Logan Price opened the blind and peered out into Mill Road, where raindrops were dancing in a frenzy across the roof of his van.

Here and there, pedestrians were defying the downpour and making a dash from doorway to car. A schoolteacher was shepherding some excited children across the street.

Then, to his dismay, he noticed a blue BMW draw up and two figures emerge. He recognised one as the chief inspector he'd met at the hospital three days earlier. The face of the second person – a young woman – was unfamiliar.

He'd been half-expecting the police to call. The chief inspector had been eager to speak to him at the hospital, but Price had been too upset at the time. Too much had been happening. Hospital staff were firing questions. Relatives were calling him. He'd tried to be as helpful as he could.

He'd even received a few calls from the press and had taken secret pleasure from telling all of them to get lost.

Now it seemed the policeman had caught up with him again and this time there seemed no escape. He would more than likely face interminable questions about Stephanie and their past life together.

But what information could he give to help them? Their marriage had been crumbling for months and, for a brief while, they'd been leading almost separate lives.

Wouldn't the detectives' time be better spent speaking to Stephanie's sister? He mumbled to himself, 'What a nuisance,' as he descended the stairs and drew open the front door.

* * *

Gavin Roscoe beamed as soon as Logan Price's face came into view. 'Mr Price. We met at the hospital. DCI Roscoe. May we come in?'

As Price nodded, the detective stepped into the hallway.

'This is my colleague, DS Roy,' he explained.

The pair had agreed in advance not to mention Stephanie's pregnancy. Paternity of the now-discarded embryo was in doubt and it seemed wrong to add to the widower's anguish.

New grief at this time might even prevent them from obtaining answers to key questions. The task would be better handled by a medical practitioner at another time.

'Please come in,' said Price. 'You'll have to excuse the mess. We'd better go into the living room.'

He led them into a small front room with a two-seater sofa, an armchair and dining table with chairs. Roscoe settled himself down in the armchair while Sunita made herself comfortable on the sofa.

'So sorry to hear about your wife's death,' she told Price, as he perched himself on a dining chair.

'Thank you. I'm still in shock. We'd been married for seven years.'

The chief inspector asked how the couple first met.

'In a pub,' said Price with a sheepish look. 'The White Swan in Shawley Green. Do you know it?'

Roscoe nodded. 'Yes, I know it,' he admitted.

'Both our families come from the area. It were surprising we'd never met before. We'd a lot in common. We were both into gardening, pub games, music, cooking and gaming.

'I was living in Birmingham at the time and she was living near the pub. We eventually got together and married. We worked and saved hard and managed to buy this house.'

Sunita nodded. 'When did you last see your wife?'

'Let me think. Ten days ago.'

She looked aghast. 'Ten days ago?'

'Yes, I may as well be straight with you both. We'd been going through a bad patch. I moved out and went to live with my mother for a while – hoping she'd calm down. She'd been talking about getting a divorce.'

'Can I ask what brought that on, sir?' said Roscoe.

'Oh, you know, just not getting on. We were arguing a lot. I thought that, if I just gave her some space, she'd come round eventually. But of course that's not to be now.'

For the first time that evening, he appeared downcast and tearful at the realisation that he would never see his wife again. It was as though he had been swept up into a cloak of sorrow.

'I'm sorry,' he said, reaching for a box of tissues in the centre of the table and taking one. 'I never expected her to be snatched away like this – so sudden, like.'

'Do you have any idea why Mrs Price travelled to the Orchard Lane Farm Shop on Thursday evening?'

'No. None at all,' he replied as he wiped his eyes. 'She used to work till six and be home by six thirty on a fairly regular basis. It were unusual for her to go over there at night. She were a bit of a home bird, you could say. So I've been puzzling over what she were doing there.'

Sunita glanced up. 'Where were you on Thursday evening?' she asked.

The question seemed to take him by surprise. He failed to answer straight away and, when he did, he stuttered and stammered a little.

'I were round my mate's place on the other side of Queensbridge,' he replied.

'Who are you referring to here, sir?' Roscoe inquired.

'Viv Tyler. He works with me at Green Magic Garden Services in Stratford.'

'We'll need his address.'

'It's 121 Temple Gardens, Queensbridge, but he's not there all the time. You'd be better off, if you need to speak to him, catching him at work.'

'And you were with him the whole evening?'

'That's right. He picked me up from my mum's in Highfield Road and we went to the Red Lion in Queensbridge for a few drinks. Then he dropped me off back at Mum's.'

'What time did he pick you up, sir?' asked Roscoe.

'Oh, must have been half past seven.'

'Can we take it that you're back living here now?'

'Yes. Me mum's knocking on, you know. I never want to be too much of a burden to her.'

Sunita was wondering whether anyone had a grudge against Mrs Price. 'Did Mrs Price have any enemies?' she asked.

'No. Not at all. Everybody loved her.'

'And she'd been her normal self in the last weeks of her life?'

'Yes, as I say, I didn't see her for the past ten days, but before that there were no unusual events, if that's what you mean. She were upset with me. I suppose I weren't the husband she'd thought I was. But that's the situation with many couples in Britain, isn't it? You marry your boyfriend or girlfriend and then sometimes you wonder if you've married a stranger. We'd have patched it up. We always had done before.'

'You don't think the divorce would have gone ahead, sir?' asked Sunita.

'No. She'd have come round. She just had her ups and downs. That's all it was.'

Roscoe stood up. 'All right,' he said. 'We've got your phone number, so if there's anything else, we can give you a call.'

But Sunita had one last question.

'Mr Price, I was just wondering. Have you got a bicycle?'

'A bicycle? No. I've got use of the company van – the green one outside. Why do you want to know anyway?'

Sunita was unsure how to reply, so Roscoe stepped in. 'A bicycle was flagged up in connection with the case. That's all,' he said, without giving too much away.

The pair walked back through the well-lit hall. Sunita stepped outside and wandered up and down the small front garden while her boss held back, explaining something to Price.

Sunita then ventured back inside. 'Mr Price, there's a bicycle in the alley between your house and the next one.'

'Oh, that old thing. I'd forgotten about that. It's hardly used.'

'Is it yours?'

'Well, it's really Stephanie's but I sometimes use it.'

Sunita shrugged her shoulders. 'I'd better take a look at it,' she said.

'Sergeant, there's a torch in the glove compartment of the car,' Roscoe remarked as he unlocked the BMW with his remote.

After fetching the torch, Sunita examined the bicycle. The only information they'd obtained from the witness Appleton was that the attacker had fled on a bicycle with a black frame. He'd been unsure whether it had been a man's bike or a woman's bike. This one was designed for a woman and – like thousands of other cycles in the town, no doubt – matched the rudimentary description.

Sunita searched the saddle and handlebars for signs of blood. There were none to be seen. But even if someone thoroughly wiped blood smears from a bicycle, she knew microscopic traces might still be discerned by forensic experts.

'Sir, I think we should impound this bike and get it examined in the lab,' she said.

Chapter 32

Sunita Roy had one final task to perform before heading home. She needed to speak to the murdered woman's sister, Isabelle.

While at the hospital, Isabelle had told the chief inspector that her sister had gone to the farm shop at eight o'clock to meet someone. Someone she knew.

That was all the sister could say. The DCI wanted her to press Isabelle on that point. He was convinced she knew more and was holding back.

'Impress on her how important it is to identify who she was meeting,' the chief inspector had insisted. 'Stress how she owes it to Stephanie that we trace the killer as quickly as possible and that this might be the only way to do it.'

Roscoe had driven off home from Price's house, leaving the black-framed bicycle in his sergeant's care.

Fortunately, the rain had stopped and it wasn't long before a uniformed colleague arrived by car and took the bike to the town's police station – to await collection by a member of the forensic team.

Sunita fetched her car from the town's supermarket car park and drove off towards Shawley Green, reflecting on their conversation with Price and how little regret he'd expressed over his wife's death. Perhaps he was one of those men who found it hard to express emotions, she decided.

In less than ten minutes, she reached the village and her sat nav led her to Chestnut Way beside the green. Isabelle's home, number twenty-seven, was a 1950s semi-detached house with a small front garden.

Sunita parked outside and followed the concrete path to the front door. But after ringing the bell twice, it was clear there was no one at home.

She called at the house next door and spoke to a young woman clutching a baby. She believed Isabelle and her family had gone away to Scarborough for a few days.

'It's not a holiday,' the woman explained. 'They're just visiting relatives. You must have heard what happened to her sister. She said she needed a break.'

All Sunita could do was write a note, asking for Isabelle to call her, and push it through the letterbox. Then she climbed back into her car and drove away.

But, as she travelled towards Warwick, she passed the Orchard Lane Farm Shop and noticed a small gathering of customers around a blue, open-top vintage car.

Out of curiosity, she drove in, found a space and stepped over to look at the vehicle, which was in the centre of the car park. As other admirers moved away, she walked round it, inspecting the gleaming bodywork and leather seating.

Then she noticed its owner walking towards her clutching two shopping bags, filled with groceries. It was Lord Culverdon's son-in-law, Rupert Faulkner.

He greeted her with the words, 'Hello, DS Roy, isn't it?'

She nodded. 'Very nice car, Mr Faulkner.'

'Do you like it?' he asked. 'It's a Wolseley Drophead Coupé.'

'British made?'

'Yes. Built in 1924. We've had it a couple of years. We went down to Hampshire for a classic car show. Stayed over and came back today. It drives like a dream.'

'So what brings you to Shawley Green?' she asked him. 'You're what – eight miles from home?'

'We came over here for a bit of shopping on the way back. Lavinia absolutely adores their organic biscuits. She'll be here in a minute.'

'I'd heard their biscuits were rather special,' Sunita agreed.

'By the way,' he said, 'it was absolutely appalling what happened to that poor shop girl. Stephanie someone-or-other.'

'Stephanie Price,' said Sunita helpfully.

'Yes, Stephanie Price. I knew her very vaguely, you know, because she was always making collections and deliveries round the farms. Terrible tragedy. If we, as a family, can do anything to help the police, don't hesitate to ask, will you?'

He zipped up his khaki shooting jacket and placed his groceries on the passenger seat. Then he removed his car keys from the side pocket of his trousers.

'People sometimes think we're out of reach and out of touch, living where we do,' he continued. 'But I can assure you we all care very deeply for our community, so if there's anything at all.'

Sunita folded her arms. 'There's just one thing,' she said. 'Mr Faulkner, do you mind if I ask where you were on Thursday evening?'

'I was in rehearsals at the Memorial Hall in East Stratford for the play *Julius Caesar*. Ask Mr Armitage. He'll tell you. Why do you want to know anyway?'

'Just routine procedure, Mr Faulkner. That's all. We need to eliminate everyone we can from inquiries.'

'Right, well, you've eliminated me. Ah, here she is now. We're going to tootle off.'

His wife, Lavinia, smiled and waved to Sunita as she approached the car with two more bags, which she placed on the back seat.

After she climbed into the front, the Wolseley's engine burst into life. Faulkner reversed from his parking space and the couple roared off.

* * *

Sunita returned to her car and was about to drive away when her phone rang. It was her colleague Tom Vickers. He informed her he had received a call from his police colleague on the fraud squad at City of London Police.

'Do you remember?' he said. 'We had a chat the other day about that guy Sarkar and his outfit called Safe Bastion Wealth Management.'

'Of course,' she replied.

'Well, I wouldn't let him have a penny of your money, Sunita.'

'Why is that?'

'First of all, the guy's not registered with the Financial Conduct Authority.'

'He let me believe he was.'

'Well, he's not.'

'What does that mean?'

'Firms offering to invest your money must be regulated by the FCA. If they're not, you won't get compensation if things go wrong. It suggests this guy's dodgy.'

'Oh, my God.'

'But I know a bit more about our Mr Sarkar because, by coincidence, he's been flagged up as a person of interest to my mate Gary. Gary's been looking into various Ponzi schemes.'

Sunita leaned back in her car seat. 'They were originally scams carried out by a guy called Ponzi in the 1920s, weren't they?'

'You're very knowledgeable. Yes, he was a guy called Charles Ponzi who paid money out to his early investors using the investment money from later investors. Gary believes Sarkar's scheme is similar. He's promising investors up to twelve per cent a month.'

Sunita was shocked. She'd been promised a sound investment by Indrani Sarkar and her boyfriend, Samir.

'Tom, I'm so grateful to you,' she said. 'I was seriously considering signing a contract with Sarkar.'

'That contract wouldn't have been worth the paper it's written on. Sports professionals, actors and singers have given money to this man, and they've regretted it. Some investors have already been made bankrupt, thanks to Slippery Sarkar. Others have lost their homes.'

Her feelings of shock were gradually being replaced by feelings of relief. She had been saved from disaster in the nick of time because of her own suspicions about Sarkar and because of her good friend, Tom.

'Do you know he spent a large part of our conversation warning me against scams?' she said.

'It's a fact that some of the greatest sharks in the world's financial oceans make a big play of the fact that there are plenty of scams around but your money is safe with them,' he said.

'Tom, I'm so grateful to you. You've saved me from giving my money to this swindler and probably having a long battle to get it back.'

'No, Sunita,' he replied. 'You'd never have got your money back. He and his cronies owe millions to their investors. So you wouldn't have been forsaking your money for a short while. You'd have been kissing it goodbye forever.'

As she travelled home after the phone call, Sunita could not stop thinking how Tom Vickers had delivered her from financial catastrophe at the eleventh hour.

But hadn't her boyfriend, Samir, strongly recommended Sarkar? What was it he'd said? 'I can assure you he is a very honest, reliable person. I've known him for more than five years.'

She felt aggrieved. Samir, whom she believed she loved and trusted, had let her down badly.

Chapter 33

As soon as Omar Khalid arrived in CID the next morning, the first of March, Sunita Roy gave him clear instructions. He had to go and find the gardener Vivian Tyler and verify Logan Price's alibi.

But she urged him not to waste time calling round at Tyler's home address in Queensbridge. He was unlikely to be there. Instead she told him to visit Tyler's works depot on the western outskirts of Stratford.

So just after half past nine, Khalid drove into Pleasant Acre Drive, a quiet residential street overlooking open fields on the fringe of the market town.

At the end of the street, which consisted mainly of red-brick semi-detached houses, he found the premises of Green Magic Garden Services.

The sun came out as he walked across to the entrance and stepped inside. The depot was an Aladdin's Cave of garden materials, ranging from bricks, stones, decking and fencing to a wide selection of plants and workmen's tools.

He knocked on a door to the right marked 'Reception', and found himself in an office in which three women sitting at desks were hard at work behind computer screens.

'Can I help you?' asked one woman in her mid-twenties who was petite and pale with spiky, blonde hair.

'Looking for Mr Tyler. I'm from Heart of England CID,' he explained, displaying his warrant card.

'He should be somewhere around. Maybe he's in the warehouse.'

One of her colleagues piped up, 'Or having a cup of tea.'

The blonde woman vowed to go and find him. She disappeared through a door and returned a few minutes later.

'He'll be right with you,' she assured Khalid.

Shortly afterwards, a smiling man in his early thirties arrived in reception.

'I think you wanted to speak to me,' he said. 'Vivian Tyler.'

'Yes,' said the detective. 'Is there anywhere we can go for a quiet word?'

'Not really,' said Tyler, who was wearing shabby blue overalls.

'Then can we just have a chat outside the door?' Khalid suggested.

Tyler nodded and they stepped into the parking area.

'You're lucky to catch me. I was meant to be in Banbury but it got cancelled because of the weather,' Tyler explained.

'Look, we're investigating the murder of Stephanie Price, your mate's wife,' said Khalid.

'That didn't take a lot of working out. Yes, I was very sorry to hear about that. Logan's in pieces.'

'We have to check all these things out, obviously,' the detective continued, taking out a notebook and pen.

'I heard it was done with a clawhammer. Is that right?' asked Tyler.

'Sorry, sir. Can't discuss that for operational reasons.'

'Oh, I see.'

'Your workmate, Logan, says he was with you at the time of the murder last Thursday. Is that correct?'

Tyler nodded. 'Yeah.'

'What time did you pick Mr Price up that evening?'

'Oh, it must have been around half past seven.'

'What kind of car have you got?' asked Khalid, who was writing in his book.

'I've got a grey Nissan Qashqai. We only went to the Red Lion in Queensbridge and then I dropped him back.'

'What time did you arrive at the pub and what time did you leave?'

'Oh, I should say we arrived at about ten to eight and left at about half past ten.'

Khalid sighed. 'You do realise we're going to be making some checks that you're telling the truth, don't you?'

'God, you sound as though you don't believe me. What's your problem? I've told you we went to the Red Lion. I'm sure the staff will remember us.'

'And you were with Mr Price the whole evening?'

'Yes, of course. He split up from his missus, didn't he? Neither of us had any idea that, soon after I picked him up in the village, she'd be at the farm shop getting attacked.'

'What did you both drink at the pub?'

'Oh, God. This is turning into the third degree. I had – what did I have? I had a few pints of cider and Logan was drinking QB Bitter.' Then he added sarcastically, 'Do you want to know what flavour crisps we had?'

'No, it's all right. There's no need for you to get annoyed, Mr Tyler. These are just routine questions. We want to eliminate as many people as we can from this investigation.'

'Well, it's hard not to take offence when someone's asking such probing questions. But I don't want to fall out with anyone. I know you've got a job to do, mate.'

'Oh I nearly forgot to ask,' said Khalid. 'Was the landlord around on Thursday evening or was it just bar staff?'

'The landlord, Dave, was around. He served us at one point, actually. There were also bar staff there, as I remember.'

* * *

After leaving the gardening firm, Khalid knew Tyler's evidence would have to be corroborated. So he drove into Queensbridge and parked in the car park of the Red Lion.

David Wainwright, the landlord, whose name was above the door of the busy town centre pub, had only just opened when the detective walked in and no customers had yet arrived.

'And what would you like, sir?' asked the burly publican as he took his stance behind the centre of the bar.

'I'm not after a drink,' Khalid explained, showing his identification. 'I'm afraid I'm after information. Do you know a couple of guys called Logan Price and Vivian Tyler?'

Wainwright smiled and nodded. 'Those two reprobates,' he said. 'I shouldn't make a joke, I suppose. Poor old Logan's lost his missus.'

'Which is why I'm here.'

'Yes, of course,' said Wainwright. 'Yes, I know them quite well. Those two boys both like a drink.'

'I just need to ask a couple of questions,' said Khalid, hoisting himself onto a bar stool and leaning against the counter. 'Were they here on Thursday evening?'

'Thursday?' said Wainwright, stroking his chin. 'That would have been the twenty-fourth.'

'That's right.'

'Yes, they were here. We had a big crowd in.'

'What time did they arrive?'

'Oh, I don't know. I wasn't here all the time.'

He walked away along the bar until he was out of Khalid's sight. He began shouting to someone upstairs.

'Rosie!' he said. 'Are you there?'

A soft female voice called back, 'Yes, dear?'

'Rosie, did you serve Logan Price and Viv Tyler on Thursday evening?'

Her voice grew louder as though she had moved part of the way down the stairs. 'Yes,' she said. 'They came in about half past nine. A pint of Strongbow and a pint of QB, like they always have. Why? What's the matter?'

'It's all right. Just a gentleman from the police. He's asking a few questions.'

Khalid was writing in his notebook as the publican stepped back to the bar.

'Mr Wainwright,' he said, 'could you ask Rosie if she's sure about the time and also what time they left?'

'Yes, certainly,' said the publican, returning to the foot of the stairs.

'Are you sure it was half past nine, Rosie?'

Mrs Wainwright climbed down the remaining stairs and appeared alongside her husband at the counter.

'Hello, dear,' said the middle-aged landlady, who had wavy, blonde hair and a friendly smile. 'Yes. I know it was nine thirty. It was halfway through *The Apprentice* and they were about to go to the boardroom. That usually happens about halfway through the programme and I know it started at nine o'clock. Logan and Viv were passing comments about the contestants.'

'Thank you, Mrs Wainwright,' said Khalid. 'That's very helpful. Do you recall what time they left?'

'Oh, they were here for the rest of the evening – till closing time.'

'Once again, that's very helpful. Thank you both.'

'That's all right, young man,' said Mr Wainwright. 'Anything to help the law. We hope you catch the person who killed that young lady. That was a terrible way to die and she was fairly young as well. Let us know if there's anything else we can do.'

Chapter 34

The chief inspector greeted his staff in a cheery tone as he arrived in CID the next morning.

Sunita Roy watched as he unlocked his room and took his coat off.

'Do you want to tell him yourself what you discovered yesterday or shall I?' she asked Omar Khalid, who was sitting beside her.

'I don't mind,' he replied.

'It's going to put an even bigger smile on his face,' she said. 'He's been convinced Logan Price is to blame for his wife's death almost since he first heard of the attack on her.'

'It's all right, Sarge,' said Khalid, taking off his brown suede jacket and hanging it on the back of his chair. 'I'll let you take the glory.'

Sunita knocked and stepped into Roscoe's room.

'I'm glad you're here,' her boss informed her as he glanced up from his desk. 'I thought we'd hold a meeting in a minute and bring everyone up to date. What is it? You look like you've got something on your mind, Sergeant.'

'Yes, sir. It looks like Logan Price has given a false alibi,' she said as she drew up a chair.

'Really? That's interesting. Tell me all about it.'

'Well, Mr Price's drinking partner, Mr Tyler, says he picked him up at half past seven and, twenty minutes later, they arrived at the Red Lion in Queensbridge. But the landlord's wife is certain they didn't get there till nine thirty, halfway through *The Apprentice* television programme.'

Roscoe leaned back on his chair. 'So why are they lying?' he said. 'That's really strange.'

Sunita shrugged. 'Sometimes people don't realise that we have to check out alibis.'

'Yes. They think we'll swallow any old nonsense.'

'I've been meaning to talk to you anyway, sir. Until now, we've been working on the assumption that the murders of Miles Kenworth and Stephanie Price were unconnected.'

He nodded. 'Yes. As Silas told us, the only link he could see was that both victims sustained severe skull injuries, which, if nothing else, points to a preference for a particular mode of attack.'

'Well, I've been thinking about the three occasions in Miles Kenworth's diary when he met up with a mystery person referred to as V. Do you remember Charles Laxton told us Kenworth had met an "amazing" woman?'

Roscoe nodded as she continued.

'He was unable to stop thinking about Vani, sir, and we wondered who that could have been. Well, I realised this morning that Vani could be short for Stephanie.'

Roscoe folded his arms. 'So what you're suggesting, Sergeant, is that Kenworth had developed a crush on Mrs Price?'

'Yes. The feelings may have been reciprocated. She spoke fondly of him when I interviewed her. The three dates are ringed in his diary as though they had special significance. The first is 10 January. He's written simply, "Meal with V." Then on 20 January he's scribbled, "Rock with V." And finally, on 5 February, he's put, "Pheas with V," which could refer to the Old Pheasant pub in Queensbridge.'

'Very smart work, Sergeant. It's all rather circumstantial, but it does mean the finger of suspicion is pointing more and more towards Logan Price. If he discovered his wife had started an affair with Kenworth, that might have presented him with a motive for murder. It also might explain partly why the arguments between him and his wife were becoming more and more bitter – culminating in her vow to divorce him. That may well have been the factor that pushed him over the edge. So we could be looking at Logan Price being a double killer.'

'Yes, sir. I suppose it's possible.'

'He only lives round the corner. If he killed Kenworth, he could have walked it in less than five minutes.'

She nodded. 'Like you said, we urgently need to speak to Stephanie Price's sister since they were very close.'

Roscoe leaned forward onto his desk. 'You told me she's away in Scarborough at the moment.'

'Yes. I'm not sure when she'll be back.'

'It's not worth interrupting her holiday. I expect she'll be home in a day or two.'

'Yes, sir.'

'All right. I've got some news of my own. Shall we go and speak to the team? I've invited Dr Ling. She's making her way over here now,' said Roscoe.

They stepped into the main CID office. He clapped his hands and beckoned the staff across.

As she waited for the meeting to begin, Sunita pinned a seventh image to the whiteboard – a photo of Logan Price. Then she wrote his name beneath it.

Within a few minutes, Brett Dawson, Omar Khalid, Wendy Hopkirk and other members of the team had gathered at the front of the office. Dr Ling had arrived and perched herself on one of the desks.

'Right, everybody. I just wanted to update you on the two murders. I'll start by telling you about the forensic tests carried out on the bicycle belonging to Stephanie Price and her husband.

'Dr Ling and her team have analysed dabs and traces of blood on the handlebars which match with Stephanie Price's, the murdered woman. No surprise there. It's her bike. Unfortunately, there were no biometrics from anyone else,' said Roscoe.

Dr Ling interrupted. 'Sir, there's no way of telling whether these tiny amounts of blood were deposited on the night of the murder.'

'Of course,' said Roscoe. 'It's quite possible Mrs Price hurt herself at some stage and there's an entirely innocent explanation as to how it got there – a nosebleed, a cut finger, whatever. So that's as far as we can take that for the moment.'

'Is this the right time for me to mention the shoeprint found in the blood in the garage?' asked Dr Ling.

'Please go ahead,' said Roscoe.

'The print consists of circles and arcs, and we believe it could be of use if a suspect was identified and some of their footwear was handed to us.'

'That's good. Slowly but surely we're getting closer to the killer, I'm certain,' said Roscoe.

Dr Ling added, 'Unfortunately, we've been unable to retrieve the attacker's DNA from the clawhammer.'

'Very well. Thank you,' said Roscoe. 'Dawson, how are we getting on with tracing the two victims' phones?'

The young detective gave the impression he had not been listening. 'What, me?' he asked. 'Sorry, the phones. Yes. We haven't been able to trace them. Mrs Price's phone was last used near the farm shop before eight o'clock on Thursday. Since then, it looks like it's been turned off. Mr Kenworth's phone was last used in Queensbridge at around six o'clock on the night he died. The phone company say they think it's been turned off.'

'All right,' said Roscoe, clearly annoyed at this development. 'DC Hopkirk, I want you to contact the media team and make a fresh appeal for witnesses. Someone else might have seen the cyclist racing away from the farm shop, apart from Appleton.'

He stepped towards the whiteboard and tapped Logan Price's photograph.

'Right, I need to tell you all that DC Khalid's made an interesting discovery. Logan Price's alibi has fallen through. He claims to have been at the Red Lion pub from ten to eight, and this was supported by his drinking buddy. But we've spoken to the landlady, who's certain they didn't arrive until an hour and forty minutes later.

'So I'm asking Khalid to apply for search warrants – one for Logan's house in Mill Road and the other for his mother's place in Shawley Green. And we're going to be bringing him in for questioning later today. That man's got some explaining to do.'

Chapter 35

A stream of pedestrians with umbrellas trooped by as the chief inspector sat in his car in a rainswept Queensbridge street on Wednesday afternoon.

'Can't be much longer now, Sergeant,' he told Sunita, who was sitting beside him. 'You can't do much landscape gardening on a day like this– Hold on. That's him now. Put in another call to forensics to chivvy them along and then join me in the house.' Roscoe stepped out of the car and waved to two constables sitting in a police car behind. 'Come on,' he yelled as Logan Price drew his door keys from his pocket.

He had barely crossed the threshold when he heard Roscoe's stern voice behind him.

'Mr Price, we've got some more questions for you,' he said.

'Oh God. What now?' asked the householder, scowling at his visitor.

'You've told us a lie, sir. You weren't at the Red Lion at the time of the murder.'

'Who says I weren't?'

'Staff at the pub.'

'It were extremely busy that evening,' he said as he stood in the hallway at the foot of his stairs. 'They're probably confused.'

'They're not confused,' the chief inspector insisted. 'I'm the one who's confused – about why you and your friend Mr Tyler are telling such blatant lies.'

'I suppose you'd better come in,' said Price.

Roscoe, his sergeant and two uniformed officers stepped in from the pavement. Price entered his front room and slumped down into the armchair.

'We've got a warrant to search your house,' said Sunita.

'What do you want to search it for?'

'Perhaps some clue as to why your wife was at the farm shop so late in the evening,' said Sunita.

'Oh bloody hell,' said Price. 'Look, my wife's just been killed. Don't you lot have any compassion? You'd think you'd leave me alone to grieve at a time like this.'

'Fascinating to hear you talk about your wife in those tones, sir,' said Roscoe. 'You didn't sound too heartbroken the other evening. Anyway, you're going to come to headquarters now and answer some questions.'

'You're joking, aren't you? I've just had a bloody hard day.'

'Are you refusing to come with us?'

'Yes I bloody am. Come back tomorrow.'

'All right. Logan Price, I'm arresting you on suspicion of the murder of your wife, Stephanie,' he said. He then recited the rest of the police caution.

Price was handcuffed and driven off to St James Street.

* * *

Two hours later, the chief inspector was making final preparations before interviewing the suspect. He called his sergeant into his room.

'Are we all set now?' he asked.

Sunita nodded. 'Yes, sir. You know that he changed his mind about having a solicitor and we put a call into Roger Sims?'

'That's all right,' said Roscoe. 'Has Sims had sufficient time with him?'

'I'll go and see.'

Five minutes later, she was back in CID, confirming that both Price and his lawyer were ready.

The two detectives walked slowly down to the ground floor and found Price and his advisor already sitting behind a table in Interview Room One.

'Good. You've had a chance to familiarise yourself with the case, have you, Mr Sims?' asked Roscoe, taking a seat directly opposite Price.

'My client only has a vague idea of why you want to speak to him,' said Mr Sims, a tall man in glasses dressed in a smart blue suit. 'He feels aggrieved because this is the third time now he's been questioned.'

'Second,' said Roscoe.

Price glared across the table at him. 'Once at the hospital, once at my home on Monday and now today,' he said.

'We only exchanged a few words at the hospital,' said Roscoe. 'Look, I appreciate, Mr Price, that you've lost your wife and you're grieving. But the wheels of justice have to keep turning and we have to understand how your wife Stephanie met her death.'

Gazing directly at Price, the chief inspector said, 'I need to point out you're still under caution, Mr Price, and an audio recording is being made. Now where were you at 7.30 p.m. last Thursday?'

Price frowned. 'I've already told you. I were just leaving me mum's place. Me and me mate Viv Tyler were going to the Red Lion.'

Roscoe shook his head. 'Mr Price, both the landlord and landlady of the Red Lion, the Wainwrights, are quite definite about this,' he said. 'They insist you didn't arrive till halfway through *The Apprentice* programme on BBC at half past nine.'

Price shook his head. He looked across at the two detectives. 'Tell me this,' he said, 'how come they are so certain two of their customers turned up at half past nine if they themselves were busy watching the television show?'

Sunita interrupted. 'Mrs Wainwright just glanced at the screen while serving you,' she explained. 'Then you and Mr Tyler began making comments about the contestants.'

'Look,' said Price, 'the pub were heaving. All the world and his bloody wife were in that pub. How the hell can the Wainwrights know who were there and who weren't? There were three rows of customers queuing to get drinks. The bloody Pope could have walked in and they wouldn't have known if he'd just arrived or been there for an hour.'

'I think they might have noticed his motorcade holding up the high street traffic,' said Roscoe. 'Anyway, the point is you've told us a lie. You weren't at the pub earlier in the evening, so where were you? You've told us you were staying in Highfield Road, Shawley Green with your mother. It would only take about ten minutes to walk to the farm shop from there.'

'Five minutes by bicycle,' added Sunita.

'This is serious stuff, Mr Price,' Roscoe continued. 'We know your wife was demanding a divorce that you opposed. You were extremely angry with her.'

'That's rubbish,' said Price.

Price lowered his head and leaned down across the table. A heavy silence hung in the air. Roscoe decided to take a chance and use this moment to inquire about Stephanie's possible extramarital affair.

'While you're thinking about that,' the chief inspector said, 'were you aware of a friendship between Stephanie and Miles Kenworth?'

Price raised his head and sat upright.

'Are you joking?' he replied.

Sunita interrupted to ask, 'Did any friends or family call your wife Vani?'

'Well, yes,' said Price, 'but it's news to me if she was friendly with Kenworth.'

'While we're on the subject of Kenworth,' Roscoe continued, 'we need to know where you were between 7 p.m. and 8 p.m. on 11 February. Phone records show you weren't far from Waverley Court.'

He sneered. 'That's probably because I only live round the corner,' he said. 'I was at home that night with my wife.'

'I need to be sure you're telling us the truth about everything,' said Roscoe.

Mr Sims looked puzzled.

'Chief Inspector, this information regarding Lord Culverdon's son is new to me,' said the lawyer. 'Would it be possible to have a brief adjournment?'

'We'll give you ten minutes. Would that be enough?' asked Roscoe.

'That should be fine. Thank you,' said Mr Sims as the detectives left the room.

* * *

More than fifteen minutes later, the pair returned.

'My client's reflected on what's been said,' Mr Sims revealed. 'He appreciates now that he should have been honest with you from the start. He admits he and his wife had grown apart in recent times, much to his regret. His wife had occasional dalliances with other men, which caused him a great deal of anxiety.'

Price stretched his bare, tattooed arms out across the mahogany table and gazed down, as though ashamed to look the two detectives in the eye.

'However,' Mr Sims continued, 'he denies knowing of any affair involving his wife and the late Miles Kenworth.'

167

Roscoe interrupted. 'This is all very well,' he snapped. 'But clearly your client wasn't at the Red Lion at ten minutes to eight, as he claimed. So where was he?'

Price raised his eyes and looked across the table at the chief inspector. 'I was with another woman.'

Chapter 36

Sunita Roy rose from her bed early after a night of restless sleep. She glanced at the clock on her bedside table, which showed it was nearly seven o'clock.

Slipping on her white dressing gown and pink slippers, she strolled into the living room and opened the blinds. Then she peered out at the grey street outside, which was shrouded in fog. It seemed as though a wispy white curtain had been draped across the county town.

After making herself a lemon tea, she glanced through some emails on her phone while sitting on the settee. But she couldn't relax. Her mind was crowded with thoughts about the two murders.

Should they dismiss the possibility of there being two killers? And if just one man was responsible for both deaths, was that man Logan Price?

She wondered if she'd been right to assume Stephanie Price and Miles Kenworth had been engaged in an affair. But if they had been, could Logan Price's discovery of that affair and his resultant jealousy have given him a motive to kill them both?

And despite his reputation for violence, did he have the intelligence and cunning required to accomplish such heinous crimes? She had her reservations. Jealousy is one thing. Murder is entirely another.

The chief inspector, as with several murder cases in the past, had become convinced more and more of Price's guilt. And the lie Price had told about his whereabouts had only reinforced that conviction, although, for the moment, Roscoe had granted him police bail and released him from custody.

At the end of the police interview, Price stated that he had lied to protect his secret lover from becoming involved with the police, and because he was ashamed of his conduct. DC Khalid had now been despatched to visit the woman concerned to see if she would corroborate Price's story.

This all encouraged the chief inspector in his belief that Price had killed both Miles Kenworth and his own wife.

But Sunita believed her boss could be making a mistake by focusing his attention on this one person and not considering some of the other suspects.

On another subject altogether, Sunita was wondering what to tell her boyfriend, Samir, who was due to phone her later that day. After learning that the investment advisor he had recommended was a conman known as 'Slippery Sarkar', she had become dismayed. Until then she had totally trusted Samir. Now that trust was gone. She felt betrayed.

Time was moving relentlessly on. She made some breakfast, showered and set off for work.

By the time she arrived at St James Street at a quarter to nine, her thoughts were still undecided about the murder cases. However, she had a clearer idea about how she should deal with Samir. She was going to speak her mind.

When she arrived at her desk, Brett Dawson greeted her and told her Isabelle King had phoned.

'She says she got your message,' he said. 'She wants you to ring her.'

Sunita at once called Isabelle, who readily agreed to help in any way she could as she wanted her sister's killer brought to justice.

So the sergeant set off for Shawley Green, arriving in Chestnut Way soon after the fog had lifted at around half past nine.

After pushing open the gate, she strode up the path and rang the bell. Within a few seconds, Isabelle greeted her and welcomed her inside.

'Would you like a tea or coffee?' she asked the sergeant, removing an apron from round her waist as they entered the kitchen at the rear.

'A tea would be nice,' said the visitor. 'No milk or sugar. Thanks.'

Without asking, Sunita sat down at the table.

'You've obviously heard that we took Logan in for questioning yesterday,' she said as Isabelle put the kettle on.

'Yes. I was gobsmacked at first. But, after I'd had time to think about it, I've got to admit he was becoming more and more violent towards Stephanie. He nearly throttled her two weeks ago.'

'He was angry over the divorce?' said Sunita.

'He was. Listen, she was my little sister and I owe it to her to help you in any way I can.'

Sunita shook her head and sighed. 'I do wonder, Isabelle, how on earth an intelligent woman like your sister got tangled up with a loutish man like Logan Price.'

'I don't know,' Isabelle admitted. 'We've discussed this countless times as a family. Stephanie loved him once. That's all I can say.'

After making them both tea and serving the drinks, Isabelle sat down at the table opposite the detective. She had the resigned look of a prisoner with a guilty secret preparing herself to be interrogated.

'There's something I haven't told anyone,' she said. 'I didn't mention this to your chief inspector when we met at the hospital because, at the time, I had every hope Stephanie would survive. Anyway, now she's passed on, I feel I've got to mention it. Stephanie had been blackmailing someone.'

Sunita looked at her in astonishment. 'What on earth do you mean?' she said.

Isabelle sipped her tea. 'She'd caught a couple who weren't married to each other having sex.'

'Goodness me,' said Sunita. 'So Stephanie decided to demand money from them for her silence?'

'Yes.'

'A dangerous enterprise.'

'Yes it was. She came round here to see me. I tried to talk her out of it. I urged her to delete the images but she insisted she needed the money to start a new life for herself without her husband.'

Sunita stirred her tea and took a sip. 'Do you know who the couple were?'

Isabelle shook her head. 'Steph wouldn't tell me, no matter how much I asked her. She said the man wasn't her employer, Gordon MacLeod. The woman was someone she vaguely knew, who was in her twenties. She wouldn't say any more than that.'

'So did she come across this couple in the course of her work?'

'I'm not sure. I know it was a Monday when she came over because I'd been doing the laundry. She said something like, "Today a bit of luck fell my way."'

'So that must have been the day she spotted the couple?'

'Yes. It must have happened at a farm because she said something about a romp in the hay. She took some pictures on her phone and told me she was going to make an anonymous call, asking the man for £50,000. In return, she'd hand over her phone with the pictures and promise not to tell his wife.'

'I'd better take a note of all this,' said Sunita, removing a notebook and pen from the pocket of her jacket. 'So we know the target of her blackmail scheme was a married man. Any other clues about him?'

'No,' Isabelle replied, 'except that she thought he'd got plenty of money.'

'So she must have known this man fairly well to have his mobile number?'

'No, she didn't know it. But she said she'd be able to find it from records kept at the farm shop. He was obviously a customer there.'

'That's interesting. That narrows it down a little. Is there any other information you can give me? What time did your sister call round to tell you all this?'

'Must have been about four o'clock.'

'So she could have taken those pictures at any time during the day?'

'Yes, except not first thing. She'd got an appointment with her solicitor then. Her boss gave her a couple of hours off at the start of the day for that.'

'So, to sum up, the incident with the couple must have occurred sometime between, say, eleven o'clock and three o'clock?'

'That sounds about right,' Isabelle agreed.

'And we don't know where this happened?'

'No.'

Sunita gazed across the table at Isabelle as she sipped her tea. She decided it was time to bring up the subject of Miles Kenworth's diary.

'You obviously know about the murder of Miles Kenworth,' said Sunita. 'After his death, we found his diary at his flat in Queensbridge and I've been examining it. He's written about meeting someone with the initial letter *V*. That's your sister, isn't it?'

Isabelle turned pale and nodded. 'How did you work that out?' she asked.

'I did some research into the name Stephanie and the short forms people sometimes use. It can be shortened to Vani.'

'Yes,' said Isabelle, sipping her tea. 'My sister revealed to me she'd fallen deeply in love with Miles Kenworth and he felt the same way about her. For some reason, he called her by the pet name of Vani. Their affair was fraught with problems. She was married and wasn't sure whether to carry on seeing him. She swore me to secrecy. Miles also wanted it kept quiet for the time being. He didn't want to cause too much upset to his ex-girlfriend.'

Sunita gulped down the remains of her tea. 'Mr Kenworth noted in his diary that he was having a meal with V on 10 January,' she continued. 'He mentioned a rock music event on 20 January and wrote about another date on 5 February, which we believe involved a visit to the Old Pheasant pub in Queensbridge.'

Isabelle nodded. 'Yes, she told me about those dates. The rock event was at Birmingham Town Hall. And you're right about their drink at the Pheasant. I think that was the night Logan found out about them.'

Sunita wrote something in her notebook. Then she glanced up. 'Really? He found out that night – six days before Kenworth's murder?'

Isabelle nodded.

'By the way, did you know I met up with your sister at the farm shop?'

'No.'

'It was a fortnight ago. She was lovely at first, but she got annoyed when I suggested she must have known Mr Kenworth very well.'

Isabelle nodded tearfully. 'She was in a difficult situation. She didn't want it known she'd been having an affair with Mr Kenworth – least of all because she didn't want her husband finding out. She still wasn't sure whether she wanted to save her marriage. But she was also extremely upset about the death of Miles and had to take time off over it.'

Sunita gave a weak smile. 'I'm sorry your sister had such an unhappy time in the last weeks of her life,' she said.

Isabelle reached for a box of tissues at the far side of the table. She wiped a tear from her right eye. 'At least she doesn't have to worry about these things anymore.'

'Yes. Let's hope she rests in peace now,' said the sergeant. 'By the way, were you aware that Stephanie was pregnant?'

Isabelle jumped up.

'What?' she exclaimed.

'The doctor carrying out the post-mortem confirmed it,' said Sunita.

'Oh my God! I'd no idea. That must have been Miles's baby.'

Isabelle sat down, again, sobbing.

'Can you be that certain?' asked Sunita.

'My sister told me she hadn't had sex with Logan for months.'

'I see. Look, I realise this is upsetting, but I must ask you this. Isabelle, you said just now that Logan found out about the affair on 5 February. How did he find out?'

'Steph told me that when they left the Old Pheasant they paused for a goodnight kiss. It turned into one of those long, passionate kisses. Steph thought someone might have seen them and told Logan. Or maybe Logan himself was travelling past on his bike.'

Chapter 37

As soon as she left Isabelle King's home in Chestnut Way, Sunita Roy phoned the chief inspector. She outlined the sister's bombshell admission that Stephanie Price had been blackmailing a married man.

'This opens up a whole new line of inquiry,' he admitted. 'I'd like you to go straight round to the farm shop and get into their computer system. If Stephanie Price used their records to get a customer's phone number, she might have left a trail. We might be able to identify that person in double quick time.

'Failing that, we need to find out how Mrs Price spent her day. Who did she visit? What farms, what suppliers, what country estates? This might involve a lot of work, but it could be highly rewarding. If you make a start, we'll see what the situation is later and I'll probably get Khalid and Dawson to join you.'

Sunita took just a few minutes to reach the farm shop in her car. She passed the meat and cheese counters before following the corridor that led to the office.

Gordon MacLeod was sitting at his desk with the door open, cleaning his glasses.

'Mr MacLeod,' she said, 'sorry to trouble you again.'

Rather awkwardly, he put his glasses on and gazed at her.

'Ah, the police lady,' he said. 'Sergeant Roy. How can I help you?'

'We believe Stephanie Price searched your computer system nine or ten days ago for a customer's phone number. Would you be able to find out which customer it was?'

MacLeod shook his head. 'Most staff have access to the computer, Sergeant. It would be a bit of a wee challenge to find out if Mrs Price had been searching through names.'

'Would you mind if we brought our computer expert down to see if he can retrieve details of her search? We think she'd have been looking for details of one particular customer and it's important to find out who that customer was. It could make a huge difference to our investigation.'

MacLeod nodded. 'If it would help track down the person that killed our poor lassie, we'd be pleased to see him.'

Sunita sat down by the door. 'There's another favour I need. Could you give me a list of deliveries and collections Mrs Price made on Monday, 21 February?'

He nodded. 'I can certainly give you a list of jobs booked in with her, but it may not be comprehensive,' he said.

'So not everything is recorded then?'

'Well, with the best will in the world, we try to encourage staff to make a note of everything but you know how folk are. Sometimes they're in a rush and matters get overlooked.'

Sunita nodded. This wasn't the first time she had learnt of staff slackness. The axe that killed Miles Kenworth had been stolen after someone forgot to lock the storeroom door. She decided not to remind MacLeod of that. She wanted to keep him on their side.

'If you could give me her Monday schedule, I can at least make a start,' was all she said.

* * *

Sunita had to wait half an hour. But her gentle persuasion and patience paid off. Gordon MacLeod made his way from the shop and found her sitting in her car. He handed her a printed list of jobs Stephanie Price had been expected to carry out on the day in question.

'She asked for an hour off to attend to some personal business at the start of the day, so she may have been a bit late seeing to her rounds,' he remarked before returning to his office.

She sat studying the list for a few minutes. It began with details of two addresses where Mrs Price had gone to collect logs: '10.30 a.m. Hartston Mill Farm, Hartston; 12 noon, Lower Wood Farm, Stratford.'

There followed six other farm addresses within a five-mile radius that Stephanie had visited during the afternoon to collect supplies of eggs, meat and vegetables.

Lastly, Mrs Price had been asked to deliver some groceries to The Kitchen at Culverdon Hall.

Sunita decided to visit the first two farms and Culverdon Hall herself and inquire about haylofts. She called Brett Dawson and tasked him with visiting the other addresses.

Calling at Hartston Mill Farm in the village of Hartston proved a waste of Sunita's time since, according to the farmer, they no longer had a functioning hay barn and hayloft.

It was nearly midday by the time Sunita began travelling to Mark Webster's Lower Wood Farm.

She began to wonder whether this was the same route Stephanie Price had taken in her van. It might have been, she told herself while passing sheep grazing alongside newborn lambs.

After rounding a bend, she saw a sign for the farm and turned onto a stony track leading to the farmhouse.

The jovial farmer, Mark Webster, was standing at his garden gate, chatting to a farmhand, as her car drew up.

The sergeant wound down her window.

'Mr Webster, I'm DS Roy from Heart of England CID,' she said as his colleague walked away.

'Nothing wrong, I hope,' said Webster, passing through the gate and stepping towards her car.

'We're making inquiries about Stephanie Price,' she explained.

'Of course. Steph. She was a lovely woman. We were both devastated to hear what happened.'

'We're visiting some of the places she went to on 21 February. It's believed she came across some trespassers at one of the farms.'

'Trespassers?' he said.

'Yes,' she replied. 'She came across a man and a woman in a hay barn who no doubt shouldn't have been there.'

'Well, we've got a hay barn,' said the farmer, casting his eyes towards the nearby building. 'But I don't know about no trespassers.

I weren't here when Steph called. One of me ewes was poorly. I was at the vet's, but I know she was here. She took the logs I put out for her.'

Sunita had noticed his sideways glance towards the barn. She cut the engine and stepped out of the car.

'Do you mind if I take a look?' she asked.

She gazed at the two tractors, the old mower, the trees and the hill beyond as she strolled across to the barn and hauled the door open. She was aware of the farmer standing a few metres behind her.

'What's this got to do with the girl's death then?' the farmer asked.

'Can't tell you, I'm afraid,' she replied.

'So Steph saw these two trespassers and challenged 'em, like – and got into an argument?'

'We'd only be guessing. This is just a small part of a much larger picture,' she explained.

'I see,' said Webster, although it was clear to Sunita that he didn't.

Then a smile replaced his confused expression like a sunbeam streaking over the horizon.

'I tell you what,' said the farmer. 'This ties up with something I found in the hayloft soon after Steph collected those logs. It was just lying on the floor by the ladder. It's a locket showing a picture of a young blonde girl with a woman who looks like her mother.'

Chapter 38

The stately home loomed up from among the trees in the distance as Sunita Roy approached Culverdon Hall. It was hard to miss because of its grey towers, which enjoyed a commanding presence over the land for miles around.

As she travelled up the gravel drive, the towers almost shimmered in the afternoon sun.

The open-top Wolseley belonging to Rupert Faulkner was parked to the left as she neared the circular water fountain that stood in front of the main house. She parked beside the marble steps and turned off the engine.

She recognised her old Peugeot might appear out of keeping in these historic surroundings. But that couldn't be helped. She had an urgent police matter to attend to on what was her last call of the day.

Sunita walked round the side of the building along the path flanked by hedges until she reached the east wing's oak door. As before, she found it partly open and was about to walk in when she heard voices. A man and a woman were arguing.

The sound was being emitted from an open window a few metres away.

Instead of entering through the doorway, she stepped along a narrow stretch of lawn until she was standing close to the window.

'I know I shouldn't speak ill of the dead,' the woman was saying, 'but Miles treated his family appallingly. After all the money his father spent on his early life and education, he threw everything back in his parents' faces. Is that any way to behave? He dabbled in drugs and angered all his neighbours, playing loud music. He brought shame on the family name.'

'You're too harsh on the lad,' said the male voice. 'He found it difficult being part of a well-to-do family. He couldn't find his proper role. Arthur was the heir, and Miles could never quite understand what sort of role he was meant to play. I far preferred Miles to Stephanie Price.'

The woman interrupted to say, 'Oh I didn't like Stephanie either. Nosy cow and she made your life hell, didn't she?'

'Yes,' said the man. 'She did everything she could to stop me from becoming manager. She even made up lies that I'd been sacked from one of my previous jobs. I'm not shedding any tears for her.'

Sunita decided she had heard enough. It was simply idle gossip – the sort that members of the public had no doubt been engaged in ever since the two murders.

She stepped through the entrance and at once realised, after noticing a sign on the wall, that the voices must have been coming from the kitchen, situated along a corridor to the left.

She took a few paces towards the kitchen door and knocked.

'Just a minute,' called the same female voice she had just been listening to.

After two or three minutes, the door opened and the trim figure of the housekeeper, Sarah Crosswell, emerged. Sunita vaguely remembered her from her first visit to the hall.

This time she paid more attention to the woman's appearance. She was tall, slim and, apart from an apron round her waist, presentable. She had well-coiffed, medium-length blonde hair and a warm smile.

'DS Roy, Heart of England Police,' she informed her, showing her identification. 'I just need a quick word.'

'You'd better come in,' she said.

Sunita found herself in a vast kitchen which included an Aga oven and cooker, two chrome hobs, a griddle and two fat fryers. Above them loomed a series of large chrome extractor fan units and fluorescent lighting.

'Would you like tea or coffee?' asked Sarah.

'No, I'm fine thanks,' the detective replied, taking a seat beside a long trestle table. 'I thought I heard a man's voice.'

'No,' replied the housekeeper. 'I'm here on my own.'

Sunita wondered why she was lying. She suspected the man was perhaps *persona non grata*. Where was he? Had he gone to a different part of the house?

'You've probably heard about the death of a lady called Stephanie Price in Shawley Green,' said Sunita.

Sarah nodded.

180

'I'm just retracing some of her last movements,' Sunita explained. 'We believe she was here on the afternoon of 21 February?'

'That's right. She was here at about four o'clock. She didn't stay long. She simply brought in some eggs, meat and vegetables, got me to sign for them and then left.'

'Do you have a hayloft here or hay barn?'

'Only at the stables.'

'I think perhaps I need to take a look there.'

Sarah sat down on a wooden chair and folded her arms. She was frowning. 'What's all this about then?'

'Well,' said Sunita, 'she supposedly met a couple of people, presumably trespassers, at some point during the day. They were chatting inside a loft, and this incident could have some link to her death, you see.'

'I don't think we'd have any trespassers here. There are people coming and going all the time at the stables and, in any case, the loft isn't very large. Difficult for people to get inside it.'

'All right,' said Sunita. 'I'm fairly certain the place concerned was at a farm I visited earlier. I just thought I'd check here so I could say I'd been thorough. Tell me, how did you find Stephanie when she called round here on that day? What sort of mood was she in?'

'Exuberant,' said Sarah. 'Something had happened to cheer her up and she told me she couldn't wait to finish work.'

'She didn't explain why she was so happy?'

'No.'

'That fits in with what I know,' said Sunita. 'You've been very helpful. We've now got a clearer picture of what may have happened to her that day.'

After she left the kitchen and went outside, natural curiosity brought Sunita back to the casement windows.

She had an inkling that Sarah Crosswell's male friend might make a quick return. And shortly afterwards, she was proved right.

The man, who must have been hiding in a side room, emerged and began asking who their unexpected visitor had been and what questions she had been asking. Their conversation became flirtatious.

'You just can't keep your hands off me,' said Sarah amid a fit of giggling.

Sunita convinced herself that she recognised the male voice and became more and more eager to confirm her suspicions. She ventured closer to the window, crouching down so that she remained beneath the sill. Then she slowly raised her head. She peeked into the kitchen.

Sarah's friend, whom she was now embracing, was Nick Halfpenny, the farm shop manager.

* * *

Sunita was still thinking about the scene she had witnessed in Lord Culverdon's kitchen as she arrived home that evening at her Warwick flat.

It had become clear to her that Sarah Crosswell and Nick Halfpenny were having some kind of affair. He was Gordon MacLeod's right-hand man at the farm shop – tasked with boosting sales among the well-heeled members of Warwickshire society. He was also a married man. She was responsible for His Lordship's culinary budget at Culverdon Hall. Did that have any significance in terms of their investigation? Perhaps not.

She was tired when she climbed the stairs to her flat and began cooking a meal. Maybe this was time for her to forget about the case for a moment and deal with the financial guru Indrani Sarkar.

So, just before eight o'clock, after she had finished her evening meal, she looked up his phone number and dialled it.

'Sunita, how lovely to hear from you,' he said as he answered her call.

'You won't be feeling like that in a minute,' she said.

'Oh, how do you mean?'

'I'm cancelling my application to invest with you. You're not regulated by the Financial Conduct Authority.'

Sarkar laughed. 'Oh such a small thing. We were registered in the past. It's just that the paperwork's not up to date.'

'I've learnt you're running a Ponzi scheme – paying investors with money raised from new investors. Eventually the system runs out of control like a runaway train. You promised me a sound investment and it's nothing of the kind.'

'My dear Sunita, these are serious allegations,' he insisted. 'I don't know who you've been speaking to. Was it one of your work colleagues? I'm afraid members of Her Majesty's police force are as ignorant of investment practices as the man in the street.

'You're doing yourself a disservice if you turn down the opportunity to place your savings with me. If you want to talk about numbers, I can assure you my investments are one hundred per cent safe and you won't obtain a better rate of interest anywhere else on the high street.'

Sunita was becoming angrier and angrier. It was like trying to reason with a street trader in a Kolkata market.

'Yes, I'm glad to talk about numbers, Mr Sarkar. I'm fairly certain your days spent conning investors are numbered. You're a crook and a charlatan and I shan't be having anything more to do with you.'

Half an hour later, her phone rang. She was not surprised that Samir Banerjee was calling her.

For a moment, she considered not replying and letting the phone go through to voicemail.

But, after a few seconds, she answered with a stern, 'Yes?'

'Oh Sunita, I've just had an anxious call from Indrani,' he said. 'Apparently you're upset with him.'

'That's right, Samir. I'm also annoyed with you. You recommended this man to me as genuine and trustworthy. I've discovered he's nothing of the sort.'

'Sunita, I'm so sorry you feel like this, but in my experience he's a totally honest and reliable man who's helped clients have amazing success with their investments.'

'You may think that, Samir. But have you had any personal experience of saving with the man? Have you placed money with him and seen its value rocketing?'

'Well, no,' he admitted.

'Sarkar isn't registered with the FCA,' she said, as she began marching up and down the carpet with the phone still pressed to her ear. 'He's running a discredited Ponzi scheme and any day now you can expect him to feel the hand of the law gripping his collar. How could you introduce me to such a fraudster, Samir? I thought I could trust you.'

'Please calm down, Sunita. It sounds as though you're exaggerating. Everyone I know has only the highest praise for Indrani. I really believe you're making a mistake.'

'No, Samir,' she said as she felt her breath quickening. 'The only mistake I made was in thinking I could trust you and that we might have a future together.' Then she hung up.

Chapter 39

Sunita Roy glanced up from her desk on Friday morning as Brett Dawson, with unkempt hair and a creased shirt, hurried into CID.

'Sorry, I'm late, Sarge,' he mumbled. 'I overslept.'

'That's all right, Brett,' she replied. 'I know you worked hard yesterday. Have you mislaid your hairbrush and your iron?'

'Sorry. I'll just go to the men's room and smarten myself up a bit.'

Five minutes later, he was back, his shirt as wrinkled as before but his blond hair neatly combed.

'Isn't the guvnor around, Sarge?'

'He's gone to see our computer guy, John Hepworth.'

Dawson studied his notebook.

'Only two farms yesterday had places for storing hay,' he said. 'The other haylofts have been converted into accommodation for bed and breakfast guests.'

'And what about the two premises still being used for hay?'

'The farmers keep a close eye on them and were sure they've had no intruders,' he said. 'But I tell you what, Sarge. When we do catch the couple who went for a romp in the hay, do you think they'll be given bail?'

'Save the jokes, Brett,' she remarked. 'Anyway, now we've got all the information about the haylofts, I'm fairly certain the place Stephanie went to was Lower Wood Farm, owned by Mark Webster.'

'I'm glad all the work has paid off. By the way, Sarge, I thought you might be interested in this.'

Dawson took a press cutting from his pocket and placed it in front of her. 'I cut it out of my girlfriend's copy of yesterday's *Daily Mirror*.'

The report, tucked away at the foot of page 12, said:

A man's body has been found at the bottom of a ravine, close to where the English peer Lord Culverdon's son went missing while hiking two and a half years ago. The decomposed body was found six miles north of the town of Nerja on Spain's Costa del Sol. An autopsy will be held. Arthur Kenworth was thirty-four and worked in the City. A spokesman for his family at Culverdon Hall said, 'We've had our hopes raised and dashed so often that his body would be found and recovered. We would prefer not to comment further at this time.' Last month, Mr Kenworth's younger brother, Miles Kenworth, was found murdered at his home in Warwickshire. Two men were arrested and released without charge.

Sunita was secretly impressed by Dawson's diligence in showing her the cutting and she began wondering about the implications of the newspaper report.

Was the dead body found at the foot of the ravine really that of Arthur Kenworth, Miles's brother? Did he fall or was there a more sinister aspect to it? And if so, did it have any connection with the death of Miles?

The legend about the witch's deathbed curse sprang into her mind. She had initially dismissed the whole idea of a chain of early male deaths in an aristocratic family as medieval folklore. But was it all a silly myth? Was it so ridiculous to consider a link between the way the two brothers had passed away?

She and Dawson spent the next hour making calls. He spoke to the mayor's office in Nerja while Sunita spoke to the town's Guardia Civil.

By the time Roscoe had returned from visiting their digital forensics expert, John Hepworth, Sunita had gained answers to many of her questions.

She knocked on his door.

'Come in,' he said. 'I'm afraid we've got a problem with the database used at the farm shop.'

'Really?' she said, finding herself a seat.

'Yes. I've just had a long conversation with John,' he said, settling himself into his high-back chair. 'He's been down to the shop, but at the moment he can't identify who it was Stephanie Price was searching for. Whoever set up the damned computer system arranged for each item of search history to be automatically deleted after nine days.'

Sunita shook her head. 'That's a nuisance. So there's nothing more he can do?'

'He's going to get some advice from someone,' he replied. 'By the way, you did a cracking job yesterday, obtaining that locket with the picture.'

He picked up the sterling silver circular pendant and chain, which had been obtained from Mark Webster. He placed it on his desk.

'I was thinking we might issue the picture to the press in an effort to trace the girl and the woman,' he said.

Sunita shrugged her shoulders. 'I don't know, sir. It's not a sharp image. May cause confusion.'

He nodded. 'I take your point, but we really ought to make a big effort to track them down. They are almost certainly connected with Mrs Price's blackmail attempt. By the way, Khalid has just returned from visiting Logan Price's secret girlfriend, Becky Morgan. She claims she and Price went to bed together on the evening of 24 February, but her evidence is unreliable. She admits she fell asleep after having sex and therefore can't vouch for his whereabouts at around 8 p.m. Khalid borrowed someone's bicycle and found you can make the two-mile journey from Miss Morgan's house to the farm shop in five minutes on two wheels.'

Sunita stroked her chin.

'So Logan would've had time to get cleaned up at his mother's and back to Becky's after murdering his wife?'

'Yes.'

Sunita nodded. 'Sir, there's something I wanted to show you. It's something Dawson's come up with.'

She handed him a photocopy of the *Mirror* news report.

'This was in yesterday's paper,' she explained.

He quietly read the news item and then remarked, 'You're not suggesting we investigate this as well as our two Warwickshire murders?'

'Well, I've found out a lot more about this since you've been away from your desk, sir. I've been speaking to the police over there using my best schoolgirl Spanish and I think we should think about looking into this incident more deeply.'

Roscoe's eyes glazed over. 'I'm tending to take the same view about this as the spokesman for the family,' he said. 'You know, it says they've had their hopes raised and dashed so often before.'

Sunita was annoyed to hear this. He was behaving as he often did – jumping to conclusions before hearing her full account.

'If I can explain,' she said, glancing down at her notebook, 'one of the policewomen in Malaga Province has told me unofficially that they're fairly certain this body is Arthur Kenworth.

'When he disappeared, it says in our file on the case that he was wearing: a blue sports top with the logo "Explorador"; some light-brown chinos; a grey waterproof jacket; a red neck scarf; some black Adidas hiking boots; and a fawn-coloured peaked cap. The clothing found on the decomposed corpse is virtually identical, according to the lady I spoke to.

'Now because the body is decomposed, it's difficult to be certain. But it looks as though this person received severe head injuries – similar to those inflicted on Stephanie Price. There's a severe indentation in the cranium.'

Roscoe sat up straight on hearing this. 'Is that right?' he said.

'Yes, sir,' said Sunita.

'Could have been caused during the fall,' he remarked.

'And I ought to mention there's been at least one other case of someone being attacked and pushed into the same ravine. Spanish police say the other victim was killed by a drug gang. Now, I'm thinking, in view of Miles's links to the drugs world, that maybe Arthur got mixed up with some villains while in Spain.

'I think it would definitely be worth speaking to Lord Culverdon about this and possibly sending me out to Spain so we could investigate for ourselves. It would be disastrous if both Lord Culverdon's sons were killed by an axe and we didn't get to know about it.'

Roscoe shook his head. He showed as much enthusiasm at the idea as a hungry diner offered half a biscuit.

'The more I think about this suggestion, Sergeant, the more I'm against the whole idea,' he said. 'This man's death was just over two years ago on the Costa del Sol. We're dealing with two deaths in Warwickshire in the here and now.'

He continued, 'There's no real confirmation that this man recovered from the Spanish mountains has any link at all with our murder cases. He could be a Spanish down-and-out who simply had a good taste in fashion. Particularly at a time like this when we've got budgetary restraints and Norris is breathing down our necks, I can't approve a rainbow-chasing expedition to the Costas.'

Chapter 40

It was nearly seven o'clock by the time the chief inspector approached his home beside the lush, green fields on the northern outskirts of Queensbridge.

He had had a long, tiring day and was feeling despondent. He was more certain than ever in his mind that Logan Price was behind both murders.

DC Khalid's discovery that Price's girlfriend, Becky, couldn't accurately account for the man's movements around eight o'clock – the time when Stephanie Price was attacked – had been an encouraging development.

But most of the evidence against the landscape gardener was circumstantial. If only they could identify the person Mrs Price had been searching for on the farm shop database. Or identify the blonde girl with the smiling eyes and the older woman with dark-blonde hair pictured in the locket. Progress seemed to be obstructed at every turn.

On top of all that, his sergeant seemed to have become obsessed with a hairbrained scheme linking the fates of

Miles and Arthur Kenworth. Surely he'd been right to deny her the chance to investigate the older brother's mysterious disappearance, hadn't he?

He firmly believed they had to focus on the investigation at home. The lives of two families were in ruins. Obtaining justice and closure for them was his priority.

The heartfelt words of Stephanie's sister kept coming back to him, 'She should be here on earth like you and me, Mr Roscoe, full of the joys of life.'

Tomorrow he faced a meeting with the chief superintendent. Would she support his stance? He was uncertain. He felt as confident as a canoeist heading for the rapids without a paddle.

He turned into the narrow lane, entered the driveway and parked in his garage.

Then he ambled over to the front door and turned his key.

Helen emerged smiling from the kitchen. She wiped her hands on her apron before reaching up and kissing him on the cheek.

'Good day, dear?' she asked.

'Not really. We're not making much headway on these murder cases,' he complained, walking into the living room.

'Sorry to hear that,' she said as he sat on their leather settee. 'Anyway we've hired the bus.'

'Oh, the double-decker to take guests to the reception? How much was that?'

'Seven hundred and fifty pounds but George and Amanda were delighted with it. Her father's paying for it.'

'Generous man,' Roscoe remarked as he leaned back. 'Oh, Helen, you'll never believe the latest news from the office. DS Roy thinks the murder of Miles Kenworth could be linked to the death of Kenworth's brother in Spain. She wants me to fork out for a trip to the Costa del Sol.'

She sat beside him. 'The girl's used her initiative well in the past. Don't you remember how she helped solve those crossbow murders and the murder of Dr Deeley?'

'Yes, but she didn't have to travel far then. This time she wants to jet off for a junket in the sun a thousand miles away.'

Helen frowned. 'Why won't you let the girl follow her instincts? She's been proved right so many times before.'

* * *

Saturday was officially a day off for the chief inspector. But he reminded himself, as he set off for his office, that rules about time off rarely meant anything for a detective of his rank these days.

Omar Khalid smiled broadly as he saw Roscoe enter the CID room through the double doors and make his way past the rows of desks.

'You're looking bright and cheerful,' he told the detective.

'I don't feel it,' Khalid complained. 'Not when it's the sunniest day outside that we've had for weeks.'

'Never mind,' said Roscoe. 'I've got a job for you which will get you out of the office. You know the picture in the locket?'

'Yes, sir.'

'I've had a few thoughts about it. One is that there's some kind of hallmark on the locket. So get yourself down to a jeweller. See what they can tell you. Maybe they'll be able to identify the maker. Meanwhile I've got to go and see Norris.'

Roscoe climbed the stairs to the second floor and knocked on the chief superintendent's door.

Within seconds, her voice roared, 'Come in.'

Norris, whose head was topped with neatly combed, mid-length grey hair, was sitting in her wheelchair at the front of her desk.

'Ah, Gavin. Just the person. Can you fill me in on the progress you're making with these two murders? The assistant commissioner was asking.'

He drew up a chair. 'We're working on the basis that Miles Kenworth and Stephanie Price were killed by the same person, ma'am. There are several persons of interest, but the main suspect is Logan Price, husband of the murdered woman. There's a huge hole in his alibi.'

'What's his alibi, exactly?'

'He initially told us he was drinking with a friend in Queensbridge at the time of the attack on his wife, but the landlady of the pub disputed this. He then admitted to us that he lied and he was with a woman friend.'

'Presumably you've spoken to the woman?'

'Yes, but she was asleep during the crucial time the attack was carried out – around eight o'clock – and she isn't a convincing witness, according to DC Khalid who interviewed her.'

She swivelled her wheelchair round until she could peer directly into his eyes. 'Gavin, this Logan Price – isn't he alleged to have caught his wife embracing Mr Kenworth?'

'Yes, ma'am. You've been reading through the files.'

'Well, he's got a very strong motive, surely.'

He nodded. 'That's right. We're nearly there. We just need a little more evidence. I need to ask you something, ma'am.'

Her eyes continued to stare into his. 'What's that, Gavin?'

'DS Roy has got it into her head that the police in Spain may have found the body of Mr Kenworth's older brother, Arthur, who disappeared there while hiking over two years ago.'

She nodded. 'Go on.'

'She's been speaking to an officer in Andalusia, who's confirmed they've found the remains of someone in similar clothes at the bottom of a ravine. Apparently, it

192

looks as though they received head injuries and she's angling for a trip to the Costa del Sol.'

'Good for her,' said Norris.

'Sorry?' said Roscoe.

She had the look of a female barrister on the point of tearing a witness apart.

'Girl's showing a bit of initiative. That's what I like about her,' said Norris.

'But, surely, ma'am, in terms of this helping the case, she must stand as much chance as a hedgehog crossing Spaghetti Junction.'

'Nonsense. I don't know why you and I didn't think of this ourselves. Two brothers, both with head injuries. This could give us a significant new lead.'

Chapter 41

Conditions in the aircraft cabin were pleasantly comfortable on Tuesday morning as Sunita Roy and Brett Dawson boarded their flight to Malaga.

Temperatures at her Warwick home had plunged to below freezing point overnight so, if their work schedule allowed, she was looking forward to spending any spare time basking in the Spanish sun.

Perspiring a little in her short, white kurti and jeans after the long walk along the boarding bridge, she struggled to keep up with her younger colleague.

'I think these are ours, Sarge,' said Dawson after his sharp eyes had scrutinised the tiny seat numbers to the left of the gangway.

She nodded. 'Yes, that's right. Yours is the middle seat of the three. I've got the aisle seat.'

Sunita waited patiently while Dawson opened the overhead luggage rack and stowed their two holdalls inside.

The pair then took their seats beside a young mother and baby occupying the window seat.

'I still can't believe the DCI approved the trip,' Dawson remarked as he clutched a set of headphones.

'I was just as surprised as you,' she replied. 'He said he'd spoken too hastily and could now see there might be something to be gained by us going.'

Their plane lurched into life and rumbled off towards the runway. Within minutes, the roar of the engines reached a crescendo and they soared into the misty blue sky.

'While you were enjoying your day off yesterday, I was hard at work,' said Sunita. 'I went through the original file relating to Arthur Kenworth's disappearance, compiled by Tom Vickers, and called Lavinia Kenworth at Culverdon Hall to check on a few details.'

'You've been busy,' said Dawson.

'Yes. I also called the hotel where Arthur stayed. Luckily for us, one of the receptionists who handled his booking still works there and I want to visit her later today, if there's enough time.'

'That's a pity, Sarge. I'd got plans for a nice, lazy time by the pool,' he said with a smile as he connected his headphones to his phone.

'There probably won't be much time for sitting by the pool. We've got our work cut out on this one, Brett,' she said.

* * *

Neither of the detectives had visited Spain before. But although their journey to the town of Nerja partly had the makings of a pleasure jaunt with its sandy beaches and cliffside coves, Sunita was determined that work should take priority.

So after hiring a Dacia Sandero from a car hire company at Malaga Airport, they headed directly into the town, which boasted four blue-flag beaches.

Sunita had booked two rooms for four nights at the three-star San Rafael Hotel but she was at pains to impress upon Dawson the need to unpack quickly.

'I'll expect to see you downstairs in ten minutes,' she said.

The streets were bustling with shoppers as the pair, in lighter clothing more suited to warmer climes, made their way across the town, which lay in the foothills of the Sierra de Almijara mountains.

They set off in the direction of the beachfront hotel where Arthur Kenworth had stayed. Sunita was eager to get there before the booking clerk she'd spoken to, Kayleigh Stevens, finished for the day.

As they turned a corner and approached the building, they realised it was far more impressive than their accommodation. It was a plush, two-hundred-room five-star hotel with a sparkling, tile-adorned walkway leading to revolving doors and a vast marble floor in the reception hall.

A woman in her late twenties with dark, curly hair was sitting behind the reception desk as they crossed the foyer.

'Kayleigh Stevens?' Sunita asked, displaying her warrant card.

'Yes. You must be DS Roy,' she replied. 'Good flight?'

'Yes, very good, thank you,' said the sergeant. 'So much easier to speak face to face, isn't it? You were telling me about Arthur Kenworth.'

Kayleigh nodded. 'Yes, he was a nice guy. I took to him straight away. He was the sort of guy who always had time for people. I'd had a problem with my car when he arrived on the Sunday afternoon.'

'The thirteenth of October?' asked Sunita.

'I think so. Mr Kenworth must have been eager to see his room, but he was very sympathetic and listened to me going on about my car. He said he was going to be spending his time hiking in the mountains and that some of his friends were hoping to join him later in the week.'

'He didn't mention any names?'

'No.'

Dawson interrupted to ask, 'When was the last time you saw him?'

'It must have been on the Friday morning just before he set out for the mountains.'

Dawson nodded. 'What time would that have been?'

'About nine o'clock. He said he was keen to see La Quilla, a beautiful village five or six miles from Nerja. Then he was going to explore the mountains to the north.'

'How did he seem?' Dawson asked as Sunita took out a notebook and began writing.

'Just his normal self – you know, friendly.'

Sunita leaned against the counter. 'I don't suppose you remember what he was wearing, do you?'

She smiled. 'The police, when they came here, asked me the same. All I can remember is he was wearing a blue top and brown chinos.'

'Did he have any kind of hat?'

'A peaked cap, I think.'

'Did you have any other guests at that time who arrived on flights from Birmingham?'

'Well, we should have that kind of information somewhere, but it might take a while to find it. I can try.'

Sunita smiled. 'That would be very helpful, if you could.'

Kayleigh shifted in her seat and shook her head. 'Oh we were so upset when Mr Kenworth failed to come back that night. The first I was aware he was missing was when someone phoned the hotel asking for him. There was no reply to his room phone and no reply from his mobile. The receptionist who was on duty spoke with the manager. They decided he might have stayed up in La Quilla for the night. But the manager became concerned by the following afternoon and notified the police.'

'Must have been a very distressing time,' said Sunita.

'Yes, it was. Lots of search parties went out but they never found him, of course. We also had his father and sister staying with us for a couple of weeks. They were devastated. So you reckon this body found near La Quilla could be him?'

'We don't know yet,' Sunita explained. 'We've got an appointment tomorrow with someone from the Guardia Civil. We hope to know more then. Thank you for your time.'

'Yes,' said Dawson. 'You've been very helpful.'

'One thing before you go,' said Kayleigh. 'I've had something on my mind. This wasn't mentioned to the police in Nerja, but a strange man came here asking for Mr Kenworth on the day before he disappeared. Dolores was on reception at the time. She left the company soon afterwards and only told me about it months later when I bumped into her. This guy just came to the desk and said something like, "Could you phone up to Mr Kenworth's room? I need to speak to him."'

Dawson frowned. 'What did this guy look like?'

'Dolores said he was tall. He had a posh voice and jet-black hair. She told him Mr Kenworth left the hotel immediately after breakfast. He asked what time that was and she said half past nine. He asked if Mr Kenworth had gone hiking in the mountains and she said, "Yes, I believe so."'

'Could have been one of the friends he'd been planning to meet up with,' Dawson suggested in a low voice.

'Yes. That's possible. Dolores asked if he wanted to leave a message, but the man said we weren't to worry and it didn't matter. He refused to give his name and hurried away.'

'How odd,' said Sunita. 'Thank you. I'm glad you brought that up.'

'Well, it stuck in my mind because Dolores said she had a laugh about it afterwards. It looked very much as though the man was wearing a wig.'

Chapter 42

The sun shone brightly over Nerja, bringing the promise of a warm day, as Sunita Roy and Brett Dawson set off from their hotel in the direction of the Guardia Civil headquarters.

The barracks were located in a side street in a whitewashed, two-storey building behind black wrought-iron gates. A Spanish flag fluttered from a pole on the forecourt.

Lieutenant Francisco Díaz greeted them as soon as a subordinate informed him the two British detectives had arrived in the reception hall.

A giant of a man, the lieutenant strode out of a side room in his dark-green uniform and shook their hands.

'Hola!' he said. 'Welcome, Sergeant Roy and Constable Dawson. Please, this way.'

He led the pair into a large office at the rear of the building, which had been built in the 1940s, after the end of the civil war. A portrait of King Felipe and three Spanish flags hung from the wall.

Díaz found them chairs before taking a seat behind his antique oak desk and removing his beret.

'I am sorry. You waste your time with this journey,' said Díaz. 'You should call before coming from England. The coroners – they find ten days ago – say is not Arthur Victor Kenworth from the Culverdon Hall in Warwickshire. It is the body of Javier López, a gentleman of the streets, who travels in Nerja and the village of La Quilla. Sometimes he works as carpenter.'

Dawson raised a hand to his mouth in disbelief. Sunita looked bewildered.

'I spoke to one of your female officers last week,' said Sunita. 'She was fairly certain it was Arthur Kenworth's body. Are you sure about this?'

'*Sí,*' he said, twirling one end of his black moustache with his fingers. 'I tell you what happens. We have an emergency call. A walker – he finds a man dead in the Municipality of La Quilla. This is the area where Señor Arthur is last seen.'

'Where exactly was the body found?' Sunita asked.

'At the bottom of a… a canyon, some miles north of La Quilla,' he replied. 'The coroner orders for the body to have autopsy. He wants to identify the person and the cause of the death. At first we think it is Señor Arthur. The body is one hundred and eighty centimetres, exactly same height. The clothes, they are similar – a blue top saying "Explorador", brown trousers, a coat that is waterproof, a scarf, black boots and a sunhat. But after some days, we discover – how do you say? – the make-up of the body is different. And some of the clothing, it is not correct. The hat and the boots with the body – they are different. We now know that it is Mr López, a character in Nerja and a drug user. He is a poor man, in trouble with police for small crimes – he takes food and drink from supermercados. He sleeps out on beaches and streets.'

'Lieutenant, that news is a great disappointment to us,' said Sunita. 'As you know, we're investigating the murder of Mr Kenworth's brother, Miles, and suspected there might be a link with Arthur's disappearance which might have helped us solve our murder.'

'So sorry it's not the news you want,' he said, getting up from his chair. 'We too share the disappointment. Don't forget we set up big rescue teams and spend two weeks searching for Señor Arthur. We want to know what happen to him also.'

Dawson rose to his feet and shook the lieutenant's hand again.

'Hold on,' begged Sunita. 'Could we have a quick look at the clothing that was found?'

The lieutenant appeared flustered. 'I'm not sure that is possible, my dear sergeant. This is important?'

'Yes,' she replied.

'Very well. Will you wait one moment?'

The two detectives glanced at each other as he left the room. Voices could be heard echoing around the reception hall outside.

A few minutes later, he returned. 'As a special favour for our visitors from England,' he announced, 'I have asked Constable Romero to show you the clothing. It is an unusual request, but you travel a long way for an unhappy result. It is all we can do.'

A solemn-faced officer in his twenties wearing a flat cap entered carrying several transparent bags containing items of clothing.

He nodded at the two visitors before placing the bags on the edge of the desk. He tugged the blue top and brown chinos out of the bags. Sunita noticed the shirt was frayed and the colour of the chinos was partly faded – probably after lengthy exposure to the sun.

'*Estás perdiendo el tiempo de todos,*' he said as Sunita inspected the chinos.

'What did he say, Lieutenant?' Dawson asked the senior officer, who was standing by the door.

'The constable – he say good luck,' he explained, although Sunita wondered if this was an accurate translation.

'I have a question, Lieutenant,' Dawson continued. 'I don't understand why a vagabond should go trekking in the mountains.'

Díaz looked puzzled. 'Vagabond? Ah, *vagabundo*. The word, it is nearly the same. *Sí*, there is some piece of information I keep from you. Señor López also has a bullet in the head.'

'A bullet in the head?' said Sunita.

'*Sí*. We think maybe Señor López making angry the people who sell him the drugs. So maybe they shoot him and throw the body in the canyon.'

Sunita raised her eyebrows but something else had grasped her attention. She was studying a label inside the chinos which was attached to one of the pockets.

'Lieutenant, do you have any further need for these items?'

'They are for – how do you say? *Incinerador*.'

'They were going to be incinerated?' she asked.

'*Sí*. You want the clothes?'

'I have an idea. They could be useful to us,' she said.

'*No hay problema*,' he agreed.

After the two detectives had left the Guardia Civil building with the clothing, Dawson, who had been tasked with carrying the bags, confessed he was mystified.

'Shouldn't we be sunning ourselves on the beach now, Sarge, or sipping sangria in a quiet beachfront bar?' he said as they walked back towards their hotel. 'It's really disappointing that this dead body has nothing to do with our case, but the world's got to move on.'

'Who said the dead body had nothing to do with our case?' Sunita asked.

'But the lieutenant spent five minutes telling us it was just one of their local junkies,' he continued. 'Sarge, I'm confused. And why did you want the dead man's clothing?'

Sunita, who was walking a few steps in front, glanced back and smiled.

'Listen, the body might not have been Arthur Kenworth's but there's a good chance the clothing is his.'

'Surely it was just similar,' said Dawson. 'Lots of people wear this kind of clothing when they're climbing mountains in Spain.'

'Have a close look at the label in the chinos. It says they were made by Langley & Sons of Queensbridge.'

Chapter 43

At Sunita's insistence, the pair spent the rest of their first full day in Spain visiting the second-hand clothing shops they found in Nerja.

Dawson was convinced the entire exercise would prove a waste of time, but realised his sergeant was becoming obsessed with the notion that the death of the tramp was somehow linked to their Queensbridge investigation.

He knew his future career might suffer if he dared to challenge her decision, but he felt there would be no harm in him posing a few appropriate questions.

'Sarge, do you think we should let the DCI know what the state of play is here?' he asked after they had showed the clothes to staff at one of the shops without anyone showing the slightest sign of recognition.

'All in good time,' she replied as they made their way to another shop.

'Sarge, it was a surprise to find the chinos were made in Queensbridge, but don't you think a lot of Brits come here – including thousands from Warwickshire every year?'

'I know, Brett. It's a long shot, but I believe it's something worth pursuing. These are good quality clothes. It's unlikely a guy on the breadline like Javier López is going to be able to afford gear like this. So it makes sense to think he'd have picked them up second-hand. We need to find out how he acquired them. Did López have the clothes because Kenworth took pity on him and offered them to him in a gesture of kindness before he died? Did López find the Englishman's body somewhere and steal the clothes? It seems to me this could lead us to Kenworth's body, so that at least the family get some closure.'

'I see what you're saying, Sarge,' said Dawson, although he remained dubious.

'This could be the only chance of finding the body, discovering how he died and whether he was murdered like his brother,' she insisted.

'I understand where you're coming from,' he admitted.

'Anyway, cheer up, Brett. It must be warmer here than back home.'

Sunita was slightly annoyed that he seemed to be questioning their mission, but tried not to become distracted by his apparent reluctance. She had also decided to ignore the continual text messages she was receiving from Samir Banerjee, who was clearly upset at the way she had ended their relationship.

During their journey, Dawson bought a copy of an English-language newspaper intended for expats called *Vida Moderna*. As soon as he opened it, he found on page three a report about the death of López which included a photograph of the dead man. He at once showed it to Sunita.

'Anything new in it?' she asked as he scrutinised the text.

'No, Sarge. It's very brief. Just says the body found in the Sierra de Almijara mountains was not Arthur Kenworth but Javier López, aged forty-six, and his family in Madrid have been informed.'

They reached another shop at five o'clock after the town came alive following its three-hour siesta. As before, they showed staff the Explorador top and the chinos and, once again, they found themselves gazing at blank faces.

* * *

Brett Dawson was not totally surprised to discover the next morning that Sunita Roy was planning for them to visit the pretty, whitewashed village of La Quilla.

After a good night's sleep, she was now wedded to the notion that the dead man might have obtained his up-market clothing there rather than in the coastal town.

It was a colder morning as they set off on their six-mile journey inland. After negotiating some winding roads through beautiful countryside, they eventually reached the hillside village with its labyrinth of narrow, cobbled streets.

As they parked outside a bar, they found plant pots brimming with bougainvillea, lavender and jasmine. Behind them, in the valley, were spectacular views across to Nerja and the blue sea in the distance.

'I've been doing some online research while you were driving, Sarge,' Dawson said. 'I don't think this place is crammed with second-hand shops.'

'No, you're right, Brett,' she replied, taking the bags containing the shirt and trousers from the back seat. 'It's more of an arts and crafts place that makes its money selling to tourists, but I've got an idea. There's a large church here, the Church of Santa Ana. We've had no luck in Nerja. Let's see if López got his outfit there.'

It took them a few minutes to climb the hill past flower-filled courtyards. They eventually reached the white, seventeenth-century church, built on the site of a mosque in the oldest part of the village. The former minaret had gained a new role as a bell tower beside the church, which stood in a quaint plaza surrounded by trees and benches.

They learned from a Christian worshipper in the church porch that the priest, Father Juan Hernández, was not about. However, if they called at a three-storey house four doors away, they might be able to find his housekeeper.t

The two detectives followed this advice. Sunita marched up to the oak door and pressed the doorbell.

Gabriela Moreno, who acted as housekeeper for two priests, was a stout, white-haired, middle-aged woman. She opened the door and tiptoed forward with the nervous tread of a doddery dowager reluctant to leave her comfortable parlour.

'Do you speak English?' Sunita asked while smiling at the lady, who was wearing an apron over her dark clothing.

'A little,' she replied with a shrug. 'Father Juan and Father Diego not here.'

'That's all right,' the sergeant continued. 'I'm sure you can help.'

'¿Qué?'

'We're police from England,' she said, producing her warrant card from her pocket and presenting it to Señora Moreno. Then, in her best Spanish, she added, '*Policía inglesa.*'

Dawson leaned forward and asked, 'Did you know Javier López?'

'Javier? Javier who works with the wood? Of course. He's well-known. We try to help him, you know.'

'I'm afraid he's dead,' said Sunita.

Dawson interrupted again. 'It's in the papers.' He reached into his trouser pocket and brought out his copy of *Vida Moderna*. He showed her the photograph of the dead man together with the clothing.

'¿Muerto? ¡Ay dios mío!' the woman exclaimed, overcome with shock. She slumped down onto an outside bench in front of the window and buried her head in her hands.

Sunita was annoyed with herself. If she had known she would be breaking the news about López to the housekeeper, she might have adopted a gentler approach.

'I'm sorry if this news has upset you,' she told Señora Moreno.

'Javier has been missing so long,' replied the woman, wiping her eyes with a handkerchief plucked from her sleeve, 'we start to believe he is taken by the Lord.'

'Can you help us?' said Dawson, pointing to the clothing his sergeant was holding. 'You clearly knew Mr López well.'

'Yes,' said Sunita. 'I know this isn't the best time, but could you look at this shirt and trousers? Did they belong to your friend?'

She pulled the chinos and shirt from their wrapping. Dawson felt almost inclined to smile. They seemed strange questions to ask at a priest's house.

The housekeeper nodded. '*Sí*,' she said. 'I think I know these clothes.'

'Are you sure?' asked Sunita. 'Have a good look.'

The woman grasped the trousers and examined the material. Then she studied the inside label.

'Yes, señorita,' she said. 'Javier came to see Father Juan and say his confession before he went missing a year and a half ago. His clothes were old. We keep a box. People in La Quilla give clothing to the church so we can give it to the ones who have need. This shirt was his size. So were the pants.'

Sunita and Dawson were excited to hear this.

'Señora Moreno, please tell us where you got these clothes,' she said.

'*Benefactores*,' she replied.

'Yes, yes. Benefactors. We know. But what was their name?'

The woman stared down at the floor of the tiled plaza as she pondered the question. Eventually, she glanced up.

'The García family,' she said.

* * *

Alberto and Carmen García and their family lived in a charming estate, or *finca,* on the far end of the village in a street called Calle Almazara.

Sunita Roy and Brett Dawson collected their car and parked by the church, as recommended by the priest's housekeeper. Then they spent the next fifteen minutes climbing the hill out of La Quilla.

After passing a hillside bar, called La Taberna, and a row of townhouses, they came to the whitewashed, detached house they sought, which was named Casa Bendita. Beside it stood a small olive grove and, beyond that, lay open scrubland speckled with bushes and small trees.

Señora Moreno had told them the family were farmers. Sunita felt sure the Garcías enjoyed an idyllic, rustic life among this rugged, limestone countryside with distant views of the Andalusian coast.

The house was surrounded by a low wall, topped with a wire netting fence. The pair walked through the open metal gates, climbed a steep pathway and approached the solid oak front door.

Sunita pressed the bell and waited. Shortly afterwards, a young woman dressed simply in a plain black dress came to the door. She had dark, sultry eyes and long, thick, dark hair.

'¿*Sí?*' she asked.

'*Policía inglesa*,' explained Sunita, producing her warrant card and showing it to the woman. 'Do you speak English?'

The woman leaned against the doorpost while studying the identity pass. 'A little,' she replied.

'Is this the house of the García family?'

'*Sí.*'

Sunita pulled the clothing from the plastic bags. 'We need to know how you came by these.'

Dawson smiled at the woman, who was in her late twenties. 'We've been to see Father Juan's housekeeper, Señora Moreno. She says the García family gave them to the church. We need to know where you got them,' he explained.

'Why? What's happened?' asked the woman, anxiously.

'They were found on the body of a dead man out in the wilderness, a few miles north of La Quilla,' said Sunita.

'*¡Madre de Dios!*' she exclaimed. Perhaps, for the second time that day, she was breaking the sad news of the tramp's death to one of his acquaintances, she thought.

'Yes,' Sunita continued, 'I'm sorry to bring sad news. The dead man was called Javier López and he was given the clothes by Señora Moreno at the Church of Santa Ana.'

An older woman appeared from within the house, asking in Spanish what the visitors wanted.

Sunita and Dawson glanced uneasily at each other as the two women held a brief conversation. Then the older woman, stout with short dark hair, said abruptly, 'No, no, no.'

The women retreated into the narrow hallway and slammed the front door.

Sunita shook her head and shrugged.

'Language barrier?' she asked her colleague as they walked back down to the road.

'I don't know what to make of it,' Dawson replied. 'I was watching the older woman's face.'

'I'm assuming that's the mother, Carmen,' Sunita remarked.

'Must be. She recognised those clothes straight away. I just don't understand it.'

'Let's go and sit down,' she said. They walked a short distance away from the finca, past the family's olive grove, where a tall figure was tilling the soil. Then they sat together on a dry, grassy bank and soaked up the view.

'Looks like we've hit a brick wall,' she said.

He nodded. 'Shall we head back to the hotel?' he asked.

'Yes, in a minute. Perhaps the boss was right and this Spanish trip has been too much of a diversion from the main focus of the investigation.'

Then her phone rang and she could tell from the number on the screen that the caller was her boyfriend, Samir.

She took a few paces along the road, away from Dawson, so she could speak in privacy.

For a few minutes, she gritted her teeth while listening to Samir as he tried to apologise for having recommended Indrani Sarkar to her. All the while, she paced about in the lane. He was imploring her to change her mind about ending their relationship.

At the same time, she noticed the young woman from the finca had entered the olive grove and was holding an animated conversation with the farmhand.

'Samir, I'm really sorry, but this isn't a good time to talk,' she told him. 'I'm in Spain. I'll phone you when I'm home.'

She ended the call and began strolling back. Dawson was no longer alone. The farmhand, a tall, tanned man in dark-blue clothing and a straw hat, was speaking to him through the fence with an upper-class English accent.

'Bloody hell, Sarge,' said Dawson, as she approached. 'You'll never guess who this is. It's Arthur Kenworth.'

Chapter 44

The chief inspector strolled across the CID office at St James Street and patted Omar Khalid on the shoulder.

'I'm sorry you missed out on the foreign trip,' he said. 'If it's any consolation, the weather right now is actually several degrees warmer over here than in Spain.'

Khalid glanced up and smiled. 'No worries, sir,' he replied. 'It was Dawson who first brought it to our attention that a body had been found on the Costa del Sol. It was only fair that he should go.'

Roscoe smiled. 'That's a very positive way of looking at things,' he said.

'In any case, my father's not too well and I promised to call round this evening to see how he is,' said Khalid.

'Sorry to hear that. I'm quite looking forward to tonight. I'm taking Helen to see *Julius Caesar* in Stratford.'

'Sounds a bit grand, sir.'

'I have to keep explaining to people it's only Stratford East Memorial Hall.'

'Still it's a night out.'

Roscoe nodded. 'It'll give me a chance to watch Rupert Faulkner in action in the role of Brutus.'

'I heard he didn't have great acting experience but agreed to have a stab at it,' said Khalid.

'I should leave the jokes to Dawson. By the way, has anyone come forward yet about the locket found in the hay barn?'

Khalid turned round in his seat to face him. 'No, sir. I've been liaising with the media team. Our computer guy enhanced the image as best he could and the picture's appeared in the *Queensbridge Gazette* and the *Birmingham Mail*. It's also been on Midlands TV. But there hasn't been much response.'

'Damn,' muttered Roscoe. 'I'm guessing the blonde girl might have been the person in the loft. But I suppose, even if she herself saw the news reports, she probably wouldn't rush to contact us if she'd been having a secret fling with a guy behind the back of her husband or boyfriend.'

'No, sir.'

'Did you get anywhere tracking down where the locket actually came from?' he asked, taking a seat beside the constable.

'I'm afraid we've drawn a blank there as well. We're talking about a sterling silver locket and twenty-inch chain that went through the Birmingham Assay office. It's valued at about eighty-five pounds and made in Worcestershire. I called the makers yesterday.'

'And what happened?'

'They told me they've sold thousands of them in shops and online. They say it might be possible to trace the purchaser, but it would probably take a long time.'

Roscoe shook his head. 'That's a nuisance,' he said. 'We might have to take that route though, if we don't trace its owner through some other means.'

'Have you heard back from DS Roy, sir, about how they're getting on?' Khalid asked.

'Yes. As I suspected, the whole trip has proved to be a total waste of energy. The body in the ravine turned out to be a tramp who went missing eighteen months ago. He just happened to be wearing a toff's clothes.'

'If he swapped outfits with a toff, it sounds as though the tramp got the better side of the deal.'

Roscoe laughed. 'Maybe,' he said.

'So they're on the plane back?'

'Not yet, believe it or not. The sergeant seems convinced the clothes found with the tramp's body definitely belong to Arthur Kenworth. After speaking with Norris, it's been decided she and Dawson can have one more day there before flying home.'

* * *

Cheers, bravos and applause greeted the actors at the end of their three-hour performance in the community hall.

Each of the one hundred and fifty seats had been filled for the fourth performance of the Avon Players' *Julius Caesar*.

The sixteen actors, in their authentic-looking Roman togas, linked hands for two curtain calls before the makeshift theatre was flooded with light and the spectators began reaching for their coats.

'Did you enjoy that, dear?' asked Roscoe, who had been sitting with Helen in the back row. He had tried to get seats for the show's opening on the previous Saturday, but all tickets had been sold.

She bent down to pick up her handbag from the wooden floor.

'Yes. It reminded me of a school production I watched many years ago,' she said.

Roscoe nodded. 'I thought Faulkner was excellent. You know that was his wife sitting in the front row, don't you?'

'Was that the blonde woman with a suede jacket and tweed skirt?'

'That's right,' he replied as they emerged into the cold evening air. 'Lord Culverdon's daughter. She seems to be the one pulling all the strings over at the estate.'

As they were speaking, the lady they were speaking about hurried through the exit door and approached them.

'Chief Inspector Roscoe?' said Lavinia, a little out of breath. 'I thought it was you.'

'Good to see you,' said the detective. 'Can I introduce my wife, Helen? Helen, this is Lavinia Kenworth.'

'Pleased to meet you,' said Helen, shaking the woman's hand.

'Likewise,' Lavinia responded.

'Lord Culverdon couldn't make it?' asked Roscoe.

'No, he's not feeling well,' she replied.

'I'm very sorry to hear that,' he said as his wife nodded sympathetically.

'Your husband put in a fine performance as Brutus, I must say,' he added.

'Thank you,' she said before her tone changed. 'Chief Inspector, I'm becoming concerned about the lack of progress you're making with your inquiries. It's been nearly a month now since my poor brother Miles was killed. No one's been caught for it.'

Roscoe frowned. 'That's not entirely true. We've made two arrests so far.'

She sneered.

'What? Charlie Laxton, who wouldn't harm a fly, and that landscape gardener, Price? It's time your CID got its act together. Did you know I'm on the county crime panel? I regularly get to see your boss, Chief Superintendent Norris. If you and your team don't make substantial progress with your investigation in the next couple of weeks, I can assure you I'll be having words with her.'

Chapter 45

While Sunita Roy stared open-mouthed at the tanned farmhand with the cut-glass English accent, Brett Dawson quickly introduced her as his senior officer.

The sergeant was inwardly battling to overcome her shock at finding Arthur Kenworth not only alive but standing a few inches away from them behind wire netting.

'You'd better tell me what this is all about,' the man told her.

Slowly recovering, she said, 'Can I say how good it is that you're alive, sir. We were led to believe you died over two years ago in a hiking accident.'

'Yes,' said Kenworth, 'so your colleague was just telling me. Everything's very hazy. I don't have a complete memory of what happened to begin with, but I'm sure I asked for a message to be sent to my family to assure them I was alive. I'm starting to worry now.'

'You think your message might not have been passed on?' said Sunita.

'I suppose it's possible.' His face was etched with concern. 'Do my family count me as missing?' he asked.

'Yes.'

'You're going back to the UK soon, are you?'

She nodded.

'Please inform them I'm very much alive,' he said. 'But tell me, how did you both come to be searching for me in La Quilla?'

'There was a report in a national paper last week,' Dawson explained. 'It said a body had been found near where Lord Culverdon's son went missing and they were holding a post-mortem. It turned out it wasn't you – it was a tramp called López.'

'That's reassuring for me,' Kenworth said with a smile. 'But how did that bring you up here to Casa Bendita?'

Sunita had been holding the shirt and chinos behind her back – partly in embarrassment on meeting the clothes' original owner. She now brought them forward with a shy smile.

Without saying a word, Kenworth looked carefully at the garments through the netting.

'Good grief!' he said. 'I got the family to throw them out as they were getting so worn.'

'We were sure they belonged to you,' said Dawson, 'so we traced them back. The old lady at the church down the hill said they'd been donated by the Garcías.'

Kenworth held up his hands in awe at their achievement in tracking him down.

'This family have been magnificent,' he said. 'I nearly died out there on the mountain. They found me, took me in and I've discovered a new way of life. Come with me. Once I've explained to them what's happened, I'm sure they'd love to meet you, and you can explain more about your visit to Andalusia.'

He bade them walk back to the double gates, where he would meet them. A few minutes later, he marched down the slope and accompanied them to the front door.

'I think Señora García might have been confused a few minutes ago when we called here,' said Sunita. 'She closed the door in our faces.'

'It's all right,' he said. 'I've explained everything to her. I'm sure she was only trying to look after my interests.'

He took a key from his pocket, opened the door and led them into a large, tiled reception hall.

Alberto and Carmen García were having tea, sitting on a leather settee at the far end of a large living room with white walls. At the heart of the room stood a traditional fireplace with images of both Jesus and the Virgin Mary hanging above.

The aging couple came forward timidly and shook hands, in turn, with Sunita and Dawson before resuming their seats.

Then the young, doe-eyed woman who had initially opened the door to them joined Kenworth, clutching his hand and smiling shyly.

'This is Maria. She and her brother saved my life,' he announced.

Sunita glanced at Dawson, who seemed rather overcome by the whole experience.

'I don't know about you, Brett, but I'm dying to know what happened to you, sir, when you set off hiking,' she said.

'Yes, definitely,' said Dawson. 'But we've been doing a lot of walking ourselves today. Can we sit down somewhere?'

'Of course,' said Kenworth. 'Forgive my manners. Look, it's turned into such a warm afternoon. Shall we go and sit outside on the terrace?'

Letting go of Maria's hand, he bounded outside like an excitable greyhound that had slipped his lead and showed the visitors onto a veranda with far-reaching views.

'This is such a lovely place,' said Sunita as she gazed across the grounds.

'We've got plums, apples, cherries, figs, almonds, apricots, pomegranates and walnuts – as well as olives,' he said proudly.

They sat down on two wooden benches on either side of a metal table.

'I get tea,' said Maria, disappearing into the house.

Beginning his story, Kenworth said, 'I set off one morning to go and explore the mountains. I've been told it was the eighteenth of October, but my memory's not good. I wanted to reach the top of El Fuerte mountain. Well, at some point, I met up with two other hikers and just after that I must have lost my footing and fallen.

'All I remember is having a terrible pain in my head and foot when I came round. I don't know how long I'd been lying there in the sun, but I was desperately thirsty.

'I realised I must have broken my foot but I managed to haul myself along the ground until I reached a stream in a rocky gorge. That's the first thing that saved me – the pure natural water from the stream. I'll never forget the moment I struggled with my hands, cupped them together and managed to sip the water.'

Kenworth's dark-brown hair, beard and moustache reminded Sunita of his father, Lord Culverdon. He spoke with a similar accent, but he was slightly taller, slimmer and appeared more relaxed.

'Were you near the tourist trails?' she asked him.

'No, this was the problem. I must have fallen twenty metres or more. I was well away from the footpaths and traditional tourist routes. It was wilderness with trees and bushes and I was there on my own for days and days.'

'How did you manage for food?' asked Dawson.

'To begin with, I had chocolate and some sandwiches I'd brought with me from Nerja, but obviously they didn't last long. I had to nibble at nearby plants until I found rosemary and certain grasses, which seemed digestible. I watched which plants the birds ate and sampled the same plants, heaving myself along the ground to reach them.'

'Blimey,' said Dawson.

'The days passed. I started to become worried that I might not survive. I'm told search parties were out looking for me with dogs and helicopters, but I never saw any of them. I've also heard a court order was taken out so the

Guardia Civil could trace the location of my phone signal, but that was to no avail. I hadn't taken my phone with me.

'As the days passed, I was starving but I must have been surviving on my body fat and muscle reserves. I tried to think positive thoughts – about Culverdon Hall and the family's history, about my work at the Stock Exchange, about my past girlfriends and my family. That way I managed to keep upbeat and avoided falling into a fit of depression.

'You know that shirt you showed me? I used it to keep myself cool on really hot days. I dipped it in the stream and draped it round myself. I later dried it in the sun and wore it at night on a makeshift bed comprising spare clothing filled with esparto grass.'

Maria returned with a tray containing a multi-coloured ceramic teapot and four matching cups and saucers. She sat down next to Kenworth and gazed at him, admiringly.

'How many days and nights were you there altogether?' asked Dawson, who had been listening intently with his head in his hands.

'I'd no idea of the time,' he said.

'So you didn't mark the days off on a tree trunk or something?'

'No. Daytime gradually turned to nighttime and nighttime to daytime. I only found out later I'd been there for twenty-two days. Do you know I lost nearly two stone?'

'How were you found?' asked Sunita while Maria poured the tea and handed the drinks round.

'It was a miracle,' Kenworth admitted. 'And it was all down to this wonderful lady's brother, Miguel. I have little memory myself but I've been told the Guardia Civil ended their official search for me after two weeks and all the volunteers were stood down. But Miguel kept looking. He spent his childhood growing up in these mountains and knows every inch of these amazing ravines and rugged crags.

'Twenty-two days after I set off on my walk, I heard him scrambling through some bushes and I shouted for help. Once he'd found me, he gave me some food and water. Then he went away and rounded up a group of villagers. With great difficulty, they put me on a stretcher and brought me here. I feel so blessed. I'm sure I'd have died if I'd stayed out there much longer.

'After that, this kind lady and her mother nursed me for weeks until I felt strong enough to get up and walk about.'

'What about your foot?' asked Dawson, who had been listening intently to his every word.

'The family's doctor said I'd broken my ankle, but I'd been lucky. It was healing well. I had to hobble about with a crutch for a while.'

He put his arm round Maria. The pair gazed lovingly into each other's eyes.

'Do you know falling into that ravine has changed my life? I wouldn't have met this beautiful lady and her exceptionally kind family. For many weeks, Maria was the only person I saw. We chatted for hours and we eventually realised there was something special between us. We were falling in love and I was absolutely ecstatic when she accepted my proposal of marriage. We're tying the knot soon.'

Sunita, who had been sipping her tea, smiled at them. 'That's wonderful news. Congratulations,' she said. 'Nonetheless, you should really have notified the authorities in Spain and the UK that you were safe. A lot of time and money was spent searching for you.'

'I suppose you must be right and for that I'm sorry,' said Kenworth. 'But I was terribly ill to start with and only had a partial memory.'

Dawson was more interested in the way a bad accident had resulted in good fortune.

'You could say that falling down a ravine led to falling in love,' he told Kenworth.

'I suppose you could put it like that,' replied Kenworth with a smile.

'You've completely put your life on hold since your accident,' continued Dawson, as though expressing his personal thoughts out loud.

'I didn't know you until today, did I, young man?' said Kenworth. 'But have you ever been in love?'

'Yes. I think I'm in love with my girlfriend,' said Dawson.

'Then you may understand,' he replied.

A heavy silence hung in the air. Then Kenworth said, 'Do you know I can't believe the police in Britain would send you both out here, years after I fell into the ravine, to search for me.'

This was the moment Sunita had been dreading. She was fairly certain Kenworth knew nothing of his younger brother's death. Now she had to shatter the happy mood at the table.

'Although we're obviously delighted to find you alive and well, our visit to the Costa del Sol is part of a wider investigation focused on your brother,' she explained.

'Miles? What's happened to him?'

'I'm afraid he's dead,' she replied.

'Dead? When? How?'

'It was almost a month ago. He was at his flat in Queensbridge when he was attacked by an intruder,' she said.

'Oh my God!' he said, cupping his mouth with his hand. 'That's terrible. Poor Miles. I haven't been following the British news at all. I must phone my family. Why didn't you tell me before?'

Sunita shrugged. 'To be honest, we were so surprised to find you alive, sir. There was so much for you to tell us...'

'You're right. I did rather hog the limelight over the past few minutes. Well, thank you for telling me. Miles and I weren't that close, but I'm in a state of shock, as you can see.'

Kenworth's face was now pale and his eyes had lost their sparkle.

'I've been selfish,' he confessed. 'I've been enjoying my life out here so much – repaying the Garcías' generosity by working hard on the farm for them. I'd almost forgotten my family back home. I must return to England.'

He paused before saying, 'I don't understand why they haven't been in contact. They must have received the messages I sent.'

He suddenly realised Maria had tears in her eyes.

'Darling, whatever's the matter?' he asked her.

'Sorry, sorry,' she cried before running inside the house.

'Excuse me one moment,' he told the detectives before hurrying after her.

A few minutes passed before he returned alone and resumed his seat.

'I've just found out why my messages never reached my family,' he said. 'Maria has just admitted she failed to carry out my instructions. She was worried I would leave, return to England and that she'd never see me again. I've got to forgive her, haven't I? She acted out of love.'

'Well, that explains that,' said Sunita.

'I can't blame her entirely,' he added. 'It was remiss of me. When I didn't hear from them, I should have made an effort to call them, but I suppose I was so wrapped up in my new life here. I don't know if you can understand that?'

Sunita nodded.

'Mr Kenworth, there's one more thing I need to ask. We came here because your brother was murdered,' she said, 'and we believed you might have succumbed to the same fate – that you too might have been murdered. You said just now you were with two other hikers at one point.'

'Yes. They appeared from nowhere. One of them came right up to me. He had dark glasses and a scarf round his neck, presumably to keep the sun's rays from his face. Moments after that I tumbled down the ravine.'

'Do you think they played a part?'

'I kept going over this in my mind during my conscious moments after the fall. I haven't said anything about this before. I was too focused on my recovery. But I don't believe it was an accident. I believe I may have been pushed. And the real reason we didn't tell the authorities, after I was nursed back to health, was that we were concerned about whether the men, whoever they were, might search for me and try again.'

Chapter 46

Sunita Roy sensed a genial presence behind her on Friday morning as she was sitting at her desk in CID. She spun round to find the chief inspector, smiling broadly.

'Welcome back,' he said. 'Good flight yesterday?'

'Yes, sir. You've heard about Arthur Kenworth?'

He laughed as he unbuttoned his coat.

'Couldn't miss it, could I? It's all over the papers,' he said as he took a chair beside her. 'The *Daily Mail* front page says, "Back from the dead."'

She nodded. 'Yes, it's all a bit unfortunate. Just before the flight home, I thought it only proper to inform our contact at the Guardia Civil, Lieutenant Díaz, of our good fortune in finding Arthur Kenworth alive. Either he or someone in his office must have tipped off the press in Nerja and, from there, the news seems to have gone global.'

'Never mind. Can't be helped,' said Roscoe. 'I don't think it'll impede our inquiries.'

'I'm just glad we took a proper statement from him before we left,' she said.

'It was a sterling job that you and Dawson did out there. I know I was initially reluctant to send you, but you followed your instincts and it's paid off handsomely. So well done, Sergeant.'

'Thank you, sir,' she said.

He paused before adding, 'What I don't understand is why, after his recovery, Kenworth didn't contact his family in Warwickshire or inform the Spanish police.'

'The woman who nursed him and became his lover failed to contact his family for her own personal reasons,' she replied. 'In any case, I get the impression he just wanted to keep a low profile. He was a man in love, and when men are in love, they can sometimes act irrationally.'

'Don't I know it,' he said before lowering his voice. 'That applies to a few people I know.'

'Just before we left,' Sunita continued 'I had a short conversation with him in private and he said, "You've seen what a wonderful country this is, haven't you? The weather, the people, the olive groves. Can you understand me wanting to stay?" I must admit, when he put it like that, I certainly began to understand his point of view.'

Roscoe shrugged. 'So is it your basic feeling that Arthur Kenworth was followed into the mountains and fell prey to an attempt on his life?'

'Yes, sir. I've got Dawson checking flight lists from Birmingham Airport to Spain around the time Kenworth flew out there. He's also checking with hotels in Nerja.'

'Good. Let me know how he gets on.'

'I hear you and your wife went to see *Julius Caesar*,' she continued. 'That's a play I studied at school.'

'Yes. Very good it was, too. That reminds me, I must go and have a word with Norris. Lavinia Faulkner button-holed me after the performance. She's getting agitated at what she claims is our lack of progress.'

'Don't worry,' she replied. 'That trip to Spain has done wonders for my thought processes. I've got a few ideas now about who might be behind both murders. I don't want to go into any detail yet – in case I'm wrong – but I feel I'm getting closer now.'

* * *

Once the chief inspector had left her, Sunita sent an email to the genealogist in Birmingham who often helped the police. She briefed him on some family research she wanted him to carry out. Then she set off in her car for Shawley Green.

It was nearly half past ten by the time she reached Lower Wood Farm. Mark Webster was chatting to a farmhand next to the hay barn.

'Good morning, DS Roy,' he said. 'I hope you're not going to take up much of my time. I'm waiting for the vet. We've got a ewe having trouble giving birth.'

Sunita cut the engine and stepped out of her car, clutching a brown envelope.

'You remember the photo inside the locket?' she asked.

'Of course. You're still having problems tracing the people in the picture, are you?'

'Yes. We've had it blown up. I want you to take another look.'

Webster frowned. 'What good's that going to do?'

'We've been having real problems identifying them. We're in no doubt they could hold the key to resolving the Stephanie Price case. So I want you to really study it.'

She opened the envelope, revealing the colour photograph measuring eight inches by ten. He took it from her and stared for a minute at the chubby, fair-skinned, freckled face of the blonde child and the straight-faced woman next to her.

'Focus on the young girl because we suspect it's she who came here and that the older person beside her is her mother,' said Sunita.

'No, still can't place them,' he insisted.

'Look,' said Sunita, 'the way I see it is the girl who left her locket behind didn't just turn up here, have a look around and turned your hayloft into a love nest. She'd clearly been here before. Probably a local girl. I want you to think carefully.'

Webster glanced again at the picture.

'Maybe she was here helping you out with farm work,' she suggested. 'Maybe she's the daughter of one of your farm hands. Maybe she works for a company you deal with.'

He shook his head. 'I tell you what I'll do,' he said after a pause. 'I'll give you a list of everyone I can think of who's been here over the past year. Will that suit you?'

She nodded. 'Of course. That would be very helpful.'

'I'll make a start now, while I'm waiting for the vet,' he said while walking towards the farmhouse door.

Sunita shouted after him, 'The girl is probably now a woman in her twenties.' As he headed inside, she returned to her car and spent a few minutes listening to a Birmingham radio station.

Ten minutes later, Webster re-emerged, clutching a scrap of paper.

'I've made it easy for you,' he said, placing the sheet in her hand. 'You've got the names there of all young women in their late teens and early twenties who have visited the farm for various reasons. I've also added some brief details about them.'

She peered at the first few names: Liz Pickford, The Grange, Hartston (Hartston Rambling Club); Janice Reeves, sales rep, Mercia Feed Company, Birmingham; Vicky Jones, Orchard Lane Farm Shop (harvest helper). Six other names followed.

'Thank you,' she told the farmer. 'Are they all blonde?'

'I honestly couldn't say,' he replied. 'Some are.'

As Webster returned to the farmhouse, Sunita spoke to both Dawson and Khalid on the phone, asking them to help by each visiting three of the women. She explained that she would herself be calling on the first three on the list. Then she set off to The Grange, four miles away in Hartston.

Liz Pickford was not at home, but her mother gave the sergeant her daughter's mobile number. After a brief conversation back in her car, the sergeant learned the young woman had no idea where the hay barn was on

Webster's farm. Despite some verbal skirmishes with the farmer over walkers' rights in the past, she claimed she had only visited the farm once over the past year — and that was to deliver a leaflet for the church.

Sunita then phoned the Mercia Feed Company and spoke to Janice Reeves. She explained she had only recently started her job and had been keen to impress her manager. As a result, she had been visiting as many farms around Stratford as swiftly as possible to win orders. She had spent no more than ten minutes with Webster and was unaware he had a hay barn close to the farmhouse.

Sunita then headed back to Shawley Green in the hope of speaking to Vicky Jones at the farm shop. But, as she travelled, she felt herself becoming disillusioned with the whole task.

Even if they could identify the right woman, how likely was she to cooperate with police? Would she admit to trespassing in a farmer's barn for a secret tryst? And would she readily pass on the name of her married lover — recognising that that might put him in the frame for murder?

Chapter 47

It was nearly midday by the time Sunita Roy reached the Orchard Lane Farm Shop.

She managed to find a space for her Peugeot among the countless rows of cars before she threaded her way through the melee of shoppers queuing for their meat, fish and cheese. She then entered the corridor leading to Gordon MacLeod's office.

As always, he was sitting at his desk. He glanced up and attempted to smile as she tapped on the door and walked in.

'Sorry, Mr MacLeod,' she said. 'I need to bother you again.'

'Nae bother,' he said. 'How can I help?'

'You have a member of staff called Vicky Jones?'

'Aye. Vicky's one of our part-timers. She helps out at weekends. Is the wee lassie in trouble?'

'No, absolutely not,' the sergeant insisted. 'But I believe she may have some information that could prove crucial. Could you tell me how to contact her?'

'I'll do my best for you.'

He scrolled through the staff list on his computer.

'Here we go,' he said. 'Victoria Jones, 41 Walnut Grove, Shawley Green. Aged twenty-eight. Father deceased – you don't need to know that. There's a phone number here if you want it.'

'Go on then,' said Sunita.

After noting the details and thanking him, she returned to her car, confident of finding her way to Walnut Grove. She remembered passing the turning while searching for the home of Stephanie Price's sister, Isabelle, near the village green.

Vicky lived in a wide street consisting of privately owned, semi-detached houses. The sergeant parked directly outside number forty-one, next to a blue Ford Focus estate, which had two toy ducks hanging from the rear-view mirror.

She opened the metal gate beside a neatly cut hedge and walked up the concrete path, past an immaculate lawn and flower beds brimming with pink camellias and mauve azaleas.

A smartly dressed, middle-aged woman with dark-blonde hair answered the door.

'Hello. Can I help?' she asked.

'I'm looking for Vicky,' the sergeant explained. In the circumstances, she was loath to tell the woman – presumably Vicky's mother – that she was from the police.

Sunita wondered if this could be the older woman in the photograph. She couldn't be certain.

'It's to do with the farm shop,' she added, a message she believed was grounded in truth if not wholly accurate.

The woman left the door ajar and shouted something out.

Moments later, Sunita saw blonde-haired Vicky edging her way down the stairs as cautiously as a cat negotiating her way down a sloping roof.

'I don't think I know you,' said the young woman.

Sunita smiled. 'Vicky, you're not in any trouble,' she said in a low voice. 'But I'm from the police and I need to ask you something.' As she showed her identity pass, she added, 'I didn't want to embarrass you in front of your mother.'

'What is it? What's it about? Is it about my job?'

'No,' Sunita insisted. 'And I must impress on you that, strictly speaking, you've not done anything unlawful. Would you like to step outside?'

Vicky stepped into the garden. The detective gazed into her eyes. There was definitely some resemblance to the girl in the picture.

'Hold on a minute,' said Sunita.

She dashed to her car to fetch the enlarged photograph. Then she returned to the garden and showed it to Vicky.

'Is that you and your mother?' she asked.

The shop assistant stared at the picture for a few seconds. Then she bore the look of someone who has just been woken by a burst of dazzling sunlight streaking across the horizon.

'Yes. Where did you get it? That picture was in my locket.'

'Your locket was found at Lower Wood Farm,' said Sunita. 'I need to know the name of the man you were there with on Monday, 21 February.'

'Oh, I see,' said Vicky, gazing down at the path. 'That's a bit difficult. That was my boyfriend, you see.'

227

'Vicky, did you know Stephanie Price, who worked at the shop?'

'Yes, of course. Everyone knew Steph. Is this to do with why she died?'

Sunita nodded. 'Yes.'

The door opened and the mother's face appeared, etched with concern. 'Everything all right?' she asked Vicky.

'Yes. It's all right, Mum. It's to do with work.'

The elder woman gave Sunita a suspicious glance. 'Well, if you're sure,' she said before slowly retreating into the house.

'We need to know who your boyfriend is,' Sunita continued.

'Was,' said Vicky.

'He's not your boyfriend anymore?'

'No. We finished. I hope you won't think badly of me but he's a married man. I know I shouldn't have been with him, but I didn't know he was married when I first went out with him, and later – well, it was too late. I found I couldn't give him up. Now he's dropped me like a ton of bricks.'

Sunita was becoming exasperated. 'Vicky, I have a vague idea of who this man might be but I need you to confirm my theory and give me his name.'

'I don't want to get him into any bother. If his wife found out about us, she'd be devastated.'

Sunita felt like responding that it was too late for any feelings of regret now. But she knew Vicky might clam up altogether if she took that approach.

Instead she said, 'Come on. You knew Stephanie. She was brutally attacked and left to die at the farm shop. We believe she'd arranged to meet someone that night. I think you owe it to her to help our investigation. Doesn't she deserve to have her killer brought to justice? We believe the man you were with at the farm can help us with these inquiries.'

'I don't see how he could be involved in any case.'

'Are you going to help us?' asked Sunita.

'What if my mother finds out I was down at the farm with him?' asked Vicky. 'I'm going to be in deep trouble. She may even throw me out.'

'You probably wouldn't have to appear in court. We could just say we received the information anonymously. This doesn't have to come back to you.'

Vicky shook her head. 'I'm sorry.'

'I don't want to be unpleasant because I can see you're a well-meaning person,' said Sunita. 'But my boss may not see things the same way as me. He may order me to arrest you and take you for questioning at a police station. Alternatively, we could take your phone away and examine it. Eventually the truth will come out.'

Vicky gazed at the ground and shook her head. 'All right,' she said. 'I'll tell you. But can I have my locket back?'

Chapter 48

The sound of a phone ringing somewhere downstairs roused the chief inspector from his sleep early on Monday.

He glanced across the bed but it seemed Helen was already up.

After hauling himself to his feet, he stepped over to the window, drew back the brown curtains and peered out.

'Is it my imagination or has it got colder overnight?' he asked Helen as he plodded down the stairs in his dressing gown. He found her sitting in the living room.

'Darling, did I overhear you talking to DS Roy last night?' said Helen. 'I've been so focused on the wedding I forgot to ask you about it.'

'Yes, the sergeant called just after eight o'clock,' he said as he started washing up the breakfast plates and mugs. 'She's been doing some extra work over the weekend without telling me. You know how obsessed she gets sometimes with these cases. She thinks she knows who killed Miles Kenworth and Stephanie Price.'

'Sounds intriguing,' Helen replied.

'She wants to check out a few things before explaining what she's discovered.'

'You should be proud of her. She's a great asset to your team,' she said. Then her phone rang.

'Oh, I wonder if that's the tailors,' she said. 'I'm meant to collect all the lads' suits later today.'

Roscoe was about to reply when she flew out of the room.

'Oh dear,' he said to himself as he looked for his coat and prepared to leave. 'I must try and keep out of her way. It's only Monday. We've got five more days of this.'

* * *

The frenzied figure darted up the stairs, her unfastened coat flapping as she ran. She pushed open the door to the CID office and hurried to her desk.

'Morning, Sarge,' said DC Khalid, glancing up from his computer. 'The boss has been asking for you.'

'Has he?' said Sunita, placing her coat and scarf on the coat stand.

'Yeah, he seems to think you've got the whole case wrapped up,' he said with a grin.

'Let's just say I've finally made some progress,' she said.

A few minutes later, Roscoe called her into his office.

'So you've got a few things to tell us?' he said as she took a chair.

'Yes, sir. I can now give you the names of the couple that Stephanie Price discovered in the hayloft.'

'Go on.'

'Vicky Jones, who works part-time at the farm shop, and Charles Laxton.'

Roscoe leaned back in his chair. 'Really? How did you find that out?'

'I got a list of farm visitors from Mark Webster, the farmer. You know, young women that might have owned the locket. I called round at Vicky's home and she admitted being in the hay barn. After some gentle persuasion, she gave me Laxton's name.'

'He's clearly the man Stephanie Price tried to blackmail,' said Roscoe. 'So that makes him a prime suspect in her murder. But there's a lot of evidence pointing towards Logan Price killing them both.'

Sunita shook her head. 'I'm afraid, sir, we'd be making a mistake if we accused Logan Price of the two murders. Let me explain.'

She sat back on her chair and folded her arms. 'Firstly, I believe there were two murderers, sir – not one.'

'How do you work that out?'

'To be honest, I've doubted all along whether one man killed both Miles Kenworth and Stephanie Price. But this theory has been reinforced by our trip to Spain. Arthur Kenworth was followed into the mountains by two men and told us, "I believe I might have been pushed." On the strength of that, I got Dawson to make further inquiries with hotels in Nerja and with staff at Birmingham Airport.

'Dawson's come up trumps. We've got clear descriptions of two men who travelled to Malaga from Birmingham the day after Arthur Kenworth travelled there. We've also got descriptions of the same two men booking in at the Nerja Palace Hotel. Those men were Charles Laxton and Rupert Faulkner.'

'Good God!' said Roscoe, slamming his hands down on the desk. 'Rupert Faulkner? That's incredible.'

'I know,' said Sunita. 'It strikes me that the murder of the younger son and what could be the attempted murder of the older son are linked. It looks like a conspiracy between the two men to take over the Culverdon Estate. I suspect Rupert Faulkner was the main player in the conspiracy. After all, he's married to His Lordship's daughter. With Arthur dead, Lavinia would inherit the house and estate. Then, through his marriage to her, he could gradually take control of the whole Culverdon empire.'

Roscoe nodded.

'That conclusion certainly has a ring of truth about it, Sergeant,' he said. 'Too much of a coincidence, isn't it – them turning up like that during his hiking trip. But listen, why do you think the pair went to all the trouble to make an attempt on his life in Spain? Why not kill Arthur closer to home?'

She shrugged. 'All I can think is that they believed they were less likely to be found out if they targeted him abroad and dressed it up like an accident.'

'I suppose we'll never know for sure. There's another thing. Why do you think they waited two years between attacking Arthur Kenworth and murdering the younger brother?'

Sunita leaned back in her chair.

'There's a clearer explanation for that,' she said. 'The reason I was a few minutes late this morning is that I received a call from Miles Kenworth's solicitor, David Walker. Miles made contact with him in December and explained he wished to make a will. Mr Walker drew up the document and Miles signed it in front of witnesses in January – just two weeks before he died.'

'Don't keep us in suspense. Who was the main beneficiary?' asked Roscoe.

'He had no wife or children and had fallen out heavily with his father, so he left everything to Lavinia and told Mr Walker he'd be calling his sister to inform her of this.'

She quickly added, 'Miles wasn't a poor man, despite living at Waverley Court. His parents set up a trust fund for him while he was a child, which paid out a huge sum of several million pounds when he reached the age of twenty-five.'

'So Faulkner learned of this from his wife and, as a result, this legacy spurred him into taking action?' said Roscoe.

'Yes, sir. It looks as though Miles's decision to bequeath everything to his sister became a trigger point for murder.'

The chief inspector cast his eyes down at the floor and was silent for a moment. Then he glanced up.

'In terms of the murder of Stephanie Price, it seems clear Laxton had the motive,' he said. 'She was blackmailing him and he was at pains to prevent his wife learning of his infidelity. Miles Kenworth's murder is a different matter altogether and, in view of the evidence about the dead man's will, it's likely Faulkner was culpable there. He obviously had the motive.'

Sunita nodded. 'We'd need to arrest them both and search their homes to learn more about the offences,' she said. 'Hopefully, that will turn up evidence. Either man could have stolen the axe from the shop as they were both regular visitors there.'

Roscoe strode to the door and opened it.

'Khalid,' he yelled. 'Have you got a moment?'

The constable hurried across the room. 'Yes, sir?'

'We're going to be arresting Charles Laxton and Rupert Faulkner. Can you apply to the bench for warrants so we can search their homes?'

'Yes, sir,' Khalid replied as he walked away.

Roscoe returned to the room, closed the door and resumed his seat.

'There's something I can't get my head round, Sergeant. I can see that Rupert Faulkner had plenty to gain from all this, but what about Laxton? I can't see why he became a partner in crime.'

'This might explain it, sir. Laxton and Faulkner are brothers,' she said.

'Brothers?'

'Well, half-brothers, to be precise. I got our family researcher working on the case last week. He's come up with some amazing facts. Laxton's mother, Rosalind Laxton, gave birth to him in 1979 as a single mother living in Oxfordshire. She came from a fairly well-off family but she was a bit of a party girl, who slept around, and she never got to settle down with her baby's father.

'A year later, she married a guy called Jeremy Faulkner in Malvern, but it wasn't a happy marriage, by all accounts, and they split up. Then she met someone else and, in September 1981, little Rupert Faulkner was born.

'Some time after this, the mother had a breakdown and the brothers were placed in foster care in Oxford. Rosalind's wealthy parents eventually paid for them both to go to a public school in Shropshire.'

'That's quite a story. But hold on a minute. You don't suspect Faulkner of murdering Miles Kenworth, do you? His alibi is sound. The stage manager with the Avon Players told us Faulkner was with them at the time of Miles's murder. Don't you remember? They were rehearsing Act 1, Scene 3 of *Julius Caesar* and Faulkner was on the stage, playing Brutus.'

'Sir, I remember the play very well from my school days in Leicester. But I realised while I was in bed last night that Brutus doesn't appear in Act 1, Scene 3.'

Chapter 49

The chief inspector listened as his sergeant gathered their team together in the CID office and briefed them.

She explained that she and DC Dawson would be raiding Charles Laxton's bungalow in Brook Lane, Hartston and arresting the estate manager.

They would meet PC Underhill and another Queensbridge constable at the address, along with a forensic team.

The DCI, accompanied by DC Khalid and DC Hopkirk together with Dr Alice Ling and a second forensic team, would at the same time head to Culverdon Hall and visit Rupert Faulkner's flat with a view to arresting him.

But, at the end of the briefing, Roscoe became distracted. His thoughts turned to the night he and Helen had watched *Julius Caesar* and were confronted by Lavinia Faulkner. What was it she'd said that had made such an impression on his mind? Lord Culverdon had been unable to attend the performance. 'He's not feeling well,' she'd told him.

He crept into his room as the meeting broke up and called Lord Culverdon's office. The number rang and rang. Finally, a woman answered whom he at first assumed to be a secretary. But as the conversation went on, he realised it was Lavinia's husky voice.

'I wondered if I could speak to Lord Culverdon. It's DCI Roscoe,' he said.

'I'm awfully sorry,' Lavinia replied. 'He's very poorly with stomach pains. The doctor's with him. He's worried he might have eaten something toxic.'

By the time he ended the call, Roscoe was fuming.

'I've been such a fool,' he told himself. 'Why didn't I cotton on that someone was trying to take down the whole Kenworth family, one by one? Why didn't I recognise that Lord Culverdon's own life might be in danger?'

Without stopping for a word with his sergeant, he hurried out of the office, got into his car and set off for the hall. Several police vehicles were already parked by the circular water fountain, when Dr Ling's car arrived.

'The family live in the east wing, don't they?' Dr Ling remarked as she got out. He nodded and then explained his fears to her.

'Are we going straight up to see the family doctor?' she asked.

'No,' said Roscoe. 'I've got an important task for you first.'

They stepped round the side of the building, following the path between hedges, until they reached the oak door. They noticed the sign on the wall inside pointing to the kitchen and found the housekeeper slicing vegetables.

'DCI Roscoe,' he informed Sarah. 'I'm afraid I'm going to have to ask you to leave. We need to conduct a search.'

'That's ridiculous,' she replied, putting her knife down and stepping over to the sink to wash her hands. 'Have Lord Culverdon or Lavinia given permission?'

'I seriously believe Lord Culverdon's life may be in danger,' Roscoe said.

'What?' she said.

'We need to search the whole kitchen,' he continued, 'and, in particular, examine any food dishes that have been recently prepared.'

Sarah showed him a beef stroganoff dish, some stewed vegetables and some chicken. Dr Ling set to work, taking samples from each.

'Who works here?' he asked Sarah after ordering her to leave the room and sit on a chair outside.

'Only me. If there's a large party of guests, we bring in extra staff,' she explained.

'Who else has access to the kitchen?'

'The door's never locked, so anyone, I suppose.'

'Over the last few days, have you worked here entirely on your own?'

'Yes.'

'No visitors that you recall?'

'Well, only Mr Faulkner – oh, and we received a delivery from Mr Halfpenny from the farm shop.'

Roscoe frowned. 'And what was Faulkner doing here?'

'He just came for a chat for five minutes, as he often does from time to time.'

'He's employed as the equestrian manager, isn't he? Why should he call round at the kitchen?'

'Well, he told me a few weeks ago, when I asked, it was to do with stock control. Lavinia asked him to keep checks, apparently. To be honest, I don't mind him coming for a chat. He's such a pleasant guy.'

And a scheming villain as well, Roscoe thought to himself.

'Did you watch him all the time he was here?' he asked her.

'Some of the time. I didn't let his visits affect my attention to my job, if that's what this is all about.'

'I'm asking these questions because your employer, Lord Culverdon, may have been poisoned.'

'Oh my God. You don't think I've had anything to do with that, do you? I love my job here and wouldn't do anything to put that at risk.'

He was aiming to carry on questioning her in this vein when his phone rang. It was DC Khalid.

'Sorry. I must answer this,' he told her.

Khalid spoke excitedly.

'Sir, Mr and Mrs Faulkner weren't around when we arrived half an hour ago. One of the windows in the flat had been left open, so we managed to get inside. We've found a container of pepper spray that could be a link to the Kenworth murder.'

'Good work, Constable,' said Roscoe.

'That's not all. Faulkner himself has just turned up and heard us talking about pepper spray and he's done a runner. Gone off in a white F-type Jag. He could be heading for the airport.'

Roscoe frowned. 'When was this?'

'Just a minute ago.'

'Let's get after him. We'll take my car.'

After ending the call, he turned briefly to Dr Ling. 'Will you be all right here?' he asked.

'Yes, sir. Don't worry about me.'

Roscoe hurried back to the front of the hall, where he found Khalid waiting for him. The chief inspector fixed a blue light to the roof of his BMW before they both climbed in and sped away.

'Was he on his own?' asked Roscoe.

'I think so. He turned right when he passed through the gates.'

'Then he won't be making for the airport. He might be heading for Stratford. You didn't get the registration, did you?'

Khalid, who was sitting beside him, nodded and read out the car number, which he'd scribbled down in his notebook.

Within seconds, they were travelling at high speed along country lanes. They then arrived at the main road and turned right towards the market town.

Using his car radio, Roscoe called the Heart of England control room.

'DCI Roscoe here. Suspect Rupert Faulkner making off at speed from the village of Hartston and heading towards Stratford,' he announced before describing the car and reciting the registration.

'This is the control room,' came the reply from force headquarters. 'Inspector Griffiths here. Message received. Over.'

'Departure from Culverdon Hall, Hartston timed at fourteen zero seven,' Roscoe continued before explaining they were pursuing a suspect in a murder inquiry, and required back-up.

'Target vehicle heading south on the A46. Any mobiles in the vicinity?' Roscoe asked.

'Negative,' came the reply. 'We'll get back to you, sir.'

The chief inspector switched on the blue light and pressed down on the accelerator.

'There he is!' yelled Khalid as, for the first time, they were able to glimpse the rear of the white Jaguar ahead of them.

'Let's hope he doesn't spot us until we get closer,' Roscoe said.

But as these words passed his lips, the distance between the two vehicles seemed to increase. It appeared Faulkner was now aware he was being chased. He was occasionally taking chances, overtaking slower-moving vehicles.

The pursuit continued across Stratford, where the Jaguar sped onto the A422 road in the direction of Banbury. Now Roscoe was no more than thirty metres behind the Jaguar with both vehicles touching speeds of up to seventy miles an hour across open countryside. They followed Faulkner across the grey, tree-shrouded necklace of lanes linking villages together on the edge of the Cotswolds.

At the village of Pillerton Priors, a motorist was attempting to pull out of a filling station. He just had time to pull back and avoid a collision with Faulkner's car as the two vehicles sped past.

The pursuit continued through the suburbs of Banbury, where the Jaguar sped through red traffic lights and joined the M40 motorway, travelling south at speeds of up to a hundred miles an hour.

'Looks like he's heading for Oxford,' said the chief inspector, as the Jaguar weaved from one lane to another while overtaking. 'He and Laxton grew up around there, according to DS Roy,' Roscoe revealed.

It was nearly a quarter to three – around half an hour after Roscoe's call for assistance – when Inspector Griffiths from force control called back. He informed him he was trying to arrange a patrol car to join them.

When Roscoe mentioned his suspicion that Faulkner might be heading for the university city, Griffiths promised to alert Thames Valley Police and ask if one of their traffic teams could assist in the pursuit.

Khalid gave his boss a worried look.

'I think we're losing him,' he said. 'I can't see his car now.'

Roscoe nodded as they approached junction nine on the motorway and prepared to turn onto the A34 trunk road, which led into Oxford.

'He probably knows the city well. We're having a job keeping up with him because I've never been trained for high-speed pursuits,' said Roscoe. 'I'm worried that, if we lose him now, he could flee the country and escape justice.'

Chapter 50

It was becoming clear that Miles Kenworth's fate had been linked to his brother Arthur's disappearance. Sunita Roy's instinct had been proved right and two very different brothers – Faulkner and Laxton – were now key suspects in the investigation.

But when her car drew up outside Laxton's rather dilapidated four-bedroom bungalow, Sunita was only too aware they still faced the onerous task of catching the two men.

There was no sign of a green Land Rover Discovery on the block-paved driveway in front of the building, two miles from the farm with the hayloft. But, as her forensic colleagues and two uniformed constables from Queensbridge joined her, she spied a light on in the front room and thought she noticed an anxious face peering out.

She asked the team to wait behind her as she approached the porch and knocked. Two dogs began to bark from inside the bungalow, which was surrounded by trees and greenery.

A timid woman in her early forties with short, dark hair came to the door.

'Police,' Sunita explained, showing her warrant card. 'I'm DS Roy. I take it you're Hazel Laxton?'

'That's right. Hold on a minute.'

The householder locked their two excitable cocker spaniels in a back room before returning to the door.

'Whatever's happened?' she asked Sunita.

'I'm afraid we need to speak to your husband. Is he here?'

The woman shook her head. 'No. He's at the estate office. Is something wrong?'

'We need to ask him a few questions. We also have a warrant to search these premises.'

'What, again? Your lot were here three weeks ago.'

'I know. I'm sorry, but more information's come to light.'

'Oh dear,' said the woman. 'I suppose you'd better come in.'

The sergeant beckoned to the group waiting on the driveway, who trooped inside.

'Can't you tell me what this is about?' asked Laxton's wife.

Sunita shook her head as she entered the shabby hallway. 'It's related to a murder inquiry.'

'What murder is it?'

'I can't go into details, I'm afraid,' Sunita said as the forensic staff started examining the living room at the front. 'Do you shop at Orchard Lane Farm Shop, by any chance?'

'Yes, sometimes.'

'Do you know a woman called Victoria Jones who works there?'

Mrs Laxton shook her head. 'Sorry,' she said. 'I know some of the faces but none of the names. Oh, hang on. Is this to do with the woman who was attacked? What was her name – Stephanie?'

Sunita maintained her blank expression. 'I'm sorry. As I say, I can't confirm anything. Mrs Laxton, does your husband have a bicycle?'

'There used to be an old bicycle that belonged to the man who lived here before, but it needed a lot doing to it,' she said.

'Do you still have it?'

'Charles threw it out.'

'When exactly?'

'Oh, two or three weeks ago,' Mrs Laxton replied as Dawson emerged from the living room, a large, bright room with patio doors leading to the back garden.

'Sarge, could I have a word?' he asked.

'Forgive me,' she told Mrs Laxton as she broke off from her conversation to follow Dawson.

'Sarge, we've found two mobile phones,' he told her in a low voice as they stepped into the centre of the room.

'Brilliant,' she said. 'Where were they?'

'One of the SOCOs noticed a floorboard was uneven. He prised up the board and there was an old chocolate box tin, which rattled when it was picked up,' he explained. 'The two phones were inside.'

'Very cunning. Using the box to block communications so we couldn't trace where the phones were.'

'It's clear they belonged to Stephanie Price,' he said.

'That's great, Brett,' Sunita replied. 'That's terrific work by the team. But listen, I'm concerned that Laxton's not here and someone might tip him off that we're at his place,' she said softly. 'I'm going to shoot over to the estate office right now. Can I leave you in charge here?'

'Sure. No problem. So long as I don't have to rummage through their rubbish,' he joked. On a previous case, he'd twice been made to delve through household waste in a search for evidence.

Sunita asked PC Underhill to accompany her and they set off together on the two-mile journey in her car.

Just as they were approaching Laxton's office along the narrow, hedge-lined lane, they noticed a green vehicle proceeding towards them at speed.

'I think that's Laxton,' she yelled, yanking her steering wheel to the right in order to block his route.

The tyres on the Land Rover Discovery screeched as Laxton slammed on the brakes and brought his vehicle to a halt, just inches from Sunita's car.

Underhill leaped out and ran round to Laxton's car door, making sure he didn't try to flee.

Sunita got out and marched across. She felt a moment of triumph.

'Charles Benedict Laxton,' she said, 'I'm arresting you for the murder of Stephanie Price. You don't have to say anything unless you wish to do so, but what you say may be given in evidence.'

Laxton got out of his car in his shooting jacket, corduroys and peaked cap. He glared at them both.

'How bloody ridiculous,' he stormed. 'Didn't even know the woman.'

'That's strange,' she said, 'because we've found two phones belonging to Mrs Price under your floorboards.'

Chapter 51

Rupert Faulkner was almost certainly becoming more desperate, the chief inspector was convinced.

As he and DC Khalid pursued the suspect's Jaguar down the A34 road towards Oxford, it was clear Faulkner had been flouting so many driving rules. He had been careering through red lights, travelling on the wrong side of the road and breaking speed limits during his fifty-mile journey.

He struck a keep-left bollard at one stage and two traffic cones as though he'd learnt to drive in a dodgem car.

The two detectives had done their best to keep up with him, but the chief inspector had not been trained in car pursuits and for a while they lost sight of the Jaguar. The stress was already beginning to take its toll.

Then their radio crackled into life and the deep voice of Inspector Griffiths, from force control, came over the air.

'Just been informed a Thames Valley traffic officer has deployed a stinger,' he told them. 'One of their cars is right behind him.'

The radio crackled again. The inspector informed them both front tyres on the Jaguar had been pierced by the tyre-deflating device. Faulkner was struggling to keep control and losing speed.

'That's him!' cried Khalid as they rounded a bend in the north Oxford suburb of Cutteslowe and spotted Lord Culverdon's son-in-law. He had abandoned his vehicle in the middle of Banbury Road and was now running off down the street in the direction of Oxford city centre with two traffic officers on foot behind him.

The detectives drew up behind the Jaguar and leaped out of their car as a text came through on Roscoe's phone to say Laxton had been arrested.

'Come on,' said Roscoe. 'Let's get after this one.'

While they ran, Roscoe could see Faulkner's balding head bobbing up and down in the distance. He watched as the fleeing man turned down a side road on the right, Beeching Drive. It consisted of a long row of detached houses on the left-hand side and a cemetery on the right-hand side, protected from view by a line of trees and bushes.

He calculated the traffic officers were now just ten metres behind Faulkner while he and Khalid were a further thirty metres behind them.

Faulkner crossed the road. He darted behind a metal security fence in the front garden of the tenth detached house along, which was being demolished. He ran past a mechanical digger and a blue portable toilet before disappearing from view.

The Thames Valley pair paused for a moment on the opposite side of the road, alongside trees and shrubs. This gave the Heart of England pair a chance to catch up.

Roscoe's open blue coat was flapping as he reached them, panting and perspiring.

'DCI Roscoe,' he spluttered, shaking their hands.

'PC Miller,' said a burly, ginger-haired officer with a broad smile. 'This is my colleague, PC Chaudhry. He's the one that deployed the stinger.'

'Well done,' said Roscoe. 'This is my colleague DC Khalid. Anyway, let's not waste any time.'

He stepped into the road and approached the demolition site, which was encased in scaffolding. A gunshot immediately rang out, striking the asphalt beside his feet. He, Khalid and the traffic officers dashed behind the trees.

'All right, lads,' said Roscoe. 'He's obviously got a weapon from somewhere. We'll have to come up with a plan.'

'Do you want us to call the firearms team?' asked Miller.

'Good idea,' said Roscoe. 'But they could be a while and we've got to manage this situation in the meantime. This is a residential area and the public are at risk. And on top of that, I want this guy kept alive at all costs. Just wait here a minute.'

Taking care to remain behind the cover of the trees, he set off down the street, his eyes trained initially on the demolition site. Once out of range of Faulkner's fire, he returned to the pavement and turned left into the next street, Chalmers Way.

Five minutes later he was back. As he made his way through the bushes to join them, a second shot rang out from the house. This time the bullet struck one of the trees.

'We're in luck,' he said, ignoring the shot. 'There's an alley behind the houses. PC Miller, if you'd like to accompany me, I think we might be able to break into the back of the house and take Mr Faulkner by surprise. At the moment, he's sitting in what used to be the front room and he's keeping his eyes on the road and the trees, where we're standing.'

'Happy to help,' Miller said.

'Don't you think that's a bit risky, sir?' asked Khalid.

'Maybe,' said Roscoe. 'But we don't have much choice. The children will be coming home from school soon. Now, Khalid, what I want you to do is, without putting your safety in danger, try and draw his fire. I suggest you duck down behind the minibus that's parked there. It's about ten metres from where Faulkner is holed up and should give you protection. Try and attract his attention in some way.'

'How do we do that?'

'I want you to shout out, "Police. Come out with your hands up," or something like that. Anything to draw his attention. But don't do it for ten minutes. So what's the time now?'

'I make it five minutes past three,' said Khalid.

'Right, set your watches, gentlemen,' Roscoe continued. 'Start drawing his attention in exactly ten minutes' time.'

He turned to Miller. 'Have you brought your taser with you?'

The traffic officer nodded.

'Good,' said Roscoe. 'We might need it.'

The chief inspector and PC Miller ventured through the trees until they felt safe to step onto the pavement and continue their way in the open. They turned into Chalmers Way where Roscoe led his colleague along a gravel footpath flanked by garden fences. They quickly found the rear of the demolition site, which they recognized from the scaffolding.

Together they hoisted up one of the heavy metal security fences and uncoupled it from its neighbouring panel.

As they stepped through the gap, they were confronted by pallets of building bricks and bags of cement on a concrete standing. Around them, the garden was overgrown with weeds and brambles.

Gingerly, Roscoe clambered through the giant opening where patio doors had once stood and peered around at the remains of the building's kitchen. All the units and flooring had been taken away.

Closely followed by Miller, he crept through the dim and dusty hallway and finally, they saw a crouching figure at the partly demolished front of the house, silhouetted against the sky.

Faulkner, wearing a khaki shooting jacket and plus-fours, was gazing out across the street from behind a wall which had once served as the base of a window. A pistol – possibly a Beretta – was resting beside him on top of the metre-high wall.

Roscoe glanced at his watch. It was nearly a quarter past three.

Exactly as agreed, Khalid and Chaudhry dashed from the bushes and headed for the minibus.

'Police!' shouted Khalid. 'It's time to give yourself up, Mr Faulkner.'

Faulkner immediately fired in their direction, which left a bullet hole in the side of the minibus.

Faulkner fired another shot towards Khalid. This time the bullet struck the road surface.

'Never!' he called back.

Miller clasped his hand on the chief inspector's shoulder. But Roscoe raised his index finger and shook his head. It wasn't the right moment to make a move, he felt. Faulkner still had easy access to his weapon. He retraced his steps to the kitchen, beckoning Miller to follow.

Minutes later, he returned to the hall and found Faulkner still squatting behind the low wall.

Roscoe took off his coat, placed it on the dusty concrete floor and watched like a tiger ready to strike. He clung to the shadows as, for no apparent reason, their quarry put his weapon down on the wall and stepped away from his vantage point. Faulkner moved into the space where the front door had once been.

Then the chief inspector seized his chance. He lunged towards Faulkner, who was slightly taller than him. Taking the man by surprise, he thrust his right arm round Faulkner's neck. He clasped his left hand onto his right hand, forcing his left elbow hard into Faulkner's back.

Having gained control over him, Roscoe forced him backwards onto the concrete floor.

'Get off me, you bastard!' screamed Faulkner.

Miller ran towards them as Roscoe pressed on top of the suspect's body with his right knee. The traffic officer stood there watching for several seconds, unsure how to help the detective.

Faulkner reached up and grabbed the chief inspector's shoulders. They grappled for several seconds together on the ground before Faulkner swivelled round and flung Roscoe off his chest.

The irate Faulkner staggered to his feet and tried to run off towards the kitchen, but Miller grabbed his arm and held him back.

'You may as well give yourself up, Faulkner,' shouted Roscoe. 'I've just heard the firearms team arriving outside. The whole house is surrounded.'

'Never,' said Faulkner, snatching his arm away from Miller and dashing into the shell of a kitchen. Roscoe and Miller raced after him.

As Faulkner reached the opening where the patio doors had once stood, Roscoe shouted, 'Stand still or you'll be tasered.'

Faulkner ignored this and ran into the garden.

Miller glanced at his superior, who nodded, and the constable fired the electronic gun at Faulkner's back. The two barbs penetrated his clothing and Faulkner fell into the brambles, where he lay writhing in agony. Miller handcuffed him and removed the barbs.

'Well done, Constable,' said Roscoe with a smile.

Roscoe stood face to face with their suspect. 'Rupert William Faulkner,' he said, 'I'm arresting you for the murder of Miles Kenworth. You don't have to say anything unless you wish to do so, but what you say may be given in evidence.'

'You've got nothing on me,' Faulkner sneered. 'This time tomorrow you'll be sorry you ever got tangled up in my plans.' Then Miller and Chaudhry led him away.

Chapter 52

A cell door along the corridor slammed shut. Charles Laxton stirred from his sleep and opened his eyes. For a moment, he thought he might be in his bedroom at Hartston with his devoted wife Hazel by his side.

He glanced around. No, he was lying on the couch in a dingy basement cell at police headquarters, still in his shooting jacket and corduroy trousers. It was one of twelve small chambers in a complex they euphemistically called a 'custody suite'.

A few minutes later, there was a knock on the door and he was greeted by the custody sergeant's strident voice.

'Laxton,' he said, 'you've got a visitor.'

The sergeant unlocked the door and Laxton's solicitor, Salman Siddiqui, stepped inside, clutching a wooden chair.

'I'm afraid none of the more comfortable rooms is available,' said Mr Siddiqui, as he placed the chair beside the couch and sat down. 'So we'll have to make the best of it in here. As I understand it, you're accused of the murder of a lady called Stephanie Price.'

Laxton shrugged his shoulders. 'Don't know her,' he said. 'This is all a misunderstanding.'

'I've had a brief conversation with DS Roy, one of the officers in the case. She wouldn't tell me much but mentioned two mobile phones.'

'Yes,' said Laxton. 'Apparently they found two phones at my house under the floorboards. Someone must have put them there to frame me.'

'Why would someone do that?' asked Mr Siddiqui.

'I don't know. Perhaps someone's got a grudge against me. There's meant to be photographs of me on this lady's phone, but what does that prove? It doesn't point to me murdering her?'

'All right,' said Mr Siddiqui. 'We'll be taken up to one of the interview rooms in a minute. What we need to do is become good listeners. We need to hear the strength of their case and my advice is for you to respond by saying "No comment" to their questions initially.'

'Fair enough. Do you know why there's been such a long wait?'

'Apparently, they're waiting for DCI Roscoe, the SIO. As soon as he arrives, we're good to go.'

At half past five, a burly custody officer led Charles Laxton up to Interview Room One on the ground floor. Sunita Roy was already sitting at a table.

'Ah, Mr Laxton and Mr Siddiqui. Please take your seats,' said the sergeant. 'The chief inspector won't be a minute.'

'I hope this won't take long,' Laxton moaned. 'I've got some unfinished business to conduct.'

'I'm not sure if you realise the seriousness of your situation,' she said. 'You're facing a murder charge and I have to remind you you're still under caution. Rupert Faulkner's your brother, isn't he?'

'Yes.'

'Why the secrecy about that?' she asked.

'It's no secret,' he insisted with a casual wave of his hand. 'I thought everyone knew.'

Sunita frowned. 'I'm not sure if that's true,' she said.

As they were speaking, the chief inspector entered the room.

'Good timing, sir,' said the sergeant. 'We're in a position to start.'

'Great,' said Roscoe, brushing some white dust off his trousers. 'We need to know exactly where you were on the night of 24 February,' he said, staring directly across the table at the suspect.

'Home with my wife,' said Laxton with a stern expression.

'All night?'

'All night.'

'You seem to remember that very clearly,' said Roscoe. 'Do you know why I'm asking about that night?'

'No, but I expect you're going to tell me.'

'That was the night someone visited Stephanie Price in the garages behind the Orchard Lane Farm Shop in Shawley and bludgeoned her to death. So I'm rather puzzled by your statement that you were at home all night. Our forensic people found a partial boot print in the blood on the garage floor. In a search of your home, we found some black, size-ten hiking boots. The pattern on your right boot matches this boot print.'

Laxton shrugged. 'Must be coincidence. Someone's obviously got the same kind of boots as me. You can't build a murder case on coincidence.'

'Maybe not, but the coincidences build up,' Roscoe continued. 'For instance, two phones belonging to Stephanie Price were found hidden beneath the floorboards at your home.'

Sunita picked up two transparent bags from the floor. Each contained a mobile phone.

'Sir, for the purposes of the DIR, I'm showing the suspect exhibit C, a Samsung phone, and exhibit D, a Huawei phone,' she said.

Roscoe gazed into Laxton's eyes.

'How do you account for these phones being in your home?'

'Nothing to do with me,' said Laxton with a sneer. 'Maybe the previous tenant put them there.'

Sunita had been quiet for a few minutes. She had been watching the accused man's face for any signs of discomfort or deceit.

Interrupting the chief inspector, she said, 'Our phone expert has unlocked both phones. He's found records of two conversations Mrs Price made to your phone number on the Wednesday of that week – the day before the murder. The first conversation lasted three and a half minutes. The second lasted two and a half minutes. And yet you say you don't know her.'

The estate manager looked as shocked as if she'd thrown him into an ice-cold bath. He hastily battled to regain his composure.

'No comment,' he replied, glancing at Mr Siddiqui.

Roscoe said, 'We've also found photographs of you in an undressed state in a hayloft at Lower Wood Farm in Shawley. You're in the company of a young lady, Victoria Jones, who's confirmed she was with you that afternoon. What this boils down to is that Stephanie Price had arrived at the scene through the course of her work. She chanced upon the pair of you cavorting in the hay barn. She took some photographs and tried to blackmail you. As a result, you decided to kill her.'

Laxton turned to his lawyer and whispered in Mr Siddiqui's ear.

'In view of your new disclosures, my client would appreciate a short break,' said Mr Siddiqui.

* * *

The chief inspector and his sergeant stepped out of the ground-floor interview room a few minutes after 6 p.m. and entered the office next door.

They then watched through the one-way glass as Charles Laxton and his lawyer became engrossed in a deep conversation.

'I don't think it'll be long now,' said Roscoe. 'I can't see him wriggling out of this.'

'Congratulations on catching Faulkner, sir,' she said, taking a seat at one of the desks.

They re-entered the interview room half an hour later.

'Have you had sufficient time?' asked Roscoe.

'Yes,' said Mr Siddiqui. 'My client would like to make a brief statement.'

The two detectives resumed their seats.

Mr Siddiqui peered down at a sheet of paper on the table in front of him. He began to read, 'This is a statement made by myself, Charles Benedict Laxton, in front of my solicitor, Mr Salman Siddiqui, on Monday, 14 March. Since being arrested and accused of murdering Stephanie Price, I've decided to tell you the truth about what happened.

'I'm ashamed to say that on Monday, 21 February I went to Lower Wood Farm in the company of a young lady I'd got to know well while visiting the Orchard Lane Farm Shop. She believed the farmer and his wife were likely to be away that morning and she knew of a place where we could go.

'The next day I received a phone call from a woman who said her name was Jackie. She had taken some photos of us at the farm. She asked me for £50,000, and if I refused, she'd send the pictures to my wife, my employer or the local press.

'I love my wife very much and any whiff of this affair would have caused her so much distress. My marriage and my job were at serious risk over what was just a few minutes of fun.

'So I followed Jackie's instructions and went to the farm shop in Shawley with the money she had demanded. I found her outside a pair of garages at the back. But she had now increased her demands. She said she'd had time to think and decided her silence and the destruction of the photographs was worth much more. I told her there was no way I could get any more money. We argued and she lost her temper with me. Without any provocation on my part, she suddenly kneed me in the groin and grabbed a hammer from somewhere. She began raining blows upon me with this hammer.

'All I could do was force her back against the wall to stop her striking me. She must have banged her head hard against the brickwork because she slumped to the ground with blood coming from a head wound. I panicked. I thought I'd hurt her very badly. I realise now I should have called an ambulance, but I was in such a state. I'm ashamed to say I rode away on my bicycle.'

Mr Siddiqui looked up. 'That's the end of the statement.'

The chief inspector leaned back on his chair and glanced at his sergeant.

'I don't believe it happened like that, do you, Sergeant?' he said.

She shook her head.

'No, sir,' said Sunita. 'We know you broke into the garage before Mrs Price arrived by picking the padlock, Mr Laxton. You got inside and came upon the clawhammer. Mrs Price didn't die from striking her head on the wall. She died from successive blows to her head by the hammer. We know this from the traces of human tissue and hair found on the weapon.

'You were so desperate to stop details of your sordid affair leaking out. You continually struck her with a series of horrific blows to the head that she had no hope of surviving, and callously left her in a pool of blood.'

Chapter 53

The two detectives watched through the one-way glass as Rupert Faulkner paced about in Interview Room Two in his grubby shooting jacket and plus-fours, staring at the floor.

Every now and then, his solicitor Magnus Huckabee, a stout, balding man in his early forties, would glance at his client and pass comment. Faulkner would glance back and either give a quick response or remain silent and peer down at the floor.

'Come on then. Let's see what he's got to say,' said the chief inspector.

They found Faulkner sitting with his arms folded at the table beside his lawyer when the chief inspector pushed open the door.

'Have you calmed down now?' asked Roscoe, taking a seat opposite.

'You'd have got excited if a bunch of idiots with blue lights had been chasing you for an hour across England,' Faulkner moaned. 'You've got no right to keep me here. You've got nothing on me.'

While Huckabee raised an index finger in an effort to silence his client, Sunita frowned.

'You'd be surprised what we've got on you, Mr Faulkner,' she said as she sat down beside her boss.

Roscoe turned on the digital interview recorder while the lawyer whispered a few words in his client's ear.

After announcing the names of those present, the chief inspector reminded Faulkner he had been arrested in connection with the murder of Miles Kenworth.

'We have a number of other matters to question you about, but we'll begin with the murder,' he said. 'You travelled to Queensbridge on the evening of Friday, 11 February, didn't you?'

'I've already told you,' said Faulkner. 'I was at rehearsals.'

'Your alibi's in pieces,' said Sunita. 'Nobody saw you at rehearsals until ten o'clock, giving ample time for you to travel to Waverley Court to carry out the murder.'

'What about Craig Armitage, the stage manager?' asked Faulkner.

'One of our team went to his home in Bidford Avenue, Stratford and Armitage has apologised,' she said. 'He was mistaken. He's confirmed he's got no memory of seeing you until the end of the evening.'

She slipped her notebook from her pocket and leafed through its pages.

'Here we are,' she said. 'His words were, "I remember buying Rupert a drink in the pub. I wrongly assumed he'd been with us earlier."'

Faulkner shrugged his shoulders.

'You've no evidence I went to Waverley Court and you won't find any. I wasn't there.'

Roscoe shook his head. 'That's where you're wrong. A pepper spray was used to subdue Mr Kenworth before he was killed. We found a pepper spray canister at your home in Culverdon Hall.'

'Doesn't prove anything,' scoffed Faulkner. 'That doesn't link me to Kenworth's murder. We've only been living in our present quarters a few months. That spray was there when we moved in. Someone else must have bought it for self-defence.'

Roscoe frowned and shook his head. 'Pepper spray is banned from public use under Section 5 of the Firearms Act of 1968, so that scenario is extremely unlikely. Our senior forensic scientist, Dr Ling, says the main ingredient in these aerosols is the irritant known as oleoresin capsicum. And traces of its residue have been found on clothing retrieved from your home – namely, a grey padded jacket and some Rutland tweed shooting breeks.

'What's more, Dr Ling has contacted a laboratory specialising in the study of these aerosols. They can predict the species, type and origin of every spray. She's confident she'll be able to prove your clothing was present at the crime scene that Friday.'

Sunita interrupted. 'Mr Faulkner, our forensic team also found microscopic traces of Miles Kenworth's blood on the ground next to one of your rubbish bins at Culverdon Hall.'

A heavy silence hung in the air before Mr Huckabee spoke.

'DCI Roscoe, I understood there were some other matters you were going to raise. Is this a suitable time for you to mention these? I'm in the dark about any other issues you may have,' said the solicitor.

Roscoe nodded. 'As you're no doubt aware, your client was in his Jaguar car earlier today and failed to stop when requested by police. After a lengthy episode of dangerous driving between Stratford and Oxford, he fired a Beretta pistol several times at police while resisting arrest and we had to use a taser. So we're looking at a charge of possessing a firearm with intent to endanger life.'

'Not to forget dangerous driving,' said Sunita.

Mr Huckabee seemed puzzled. 'My client informs me he was in the process of surrendering himself to police when the taser was deployed.'

'That's incorrect,' snapped Roscoe. 'He was tasered when he refused to submit to being arrested. We also need to question Mr Faulkner about the attempted murder of Miles Kenworth's older brother, Arthur.'

'This should have been brought to my notice earlier,' said Mr Huckabee indignantly.

'As you know, we've only managed to arrest Mr Faulkner this afternoon,' said Roscoe. 'The allegation is that Mr Faulkner travelled to Spain on an EasyJet flight on

Monday, 14 October 2019. He was accompanied by his brother, Charles Laxton. The reason for their trip was that Mr Faulkner's brother-in-law, Arthur Kenworth, was on holiday on his own in the town of Nerja. It's our contention that the brothers followed him into the mountains, no doubt in disguise, and pushed him into a ravine. You've probably seen on the news that Arthur Kenworth survived the attack and has fortunately been found alive.'

'What an extraordinary allegation,' said Mr Huckabee. 'Have you any evidence of this?'

'No,' said Faulkner. 'They've got no evidence at all.'

'We've got detailed eyewitness descriptions of Mr Faulkner and Mr Laxton boarding a flight from Birmingham and checking into the Nerja Palace Hotel,' said Sunita. 'We've got a full witness statement from Arthur Kenworth and a statement from a receptionist at Mr Kenworth's hotel about one of the two men who had been searching for him.'

Faulkner glared at the detectives and sneered.

'That's nonsense,' he said. 'Must be a coincidence. Just two men who look like us. Why would I want to kill my brother-in-law?'

'We can only assume you wanted to get rid of all claimants to the Culverdon Estate so that you and your wife Lavinia would inherit everything,' said Roscoe.

Faulkner sneered again. 'Don't be so ridiculous, man. We're very happy as we are.'

'We should also mention the sudden decline in Lord Culverdon's health,' said the chief inspector. 'He's been complaining of stomach pain over the past two weeks. Our Dr Ling's confirmed that she's found traces of the herb aconite in curries and other spicy dishes being prepared for His Lordship. This is a deadly poison also known as monkshood or wolfsbane. It could easily have killed your father-in-law and there were traces of it in your bedroom. Fortunately, His Lordship has survived – but it's no thanks to you.'

Sunita intervened to say, 'The housekeeper and cook, Mrs Crosswell, says the only person apart from herself to be present in the kitchen at Culverdon Hall on several occasions over the past fortnight has been you, Mr Faulkner.'

'This is a tissue of lies,' screamed Faulkner. 'Anyone with access to Culverdon Hall could have sneaked into the kitchen.'

'Not according to Mrs Crosswell. She says you're the only person she's seen there repeatedly. She's convinced it was you who's been poisoning Lord Culverdon's food.'

'She would say that,' said Faulkner. 'She's the cook. Maybe it was her.'

'No, Mr Faulkner,' said Roscoe, 'it was you. Both you and your brother Charles are going to appear in court later this week, charged in connection with both murders, and I hope the judge and jury have the good sense to send you both away for life for these cold-hearted crimes.'

Chapter 54

Chief Superintendent Norris was sitting hunched over her laptop when the chief inspector was summoned to her office on Tuesday morning.

She glanced up and gave a weak smile before beckoning him in.

'I hear you've charged the two men,' she said.

'Yes, ma'am,' he said. 'Laxton with the murder of Stephanie Price; Faulkner with the murder of Miles Kenworth and the attempted murder of Lord Culverdon.'

'What about the attempted murder of Arthur Kenworth in Spain?'

Roscoe shook his head. 'Since the incident took place in Spain, we're waiting to hear from the Spanish authorities, but we've been advised the evidence may not be strong enough for a prosecution. Arthur had problems remembering exactly what happened before he fell and there are no witnesses that we know of.'

'I'm very pleased about the other charges,' she admitted as she leaned back.

'Yes,' he said while finding a chair to sit on. 'It's a relief to have resolved the two murder cases.'

'That man Faulkner was clearly trying to wipe out the whole Kenworth family,' she observed. 'You're absolutely certain the poison used in Lord Culverdon's food was aconite?'

'As sure as we can be at this stage. As you know, full toxicology tests aren't available for ten to twelve weeks.'

All at once her expression changed to that of a headmistress interrupting a disruptive pupil.

'Gavin, I'm meant to be reprimanding you this morning,' she said with a frown.

'Whatever for, ma'am?'

'Failing to wait for armed back-up when you confronted Faulkner in Oxford,' she replied. 'You put your life and that of a Thames Valley officer in jeopardy. The assistant chief constable said you should be disciplined. You and PC Miller could have been killed, Gavin.'

Roscoe frowned. 'There was no time to wait, ma'am. The local school bells were about to ring. People were due home from work. I wanted to act quickly and nip things in the bud.'

'Well, perhaps, on this occasion, we can deal with it in terms of a friendly warning. By the way, I was personally very impressed by the bravery shown by both you and PC Miller.'

'Thank you.'

'Do you believe anyone else was involved in this murder spree – the wives of Faulkner and Laxton, for example?' asked Norris.

He shook his head. 'There's no evidence of that at this stage.'

'I've had Lavinia Faulkner on the phone this morning. Did you know she's on the police and crime panel? She's obviously delighted to learn Arthur is alive but she's furious we've arrested her husband and she's making all kinds of allegations against you.'

He shrugged his shoulders. 'That can't be helped, ma'am. We're convinced we've got the right offenders.'

'Gavin, I just wondered if Lavinia Faulkner could have been involved?'

'No evidence of that. Of course, we'll need to bear that possibility in mind as we complete our investigation. But her name didn't crop up in any of the inquiries made by DS Roy and members of the team.'

'How did that man Faulkner get hold of the pepper spray, by the way?' she asked.

'Apparently he's got a friend in the Army Reserve who got hold of it through the military police.'

'What exactly did the two brothers hope to gain by their actions?'

'Well, ma'am, Lord Culverdon is a wealthy man. All I can think is they wanted control of the Culverdon Estate and His Lordship's money. With Miles, Arthur and their father out of the way, Faulkner and his wife would have inherited the lot. Of course, they had no idea Arthur was still alive – no one in Britain did, until DS Roy found him.'

She nodded. 'Bright girl, that one. She's done well, Gavin. If I hadn't sent her to Spain with young Dawson, we might never have discovered the murder attempt on the older brother. Wasn't it she who first realised Faulkner and Laxton were half-brothers and acting in league with each other?'

'Yes. That's right.'

'Did you ever find out which of the brothers stole the axe from the farm shop in Shawley Green, Gavin?'

'No, ma'am. Both Laxton and Faulkner were regular customers. It was during his many shopping trips that Laxton got to know Vicky Jones, the woman he was caught with in the hayloft.'

Norris scowled. 'That was a rum old business,' she remarked.

'But Faulkner was also a frequent visitor, so either of them could have stolen the axe. I suppose, at the end of the day, how the killer acquired the murder weapon is unimportant. What's important is that these two men are now behind bars and the Midlands is a far safer place. Incidentally, the brothers have fallen out with each other spectacularly, with each claiming the other was responsible for the murders.'

'What was their reaction when they heard Arthur Kenworth was alive?'

'Both were taken aback,' he said, 'and then denied being in Spain at the time he disappeared.'

There was a pause while she digested this thought. Then she said, 'Did you see what the *Queensbridge Gazette* said this morning on their website? They said you're to be congratulated for making these arrests so quickly. It's almost exactly a month since the axe murder.'

'Yes, ma'am. I was waylaid by members of the press last night when I left the building. They'd been tipped off that we'd made some significant arrests. I gave them a brief statement. Yes, it's been quite a fast-moving investigation this time.'

She smiled. 'You've timed it very well. You've got a big family wedding on Saturday, haven't you?'

'Yes. George is getting married and we were wondering if you might be able to join us.'

She manoeuvred her chair round the desk until she was little more than a metre away.

'I was flattered to receive the invitation, but I'm going to be very busy this weekend,' she said. 'There's an equestrian event near Rugby which I'm bound to attend. That said, I hope the weather stays fine for them and I'll be sending a card.'

* * *

Sunita Roy was replacing batteries in the television remote when the chief inspector returned to CID after his meeting with Norris.

'Sir, have you heard the news?' she said. 'Arthur Kenworth is back in Britain. He's just arrived at Birmingham Airport on a flight from Malaga.'

'I imagine Lord Culverdon will be delighted,' he remarked as he opened the door to his room.

'I wonder how Maria García is going to take to spending a couple of weeks at Culverdon Hall,' she continued. 'It's all going to be rather strange for her.'

'Apparently, the couple have sold their story to a celebrity magazine and they're going to use the money to develop their olive grove.'

Half an hour later, Sunita turned on the office television for the ITV lunchtime news. Staff gathered round to watch as a heavily tanned Arthur Kenworth was surrounded by a press posse in the arrivals hall.

Cameras flashed and journalists fired questions as he waded through the crowd. An ITV correspondent reported:

> The heir to the Culverdon family fortune flew into Britain today after being missing for more than two years and announced, 'It's great to be back.'
> Arthur Kenworth, elder son of the twelfth Viscount Culverdon, was mobbed by the press as he arrived at Birmingham Airport.
> 'I can't say too much about what's happened to me as it's the subject of a police investigation,' he said. 'All I'll say is that it's been difficult being apart from my family all this

time. I'm very much looking forward to being reunited with them.'

The colourful former financier, who celebrates his fortieth birthday next month, vanished in October 2019 near the town of Nerja on Spain's Costa del Sol while on a hiking trip.

Despite an extensive search being launched amid fears of a climbing accident, a body was never found and his disappearance became shrouded in mystery. Then a few days ago it was reported he had been found alive and well in the mountain village of La Quilla, a few miles north of Nerja. He is believed to have been staying there since surviving injuries received after falling into a ravine.

Remarkably, he was taken in by the García family, whose twenty-six-year-old daughter Maria nursed him back to health.

It is understood Maria, now his fiancée, flew in on an earlier flight with journalists from a national magazine, who have paid the couple a substantial sum for their exclusive story.

Mr Kenworth was met at the airport by his sister, Lavinia, who is believed to be driving him back to the family seat in Warwickshire later today.

The chief inspector smiled and shook his head. 'I don't suppose the guy was expecting such a huge welcome-home party at the airport,' he said quietly.

'No, sir,' said Sunita. 'Just shows the excitement his reappearance has caused. I imagine Lord Culverdon may have to lock the gates to keep out roving reporters.'

'Oh, for Heaven's sake,' said Roscoe as his smile vanished. 'I hope Arthur's return doesn't have any impact on my son's wedding on Saturday.'

'Don't worry. That's four days away,' she said. 'I'm sure all the fuss will have died down by then.'

Chapter 55

The wedding guests were in a boisterous mood as the double-decker, festooned with balloons and bunting, wound its way along the narrow country lanes of West Warwickshire.

The seventy-five guests on board were swapping memories of the happy couple's childhoods and laughing about poor George, who had dropped the wedding ring during the service – sparking a five-minute break in the proceedings so a search could be conducted.

Eventually, after scrambling about on his hands and knees, the vicar recovered it from beneath one of the pews.

Shortly after half past twelve, the driver passed through the wrought iron gates of Culverdon Hall. Guests who had travelled earlier watched as the bus, emblazoned with banners saying, 'Congratulations Mr & Mrs Roscoe,' trundled up the drive to the hall, where the chattering passengers scrambled out.

Sunita Roy climbed off the bus cautiously in her pale-yellow sari and stood for a few moments beside the fountain, staring up at the light-grey walls of the historic house. Tom Vickers came to join her, still clutching his order of service from the church.

'You all right, Sunita?' he asked.

She smiled. 'Yes. I was remembering the first day I came here with the DCI,' she said. 'It wasn't a fine day like today. It was raining. We met His Lordship and members of his family in their sumptuous rooms in the east wing. I'll never forget it.'

He gave her a broad grin. 'I think you've done amazingly in finding the missing son and solving the murders. And don't give me that line that it was all down to teamwork.'

She shrugged. 'But it was.'

The chief inspector clambered down the stone steps and patted Vickers on the back. 'Are you two going to stand here all day chatting? Come and have a brief word with the happy couple, and I'll show you both to the table. Helen's got you sitting together. I hope that's all right.'

Roscoe led them through the vaulted hallway, past groups of guests who were milling round, locked in conversation. They entered a grand dining room where a dozen tables had been arranged for more than a hundred guests. Ornate chandeliers hung from the high ceilings, while tall windows along the wood-panelled walls afforded views of the lake and trees beyond.

The pair spent a few minutes congratulating George and Amanda, who was wearing an ivory lace dress.

Then Roscoe led them to their seats in the middle of the room.

'Let me go and get you both something wet and fizzy,' he said before disappearing into the crowd.

Sunita turned towards her colleague and smiled.

'It's so good to see you again, Tom,' she said.

'It's good to see you, Sunita. I've been so busy over in Summerstoke, I haven't had a chance to call you.'

'What have you been up to?' she asked as Roscoe placed their drinks on the table and rushed away again.

'Nothing major,' Vickers replied. 'I've been out with the lads a few times, celebrating my divorce going through. Otherwise, it's been the same old, same old. Oh, I nearly forgot to tell you. You remember Slippery Sarkar, the investment guy?'

Sunita sighed and rested her arms on the table. 'How could I forget him?'

'I was having a chat with my pal Gary from the fraud squad the other day. Sarkar's been arrested along with some other guys. He's going to be up in court soon.'

'Thank God I sought your advice,' she said, gazing fondly into his eyes.

As Roscoe was returning with their drinks, an unexpected visitor was emerging from a door in the corner, dressed unobtrusively in waistcoat, shirt and trousers as though he was one of the waiters.

'I'm not intruding, am I, Chief Inspector?' said the newcomer.

'Not at all,' said Roscoe. 'Lord Culverdon, how good to see you. You're better now?'

'Yes. I've found the meals served in our kitchens much more palatable these last few days – since that rascal Rupert was put under lock and key. Thank you so much, Chief Inspector, for your prompt actions. I believe you saved my life.'

'Not at all, sir,' said Roscoe. 'Just part of normal police work. You've met my sergeant, DS Roy, haven't you? And this is DI Tom Vickers, one of my closest colleagues.'

The peer smiled as he shook their hands. 'I didn't want this event to pass off without me seeing you, Chief Inspector. I wanted to give you my warmest thanks for the way you handled the investigation into Miles's death. It was a first-rate job. I also need to thank you for finding Arthur as well as saving my life. I've made a substantial contribution to the police benevolent fund and, if any of you are so minded, I'd be happy to show you and your families round Culverdon Hall at any time.'

'That's incredibly kind of you, sir,' said Roscoe. 'DS Roy is the detective who took a particular interest in your son's disappearance.'

Sunita stood up and smiled at Lord Culverdon. 'I was intrigued that clothing matching Arthur's had been found on a dead body near La Quilla,' Sunita explained.

'Yes,' said Roscoe, 'as a result of her persistence, she found the García family.'

'I'll be eternally grateful, DS Roy,' the peer said. 'We threw a family party the moment Arthur came back and the lad's told me everything – including the kindness you showed him while you were in his company out there. Of course, there's a downside to all this. My daughter is devastated by what's happened. I'm afraid I was never in favour of her marriage. Rupert was a spoilt brat who grew up always wanting his own way. But you know what they say in France, don't you? *Comme on fait son lit, on se couche.*'

'You make your bed and you lie in it?' suggested Roscoe.

'Precisely,' Lord Culverdon agreed.

'Will we have a chance to see Arthur today?' asked Roscoe.

Lord Culverdon shook his head. 'He's decided to keep a low profile today, what with these blighters from the press hanging around. He and Maria are having their pictures taken somewhere in the building after signing some kind of deal with a glossy celebrity magazine. My old father is probably quaking in his grave at the whole idea. It's not my choice but it's what they want to do. I'll just have a quick word with your son, Chief Inspector, if I may – just to wish the happy couple well. Then I must dash off.'

The three detectives watched as the peer strolled across to the dining-room door, where George and Amanda were greeting guests. He shook George's hand and gave the bride a peck on the cheek.

Roscoe's attention was distracted by the sight of two female wedding guests running after a toddler. When he turned back, Lord Culverdon had slipped away.

'I wonder,' he remarked.

Sunita glanced up at her boss. 'You wonder what, sir?'

'I just wonder if there was more in it – this business of Arthur Kenworth vanishing. I wonder if His Lordship knew Arthur was alive and well. It beggars belief that he was being nursed and growing olives all that time.'

'I know,' she said. 'But it's like a lot of our cases. There's often more going on beneath the surface that the police never get to know about – no matter how hard we try.'

THE END

If you enjoyed this book, please let others know by leaving a quick review on Amazon. Also, if you spot anything untoward in the paperback, get in touch. We strive for the best quality and appreciate reader feedback.

editor@thebookfolks.com

www.thebookfolks.com

More fiction in this series

MURDER ON OXFORD LANE (Book 1)

A budding chorister doesn't return home from practice but his wife doesn't appear concerned. DS Sunita Roy becomes convinced he has been murdered but she has her own problems in the form of an ex-boyfriend who won't take no for an answer. Will she keep her eye on the ball when all expect her to fail?

THE CROSSBOW STALKER (Book 2)

When a serial killer armed with a crossbow terrorises the West Midlands, Chief Inspector Gavin Roscoe suspects a motive of jealousy and revenge. But as the number of victims increases, the connection initially established between them wears thin. DS Sunita Roy has a different theory and resolves to pursue her own instincts, come what may.

MURDER OF A DOCTOR (Book 3)

Police search for the identities of people seen near the scene of a doctor's murder. And it seems like an open and shut case when a father with a grievance against him can be placed nearby. But DS Sunita Roy wants to dig deeper, and with an internal affairs investigation ongoing, she'll have to tread carefully.

OUT FOR REVENGE (Book 4)

There's a noticeable change of atmosphere in the city when a dangerous prisoner is released. He has plans to up his drugs business. But someone will quickly put an end to that, by putting an end to his life. Detective Sunita Roy has the unenviable task of hunting down the gangsters who were likely responsible. But when the cops close in, they'll have an even bigger problem than they first imagined.

All FREE with Kindle Unlimited and available in paperback.

More fiction by Tony Bassett

SEAT 97

Journalist Nick Colton lands the scoop of his career when a concertgoer sitting next to him is shot dead in front of his eyes. But the gunman escapes amidst the chaos, and Colton's investigation into the murder will see him treading a dangerous line through London's unforgiving streets.

FREE with Kindle Unlimited and available in paperback.

Other titles of interest

MURDER ON A COUNTRY LANE by Jon Harris

After the shock of discovering a murder victim, young barmaid Julia isn't too perturbed because local garden centre owner Audrey White was a horrible so-and-so. But when her fingerprints are found all over a death threat, Julia becomes the police's prime suspect. Equipped with an unfetching ankle tag she must solve the crime to prove her innocence.

THE FERRY PORT MYSTERY by David Pearson

Smarting after taking the rap for a botched investigation in Dublin, Detective Inspector Vikki Kirkby is stationed in the county town of Wexford in the sleepy south of Ireland. But she is soon up against her bosses and the distrustful local Garda, when they don't agree with her that the death of a local couple is suspicious. Will a handsome local businessman become the ally she needs?

All FREE with Kindle Unlimited and available in paperback.

www.thebookfolks.com

Printed in Great Britain
by Amazon